The Body Brokers

Also by Brian Cuban

The Ambulance Chaser

The Addicted Lawyer:
Tales of the Bar, Booze, Blow, and Redemption

a thriller

Brian Cuban

Post Hill
PRESS

A POST HILL PRESS BOOK

The Body Brokers
© 2024 by Brian Cuban
All Rights Reserved

ISBN: 979-8-88845-158-8
ISBN (eBook): 979-8-88845-159-5

Cover design by Cody Corcoran
Interior design and composition by Greg Johnson, Textbook Perfect

Post Hill Press
New York • Nashville
posthillpress.com

Published in the United States of America
1 2 3 4 5 6 7 8 9 10

To my late mother, Shirley Cuban,
who taught me the meaning of grit and resilience
as she faced cancer down on her own terms.

Chapter 1

*C*offin duty is a nightmare. I'm not claustrophobic, but standing for eight hours in an unventilated wooden box makes me feel like a vampire in training. This evening's anniversary date with Emily can't come fast enough. Ten minutes before my shift ends, the two-way glass allows a perfect view of a woman in her fifties concealing a half-ounce bottle of Chanel No. 5 perfume in her Birken handbag. I whisper into my walkie-talkie, "Code two, section five," and then inch open the door, creeping up behind her, handcuffs out.

"Ma'am, store security. I'd like a word."

She responds swinging her fist. It glances off my jaw, igniting painful shockwaves down my spine. I drop to one knee and sputter, "Shit," as she bolts out the exit.

As I push myself to my feet, humiliated and face throbbing, Senior Loss Prevention Manager Mark Mazansky says, "For Chrissake Feldman, why didn't you wait for backup?"

Massaging my neck, I say, "When will The Old Man mothball these antiquated two-way mirrors and install more video cameras? This is ridiculous."

Maz bristles. "For a lawyer, you're not too smart. I already explained. Real-time surveillance is proactive. We catch them in the act. Covert security cameras are reactive. They're out the door before we have a chance to do anything. The coffin ain't going nowhere."

As I turn and head for the exit, he says, "Keep it up, and you'll be back on the unemployment line."

The warning, while pure Maz bluster, conjures a past I'd prefer not to relive. Falsely accused of a three-decade-old murder. Indicted and jailed. The indignity of skipping bail to prove my innocence. A fugitive.

The back of my skull might as well have an ice pick embedded in it as I walk to my car, past the downtown courthouse where I tried auto accidents, slip-and-falls, dog bites, and whatever else walked through the door of my strip-mall office. The Pennsylvania Board of Disciplinary Procedure revoked that privilege for two years via suspension of my law license.

After a hearing, they decided my making false statements to the FBI merited punishment. I can't disagree, but waking up the day after with no family, clients, or purpose triggered a cocaine and Jack Daniels binge that would make *Scarface*'s Tony Montana proud. A new rock bottom. Then came detox, a month of rehab, and a reset of the sobriety clock. If there's any upside, it led to meeting Emily. We attended the same Alcoholics Anonymous meetings. However, we didn't get to know each other beyond the usual story sharing until a crew from the group, the two of us included, enjoyed a night out at the Dry Hump Mocktail Lounge in Lawrenceville.

Six months after that first night, we've progressed to talk of cohabitation and the L-word. Emily restored a long-dormant butterfly nest in my stomach. Excitement for each day reignited by anticipation of holding hands, Schenley Park picnics, and the bedroom.

As I drive to her place, thoughts of a quiet dinner celebrating our half-year anniversary, then late-night karaoke, soften the right-hook headache. I pull to the curb behind the chair Emily placed on the street to reserve me a parking spot. When she doesn't answer her doorbell, I text: *Out front, need aspirin.*

Continued silence after I knock on the locked door draws worry into the equation.

I sprint to the living room window and look through the curtain slit. Emily is on her back, motionless.

I bang on the front window, but she doesn't move.

"Emily!"

Her index finger twitches. I rush to my car and grab the tire jack. Then I smash the window glass.

"Emily!" Her right hand contracts into a claw, then goes limp.

The jagged opening is wide enough to maneuver my way inside. I kneel and run my hand along every inch of her scalp. I then press two fingers on her carotid artery, which offers no pulse. The room spins as I straddle her and perform CPR. Milky liquid seeps from the corner of her mouth, forming a half-dollar-sized puddle on the hardwood floor. I fumble with my phone, dialing 911.

"What is your emergency?"

My breaths are short and shallow. "I found my girlfriend unconscious."

"Try to stay calm, sir. What is your name and address? Help is on the way." What's the address? I rush to a stack of mail on the breakfast bar and snatch the top envelope. "Jason Feldman. I'm at 2020 Carson Street on the Southside."

"Has she ingested any drugs?"

"No. She's in recovery and wouldn't use an illegal substance."

"What's her name?"

"Emily Wilson."

"If she's not already, please turn Emily on her back."

"She is. Please help her."

"Try to calm down. The ambulance should be there any minute. Have you checked her vitals?"

"Yes, and I performed CPR. It didn't work."

Time seems to stand still as I wait for help. I'm about to try CPR again when sirens screech into earshot, then snap off in front of Emily's condo. An EMT enters, kneels beside her and says, "Possible overdose." He reaches into his bag and takes out a device resembling an oxygen mask. Emily had shown me one and said it was for clearing the airway to resuscitate an overdose victim. He sets it on her face and blows into an air valve. Emily's chest expands and contracts. Maybe she's going to be okay?

"Is she breathing?"

He ignores me and continues forcing air into her lungs. Then he inserts the plastic tip of Narcan nasal spray up her left nostril, then her right. After shining a flashlight pen into each eye, he takes her pulse for endless seconds. He repeats the procedure with a new spray container. After checking her vitals again, he says, "She's gone."

"She's not!" My voice cracks as I scream, churning my head from side to side in denial.

He takes a white sheet out of his backpack and covers Emily with it. "I'm sorry for your loss."

His condolence pounds my chest like a sledgehammer. Last month was Emily's one-year sobriety anniversary. She had struggled with heroin addiction, then fentanyl. Binge drinking was also a problem. But with the help of Suboxone and our AA group, she eventually got clean.

A rap on the wood door spins our heads to Emily's housemate, Delaney, standing in the foyer. Her gaze shifts from the EMT to me. "Jason, what's...? What's going on here? Where's Emmi?"

I move to block her view as if to forestall the inevitable.

"My god, what happened?"

Before the response makes it past my lips, the paramedic blurts in a monotone of someone who routinely delivers bad news, "She's deceased. An overdose."

Delaney pushes past me and kneels next to Emily. Like the paramedic, she checks her vitals. She then glances at the empty Narcan containers and says, "It didn't work?"

"I'm sorry, no. I tried twice."

Delaney's chin drops, and her eyes close. She runs her hand across Emily's forehead and stands. After two steps toward me, her legs buckle.

I guide her to the couch, supporting her body weight as she crumples onto the cushion and draws her knees to her chest. Her sobs echo through the room.

"When was the last time you saw her?" the paramedic asks.

Delaney struggles to compose herself between breathy gasps. "When she left for work yesterday morning."

The EMT's eyes narrow. "We've met before. Where do you work?"

"I'm a physician on the ER staff at University Medical Center."

A Pittsburgh police officer enters and surveys the scene. He then stands over the body and rubs his unshaven face. "This is the third one tonight. I'm Officer Sunseri. Who lives here?"

I point to Delaney. She's motionless, with her head down, eyes closed, and hands folded, as if in deep meditation.

Sunseri taps onto a black iPad, and then jabs his stylus at me. "Who are you?"

"Jason Feldman."

"Do you live here?"

"No, I'm a friend of Emily's. Well, we were dating."

"Is she the deceased?"

The articulated word is surreal, like it's happening on a Netflix crime show, and I'm an actor. "Yes, I found her this way."

Sunseri bends over Emily's body and taps his tablet again. "When did you last see her alive?"

I fight through brain fog for a memory that is less than twelve hours old. "She stayed at my place last night and left early this morning. This doesn't make sense. Emily was zealous about her sobriety."

Sunseri kneels on the floor and examines Emily's fingers. "Fentanyl is in everything now, even cocaine."

I flash to my last relapse, and a shiver runs down my spine. It's a whole new ball game from my struggle with addiction when the biggest worry was a cut of speed or baby laxative contaminating my blow.

Sunseri swings the sheet off Emily's pale corpse like a bullfighter waving his cape. I was too caught up in trying to save her to notice, but she's wearing the same outfit as on our first date: a white button-down blouse and jeans. Her brown hair is cut to just above the shoulders. This morning it was longer. She told me she was having it done today. I swallow back tears and fight the urge to shake her by the shoulders as if she's napping.

Sunseri motions to the paramedic. "Any thoughts on the time of death?"

The EMT clears his throat and says, "Her body is still warm, and there's no sign of rigor or blood pooling. The medical examiner will make the official determination, but we could be talking less than thirty minutes."

I think back to the twitch. "I saw her right index finger move before I smashed the window glass."

As if he feels my guilt, The paramedic nods and says, "It doesn't mean she was alive. The post-mortem chemical release from the body can cause that."

But what if she was? I could have driven faster or called during the day. Emily was her usual cheery self when she left my house this morning. What could have happened in the interim that would have taken her down this dark road? No one knows better than me how fast life can turn on a dime from sobriety to relapse, but there are often signs. Did I miss them? Emily's right eye, half shut, stares back at me, passing judgment.

Sunseri presses on a bulge in Emily's front right pocket, then turns to the EMT. "Do you have any extra nitriles? Mine are in the car."

The paramedic tosses him the gloves. After putting them on, Sunseri reaches inside. When his hand withdraws, his fingers are pinching a Ziploc baggie filled with a white substance, along with round, blue pills stamped with the letter "M" on one side and the number "30" on the other. I close my eyes and process the sickening visual. I've transported enough cocaine in baggies to know that the white powder isn't Sweet'N Low.

He breaks the seal with his pen and inserts a thin black tube resembling a straw with an angled, shovel-like tip on one end. He maneuvers it until a raisin-sized mound of white powder collects in the scoop. Delaney raises her head and watches intently.

"What are you doing?" I ask.

"A presumptive field test." Sunseri inches the instrument out. He then upends the substance into a transparent plastic pouch the size of a credit card. "The reagent will change color if this is fentanyl."

He runs his thumb and forefinger across the top, sealing the bag. He jiggles it, and the liquid inside changes color from clear to orange.

"This is fenty—" The test kit falls to the floor as Sunseri clutches his chest, wheezing. "I can't feel my arms. My heart is racing. It's fentanyl, airborne. Evacuate the premises."

Sunseri's eyes roll to the back of his sockets. He drops to his knees and flops forward. His forehead smacks the floor with a dull thud. I backtrack three hurried steps toward the front door.

Delaney rises from the couch and crouches alongside him as the paramedic checks his vitals; then, as he did with Emily, administers Narcan.

"Shouldn't we leave?" I say, terrified by the specter of suffering the same fate.

Delaney is impassive to the detective's predicament. "No need to panic. He fainted."

The EMT shines his flashlight pen into Sunseri's right eye, then the left. "Pupils are normal and reactive."

"Fentanyl is *not* airborne," Delaney says. "In all likelihood, the officer experienced a panic attack and passed out. Give him a minute, and he'll be fine, besides a possible concussion. He should be evaluated for that."

My back is against the front door in case I have to escape before breathing the dust of death. "Are you sure? I've read stories about a granule of this stuff having the ability to kill tens of thousands."

"Yes, I'm sure. None of us are in any danger."

"My head." The exclamation coupled with a groan signals Sunseri's return to consciousness. He pushes himself into a sitting position and rubs his forehead, squinting around the room.

"Did I overdose?"

The EMT checks his pulse and says, "Take it slow." He then presses the bulge on Sunseri's forehead. "Your head bounced off the floor like a tennis ball. We'll run you to the hospital for a once-over."

"I'm okay." Sunseri leans backward, his palms on the carpet, supporting his weight. "Help me to my feet." The EMT bends over and hoists him upright.

Sunseri presses on the growing bluish bruise and winces. "You saved my life. Thank you."

Delaney expels a snort as if she told herself a joke.

Sunseri stands and executes an unsteady pivot in her direction and then bends forward, both hands flat on the dining room table. "Do you find this funny? We all could have died."

"This is tragic for me and all who knew and loved Emmi, but you passed out. It's a scientific impossibility to overdose from passive fentanyl exposure."

Please let it go, I beg silently. Emily told me Delaney is a doctor, but I'm skeptical of her opinion on this. It seems like every other day, I read a story about a cop going to the hospital because of fentanyl exposure. I want to run out the door, but my feet are anchored to the floor. If Delaney is right, I don't want her to think I believe Sunseri over her.

"Missy, I've been on the force since you were an itch in your daddy's pants. Leave these things to experienced professionals. The baggie contains enough fentanyl to wipe out the entire city." His tone is sarcastically smug, as if no one could possibly know more than he does.

"Please address me as Dr. Martin," Delaney says. "I'm an emergency room physician. I also teach toxicology at Pitt Medical School. You were hyperventilating. Opioids suppress breathing."

She now sounds more credible than Sunseri. I allow myself normal breaths, less concerned about breathing in the powder.

Sunseri eyes her up and down. "You're a doctor?"

"I understand the skepticism. You're more likely to believe that a Black person around drugs deals them or robs to get them."

His pale cheeks morph to blood red. "I didn't mean—"

Delaney's arm pistons forward like a crossing guard. "Please, don't. Of course, you did."

Sunseri gestures to the paramedic. "Tell these two how dangerous fentanyl is. If not for the Narcan, I'd be a corpse."

The EMT picks at a piece of lint on his uniform and readjusts Emily's limp arms across her chest in a mummy position. "It's standard procedure to administer Narcan. I'm not a doctor, but you might have experienced a panic attack."

Sunseri, his face flushed, belches an annoyed grunt and swats at the air as if dispatching a fly. "I know what happened." He then shuffles to a chair and slowly lowers himself.

"Are you sure you're okay?" I ask. "You slammed the floor hard."

"Never mind. Plant yourself on the couch."

Grateful to be off my feet, I comply, doing my best to suppress tears as Delaney's muted sobs float through the room, interspersed with the low hum of the air conditioner. This isn't a movie. I'm not dreaming. Emily is dead.

Sunseri points at Delaney. "What was your relationship with the deceased? Were you aware she was a junkie?"

What is this guy's problem? I get that he's embarrassed over his face-plant, but a little empathy and professionalism would be nice. He wouldn't speak that way if it were his girlfriend, wife, or child.

Delaney goes rigid and scowls. "Please don't dehumanize her. Emmi was a person like you."

"Not me, honey."

Delaney flashes Sunseri a death stare while I wonder if he was born a misogynist prick or had to work at it.

A knock on the half-open door interrupts the caustic interrogation. I double take, and my heart dances an arrhythmic rumba. It's a person I hoped to never see again—Detective Jeanette Keane. Her once shoulder-length blond hair is now a pixie cut, but the brown plaid blazer is the same one she wore when arresting me two years ago. She walks toward Emily's body and bends over it. Maybe she doesn't recognize me? I'm sure as hell not saying a word to jog her memory. Then she looks back over her shoulder, and I know she does.

"Jason Feldman, what a surprise."

Sunseri jerks his thumb at me. "Is this guy a friend of yours?"

"We have history. What happened to you? Your forehead is black and blue with a bump the size of a golf ball."

He points at Emily and says, "She had a fentanyl baggie. I may have inhaled a whiff."

Keane picks up an empty Narcan spray bottle off the floor. She squeezes the plastic, and the nozzle hisses air. "This city goes through a truckload of these a week."

I back away from Keane as she snaps on a pair of nitriles and picks up the baggie. Unlike Sunseri, she doesn't appear concerned about our proximity to the fentanyl powder. Delaney must be right. He fainted.

She extracts a pill and rolls it between her fingers. "These are almost certainly counterfeit." She then drops the baggie in an evidence bag and seals it. "If these had made it to the street, a lot of people might have died."

Is Keane insinuating that Emily was dealing? Impossible. I rise from the couch, shaking my head so hard that the room spins. "Emily was not a drug dealer."

"Calm down. I didn't say she was." Keane motions to the couch. I draw a deep breath, release it, and then retake my seat.

"This is a waste of our time," Sunseri says. "Just another OD."

"How dare you?" Delaney jumps to her feet. "She was my best friend."

Emily said they were close but rarely talked about Delaney. Until today, I didn't know she taught at Pitt. Emily and I were doing great in our little world. She didn't seem eager to tell me more. Why rock the boat?

Keane raises her hand. "Let's backtrack. What's your name?"

"Delaney Martin. Emmi and I are roommates." She tears up again. "Were."

Keane jots in her spiral notebook. "Did you see or talk to her today?"

"No. The last time was when she went to work yesterday morning. I left not long after her for a double shift at the hospital."

That confirms that Emily went home after she woke up yesterday, but I can barely remember the evening before. Has the trauma impacted my short-term memory? Even if I could recall everything we did, why would I check her pockets? I had no reason to suspect she was using again.

9

"Ms. Martin, where do you work?" Keane asks.

"As I told the other officer, I'm an ER doctor and toxicology professor at Pitt Medical School."

Keane's brows arch, but there's no hint of the supercilious disbelief Sunseri exhibited. I can tell she's impressed.

"That would make you well-versed on fentanyl, wouldn't it?"

"Yes. I treat overdoses every day in the ER. Emmi also knew the risks. I can't fathom..." Delaney's voice trails off, replaced by more quiet sobs.

Keane turns to me. "Did Emily appear out of sorts? Were you aware of problems at work, family, or a relationship?"

How do I answer that? Emily and I had disagreements and a few heated arguments, but all couples do. Things were the tensest when I questioned her reluctance to open up about her past. She only said that her parents died young. I didn't press because I understood not wanting to talk about painful events. I also didn't want to push her away.

"Emily and I were dating and doing fine. What's the relevance to what happened here?"

"Besides an accidental overdose, the possibility of suicide is something we must consider," Keane says.

I shoot Keane a *What the hell are you talking about* glare. "Emily was not suicidal."

"You might be right, but it's easy to miss the signs," Keane says. "Was she facing any unusual struggles?"

"Nothing I'm aware of. We had dinner plans. I was here to pick her up."

Keane continues taking notes. "What about you, Dr. Martin?"

Delaney ponders the question. Then she says, "Emmi didn't tell me anything, but my schedule has been hectic. There wasn't much time for chitchat."

"Where did she work?"

"Sunny Awakenings Addiction Treatment Center," I tell Keane. "She is—was—a marketing representative.

Keane nods. "The King of Clean, King Fox. He runs morning and late-night-television rehab commercials. I'll pay them a visit."

Good idea, I think. Someone at Sunny Awakenings had to have noticed something different in Emily's behavior. That's what they do. Help addicts who want to get sober.

Keane turns to Sunseri. "Did you find identification? I don't see a purse, backpack, or wallet lying around."

Sunseri rubs his forehead and says, "Only the baggie with pills and powder."

Keane walks toward the kitchen. "If you don't have any objection, I'll look around for anything that might hint at what happened."

Past dealings with her trigger my legal reflexes. "Don't you need a warrant unless Delaney consents?"

Before Keane can respond, the paramedic says, "I've got to get back on the street. It's a busy night." We all glance toward him. He's standing with his arms crossed, tapping his foot.

Sunseri stumbles toward the door as if he's about to hit the deck again. "I'm woozy. Drop me at the hospital."

"Take care of yourself," Keane tells him.

Sunseri grunts and leaves the condo with the paramedic as two individuals enter with a gurney. Both are wearing dark blue windbreaker jackets with "Medical Examiner" imprinted in yellow on the backs.

Delaney and I watch in silence as one unfolds a silver body bag. Her chest heaves while I bite my lower lip to keep from losing it in front of everyone. They roll Emily's body onto her side and slide it halfway under her. After repeating the process on her other side, they each take hold of the black grip straps and lift her onto the gurney.

"We'd like her mobile phone and laptop," Keane says. "The data may tell us who supplied the narcotics."

My mouth goes dry as images of intimate photos we shared run through my head.

"I'm uncomfortable with you traipsing through my private communications with Emily." I walk to the kitchen and pour myself a glass of water. "If the cell turns up, we'll reach out, but you'll need a warrant to go through it."

When I'm back on the couch, Keane drags a chair from the dining room table, the legs screeching against the floor like nails on a chalkboard. She turns it around, and then straddles the seat with her arms crossed over the backrest. "It's not your phone, counselor. You don't have standing to contest a search. Regardless, this is about more than one dead girl. If a batch of counterfeit opioids are in circulation, we could end up with a mass fatality situation."

She's spot-on about my lack of legal standing. A first-year law student would know how stupid I sounded with that half-ass legal opinion. I also don't want to look like an idiot in front of Delaney. Who knows what she's thinking about me.

"I have no idea where her devices are," Delaney says. "I'm traumatized, exhausted, and have difficult phone calls to make."

Keane frowns. "I'd like to search the condo and understand it's a brutal night for both of you. Crime Scene should be here soon. They will wrap this up as fast as possible."

I'd prefer that Delaney and I look around first, but like with Emily's phone, I'm unable to do anything but sit here with my mouth shut. Also, if I make a fuss again, they might think I'm hiding something.

"You have my permission," Delaney says.

"I appreciate the consent, but we still need a warrant for Emily's room."

"Why do you need one if I said it's okay? This is my home."

Keane nods in agreement. "That's correct, but as a tenant, Emily has an expectation of privacy in her bedroom. We, therefore, need judicial authorization to search that area. Neither of you have an idea where her cell phone is? I'd expect it to be nearby."

"I'm not sure," Delaney says. "She always carried it with her. I can go to her room and look."

"That won't be necessary. When the warrant arrives, Crime Scene will take care of it."

"What about you, Jason?" Keane says. "Any idea where it might be?"

"If it's not on her person, I don't have a clue. She texted me this afternoon, around two, so she had it then."

"What about?" Keane asks.

I open my texts to our last communication. "She was handing out free Narcan in Homestead and then going home early to change for our date."

"Do you mind?" Keane extends her hand, the fingertips almost touching mine.

The hell if she's snooping through my phone. I step backward. "I'd rather not give you carte blanche into my private moments. I'll mine the messages and screenshot anything relevant."

Keane shakes her head and scribbles. I have no doubt she's memorializing my reluctance to cooperate. I hope she also writes down that we've done this dance before, and it didn't go well for me.

"Don't you want to help?" Keane asks. "She was your girlfriend, after all."

"At the appropriate time, we can go through the texts together without breaching my right to privacy," I tell her. "It's not happening tonight."

"Have it your way." Keane unleashes an exaggerated sigh. "Did Emily keep Narcan here?"

Delaney points to the bedroom. "It's in her closet. She volunteered with a local harm- reduction organization, handing out free sprays as well as fentanyl test strips."

Keane again picks up an empty container left by the paramedic. "Did you administer it, Jason?"

"The EMT left those."

"You didn't know it was in her closet?"

I'm unsure how much time elapses before I manage, "I didn't, but keep a box in my glove compartment."

"You were first on the scene and didn't use it?"

Keane's statement bites like an accusation of wrongdoing. Why didn't I take the Narcan inside with me? All I had to do was open the glove compartment and remove it. A maneuver that takes seconds. Instead, my thoughts were about my pounding head.

"When I arrived, I had no idea she'd overdosed, so I didn't bring it from my car."

Delaney's glare bores a hole in the side of my head. I don't have to be a mind reader to decipher what she's thinking. I could have saved Emily.

The front screen door opens, and another uniformed officer steps inside, waving a piece of paper.

"I come bearing warrants," he says and hands it to Keane. "Are you ready for us to tear this place up?"

"What do you mean?" Delaney jumps to her feet. "This is antique furniture bequeathed by my grandma. You will treat me and my home with dignity and respect, or I'll be at the Office of Municipal Investigations filing a complaint at 9 a.m. tomorrow."

I'd have ripped the cop a new one as well, and I can already tell Delaney Martin is not the type to back down.

Keane glares at the blond-haired, blue-eyed crime scene officer who could have adorned a Hitler Youth propaganda photo in a past life. His shoulders slump, and he says, "Ma'am, I'm sorry. It was a joke in poor taste. If you take a seat, I'll explain the process."

Delaney doesn't budge, arms crossed. "I prefer to stand, thank you."

"As you wish. My name is Officer Franko with the Crime Scene Unit. We will search the premises and collect forensic evidence. Do you keep any weapons in the domicile?"

"I don't own one," Delaney says, jaw quivering. "I've seen too many gunshot wounds in children of this community. Children of color."

I glimpse the holstered 9mm automatic inside Keane's jacket. She once threatened to shoot me with it.

"What about Emily?" Keane asks.

"She hated guns," Delaney responds.

Keane nods and jots more notes. "Did she have friends besides you and Jason?"

Her question drives home an unsettling epiphany. I don't know who her friends were. There were the people in our AA group, but after we met that night out, we retreated to our dating bubble.

"My work schedule doesn't allow for much socializing," Delaney tells her. "I got the impression if not with Jason, she spent most of her time working or volunteering. She also attended out-of-state conferences as a rep for her company."

"Delaney is correct," I say. "I sometimes traveled with her. Emily handed out business cards, free pens, candy, and stuff."

"Excuse me. I'm using *my* restroom," Delaney says. Her overemphasis on the possessive doesn't escape my attention.

Keane shrugs. "It's your condo, but once the search begins, you both have to wait outside."

"I'm not leaving my home." Delaney puffs her chest and anchors her legs to the floor in a "V" stance, as if she's daring anyone to move her.

Keane's not budging either. "Dr. Martin, I empathize with the challenge of the situation, but you both must leave the condo until the search concludes. We now have a warrant and can remove or arrest you for obstruction of justice."

Keane's aggressive turn only intensifies Delaney's resolve. "I'm not going anywhere, and you're treating me like a criminal."

I pat her arm, but she swings it wide, hurling my hand off like polarized magnets. "Don't touch me. I want you all out of my home."

Keane must sense the confrontation spinning out of control. She backs away and says, "How about this? We'll start with the couch. When the officers are done, you both can sit and wait for us to finish."

"Okay." Delaney's body posture relaxes. "That is acceptable."

I breathe a sigh of relief. Keene was right, but if I took her side, Delaney might hate me. My gut tells me that earning her trust won't be easy.

Keane motions to the CSI officer. "Begin with the sofa."

Delaney and I are motionless and tight-lipped as they squeeze cushions and delve fingers into every crevice. After a hushed dialogue with the Hitler Youth cop, Keane announces, "You can both sit."

Another hour passes as we listen to Emily's drawers open and slam shut. An officer exits the room carrying her backpack. He whispers to Keane, and they move to the kitchen, out of earshot, continuing the discussion.

They finish their conversation, and Keane enters the living room. "We're finished. Her backpack contains keys, makeup, and two Narcan nasal sprays, but no cell phone or wallet."

Before Keane can get another word out, Delaney says. "Emily wasn't using. That Narcan wasn't for her."

Keane sets the backpack down. "It's not my intention to upset you, but how can you be sure?" She glances at her notebook. "You said, and I quote, *my schedule has been hectic. We had little time for chitchat.*"

I interject to diffuse the escalating tension. "Dr. Martin is correct. Emily always carried it with her in case she had to reverse an overdose. What about her phone? It has to be here."

"Have either of you tried calling her cell?" Keane asks. "If it's in this condo, we may hear the ringtone."

Delaney and I give each other a *Why didn't we think of that?* look. She takes her phone out of her handbag.

"Be sure to put it on speaker," Keane says.

We edge close to Delaney as she makes the call. It goes straight to voicemail.

"This is Emily Wilson with Sunny Awakenings Treatment Center. Please leave a message or call our toll-free number for assistance. If this is a medical emergency, call 911."

Emily never turned her phone off or forwarded calls straight to voicemail. Even in the bedroom, she left it on, worried that an addict in crisis would not be able to get a hold of her.

"Her phone was never out of her sight," I say. "It has to be here."

"She might have met her dealer here," Keane says. "Tried the product, overdosed. Her dealer then took the items to scrub the scene. It's happened before."

That's an insane theory. Emily used while I was on my way here? I can't fathom that possibility. But then again, I did cocaine in the courthouse bathroom stall with cops and judges walking in and out. It's how addiction works. Consequences become secondary to the dopamine fix.

"No," Delaney spits out. "I don't believe a word."

"I understand, but it's my job to consider all possibilities," Keane says with sympathetic softness. "Does Emily have family we can contact?"

"Her parents are deceased, and she has no siblings or children," Delaney says. "I'm her family." The weariness in her voice is palpable. "Can we pick this up tomorrow? My next shift begins in less than six hours."

I'm right there with her. My eyelids are heavy, and my ability to focus diminishes with each passing moment.

"We'll get out of your hair so you can sleep," Keane says.

"What happens next?" Delaney asks.

"The medical examiner will conduct an autopsy, and assuming toxicology confirms an overdose, we'll continue our investigation to figure out how she came into possession of the drugs. Hopefully, we'll then arrest her dealer."

I lean forward and rest both hands on the couch backrest. The déjà vu tugs so hard it resembles vertigo. The only woman in my life is dead, partly of my doing. Moments mattered, and I failed.

When Keane leaves, Delaney says, "Sunseri is a major asshole. The detective, not so much. How do you know her?"

I contemplate a range of responses amid a modicum of surprise at Delaney's ignorance of my backstory, given that Emily knew most of it.

"It's a long monologue for another time. Let's call a glass installer to fix the window."

As I'm giving a twenty-four-hour emergency service the address, Delaney's phone goes off.

"It's my father." She disappears into her bedroom and shuts the door. Snippets of dialogue over sobs penetrate the thin wood. "Daddy, it's awful, and I'm devastated. No, you don't need to come over. I'll be okay. Yes, I will. I love you too."

She exits the room and slumps onto the couch, head buried in her hands.

I sit beside her. "As much as it pains me, we should acknowledge the possibility that Emily relapsed."

Why did I say that? Of course she understands addiction.

"I'm not an idiot, and I don't deny that potential scenario," she tells me. "You know as well as I do Emmi was fanatical about harm-reduction safety. It's inconceivable that she would use alone or not utilize a test strip."

How can I be sure Emily practiced what she preached? There were times when she cried about someone in the recovery community dying from an overdose. They were advocating for the same drug safety principles she was. Why was Emily any more immune to relapse than they were?

"This makes no sense," I tell her. "Where could her phone be?"

Delaney stretches out and drapes her arm over her eyes. "I wish I knew. I'm exhausted and can't think."

She needs sleep. We both do. Most of all, we need answers.

Chapter 2

Delaney sleeps through the glass replacement. Once the two workers leave, I jiggle her shoulder. She rolls onto her back and opens her eyes.

"How long have I been asleep?"

"Over two hours." I draw back the window curtain, exposing clear, smudge-free glass. "You were lights out, and I didn't want to wake you."

"You should have." She jumps to her feet. "How much was the bill?"

I flick my hand in a dismissive wave. "Don't sweat it. We'll settle up later. I'm headed home to close my own eyes."

"I'm not staying here tonight," she says. "I'll book a hotel or stay with my dad."

"My house in Squirrel Hill has three bedrooms," I tell her. "The place is a bit untidy, but you're welcome to spend the night."

Part of me wishes I could yank the words back. Will she decide I'm a pervert, hitting on her amid unimaginable tragedy?

"I don't want to put you out. A hotel is fine."

The tensive undertone of her response carries vibes of me politely declining a party invitation from someone I secretly don't like. She'd rather not come to my place.

"You're not putting me out. I wouldn't want to stay here either. It's late, and I live ten minutes away."

She mutters something to herself and offers a feeble smile. "Thank you. I'd rather not go through the hotel hassle, and don't want to burden my father."

Delaney packs an overnight bag, and as we leave, I can't help but glance at the spot where Emily's life slipped through my fingers.

The moment Delaney is in the car, she edges herself toward the passenger door and clutches the handle as if she's getting ready to jump from an airplane. I'm not sure if it's the stress of tonight's tragedy or she's afraid of me for some reason, but it's best left alone for now.

We enter my home, and I flick on the lights. The thick plastic couch covering squeals and crinkles as Delaney sits.

"I've been meaning to remove the Jewish furniture covers."

"My dad has the same." She manages a weak giggle. "I nag him to let the furniture breathe. When I complain, he'll say, 'This is how your grandparents kept the furniture spic-and-span. If it was good enough for them, it's acceptable for us.'"

"I'll tell my pops you approve," I say, grateful for a moment of tension-relieving humor, however brief. "Follow me to your bedroom."

Delaney stands and looks around the living room as if she's reassuring herself that I'm not a mass murderer. She then glances at the front door. Nothing I say will convince her that this is a safe space. If she wants to go to a hotel, I'm happy to drive her.

"I don't think I'll fall back to sleep." She checks her watch. "On the bright side, I'm accustomed to running on fumes and caffeine in the hospital."

I point to the guest bedroom door. "This is yours. The bathroom is down the hall. Fresh towels are in the cabinet above the toilet."

"After a few hours' rest, I'll be out of your hair," she says.

I step across the bedroom threshold but catch myself and reverse, staying in the hallway. "Have I done something wrong? I can't shake the feeling that you're afraid of me. I'm not going to try anything, if that's what you're worried about."

Delaney sits on the bed. "That's not it."

Then what is it? Does she believe I gave Emily the drugs? As crazy as it sounds to me, I might wonder the same in her place.

"Is it something you want to talk about?"

"I'm tired and need a quiet space to process, that's all."

If she believes I'm involved, nothing said a few hours after Emily's death is going to change her mind. Sparring over it tonight is pointless.

"Try to sleep," I say. "We have a long and emotional day ahead."

I go to my room and sit on the edge of the bed. Who can I share my grief with? There's no one. I've never felt so alone.

Chapter 3

"Alexa, what time is it?"

"The current time is 4:30 a.m."

There's no point in trying to sleep with the nonstop parade of thoughts in my head. Multiple cups of coffee will help sustain me through the morning, but I haven't eaten since breakfast yesterday, having skipped lunch. The closest place is open all night and only a ten-minute walk. However, it's also a mirror of my past. The Squirrel, a onetime hangout.

I throw on my coffee-stained Pitt Law sweatpants and a frayed Billy Joel concert T-shirt and then head out into the humid, dark morning. Each step through streetlight-illuminated haze feels like pushing against gravity. The mechanical squeak and hum of a sanitation truck raising a steel dumpster bin reminds me it's trash day. I wrinkle my nose at the pungent odor of rotting fruit and french-fry grease.

Emily. What happened? You could have come to me if the compulsion to use was overpowering.

As I step off the curb, the blast of a car horn shatters the early-morning quiet and staggers me back to the sidewalk. A cab blows by within inches of kneecapping me. The driver pops his head out the window and shouts, "Do your sleeping at home."

Sleepwalking is more like it, unable to make sense of what's happened.

I'm a few feet from The Squirrel's entrance when a black Lexus rolls up to the curb. The window lowers, revealing a guy with what appears to be a crew cut, though the morning darkness makes it difficult to be sure.

"How's the chow there?" he asks.

"It's been a neighborhood fixture for decades," I tell him.

"I didn't ask how long. What do they serve?"

The abruptness of his retort is off-putting, and I'm in no mood for it. I shoot back,

"Food."

Cindy, who has waitressed here since my law school days, circles from behind the counter in her white T-shirt emblazoned with a rodent eating a french fry above the tagline "Go Nuts at The Squirrel."

She bear-hugs me and says, "Look what the cat dragged in. I thought you might have died or something."

"I thought it best to stay away with everything that happened."

She puts her lips to my ear and whispers, "Communities heal, and forgiveness is a blessing. Come sit at the counter."

The knowing glares from the few customers unsettle me. Each set of eyes is an accusation and reminder that the past is immutable.

Cindy hands me a menu and says, "Can I start you with coffee? The circles around your eyes would make a two-hundred-year-old redwood blush."

"Sure. I'll also have a lox and bagel for me and some scrambled eggs to go." I tap the rigid plastic and do my best to ignore the stares. "Your customers are eyeball-gutting me. I'll take my food to go as well."

She squints over my shoulder. "Hon, it's your imagination. Herb is at table three. He's the salt of the earth and a foreman at the Edgar Thomson Works. The bald gentleman reading the newspaper by the window is Phil. He's been a regular for decades. I'm surprised you don't recognize him. His wife is battling breast cancer. We took up a collection. The jar is at the end of the bar if you want to contribute."

"That's tragic," I walk to the jar and drop in ten dollars.

I'm almost finished eating when a sharp bang vibrates the window, reverberating through the diner.

Cindy rushes from behind the counter and shouts, "What in the world happened?"

We hurry outside, where a massive blue garbage dumpster is on its side, blocking the sidewalk. A city employee is screaming at his driver about not securing his load, allowing it to come loose and plummet to the street.

As I watch the argument, a vehicle maneuvers around the trash receptacle and rolls to the curb about fifteen yards from me. It might be the dickhead driving the Lexus, but with only a hint of the rising sun, I'm not positive.

I rush back inside to get Delaney's order and pay.

Outside, a digital bank clock across the street reads 6 a.m. and eighty degrees. A reminder that I haven't slept in almost twenty-four hours, and it's going to be a sweltering, dog-ass day. A few more degrees of daylight illumination confirm that the car is a black Lexus, but the driver is gone. The sidewalks on both sides of the street are also deserted. I've had more than enough experience with being followed to trust my gut, which is screaming that until today, the number of times a random person in a car asked me for a restaurant recommendation is zero. The axiom that there's a first time for everything is also overrated. I use my phone to snap the license plate.

Back in the house, I put Delaney's eggs in the fridge. There's no point in waking her. She's earned as much sleep as possible. After changing, I power up the big screen. The first commercial tears at my heart as if the television gods are looking down.

A teenage girl in ragged jeans and a gray sweatshirt is navigating a dark hallway, her hands outstretched. She reaches a door and pushes it open to a blast of sunlight over a plush green field, where an adult woman, young boy, and golden retriever await. The dog barks, raising a paw. A calming female narration follows. Her voice reminds me of my mother telling me everything would be okay when I woke up screaming after a nightmare.

"Are you or a loved one struggling with opioid addiction? Do you feel lost in the dark, struggling to find your way? We offer a new beginning, as we have for thousands of people, with a 90 percent success rate. Call now at 1-800-4ASUNNY to schedule a free, no-obligation assessment. Phones answered twenty-four hours a day. It's time for your Sunny Awakening."

"Have you slept at all?" Delaney stands in the hallway, the overnight bag slung over her shoulder.

"You startled me. Are you leaving?"

"I didn't mean to. The television is on, so I figured you were up and about. My shift starts in a few hours."

Should I tell her about the Lexus? If she believes I played a role in Emily's overdose, she may see it as me creating more drama to deflect blame.

"Sleep was a hopeless endeavor. I went out for food and brought back eggs for you."

"That's kind, but I'm not hungry. I need to go home and change for work."

It's more like you want out of here as fast as possible. She's more stand-offish than last night, and I need to thaw some of the ice. I want her to believe me.

"Please stay a few minutes. I'll make coffee. If I were in your place, I'd be thinking what you are."

"And what is that, Jason?"

"You're not positive but still considering the possibility that I provided the fentanyl. For the record, I'd never even seen that particular drug prior to yesterday."

She opens the front door, then turns to face me. "We're strangers. I shouldn't have come here."

"Why did you?"

"I was confused and traumatized. Also, Emily had only said positive things about you."

That means Emily never told her about my legal problems. Regardless, we'll never develop any level of trust without discussing my past.

"Please stay for one cup of coffee so we can have an actual conversation."

She sighs and drops her overnight bag on the floor. "I guess that's not a terrible idea."

I head to the kitchen and slap a dark roast K-Cup into the machine. "Can't you call in for a day off?"

"We're short-staffed in the ER. I've been working a lot of double shifts. To top it off, I teach my toxicology course this evening."

"A busy schedule," I say, and set the coffee mug in front of her.

"The life of an ER doctor." She stares into the caffeinated darkness while tracing her finger along the ceramic edge.

What is going through her head? That she's across the table from the man who killed her best friend? The longer the elephant stays in this room, the worse things will get.

"Would you like me to take you home and walk the condo before you go in?" I ask.

"That's unnecessary," she says, and seems to relax a little. "Please check when we can claim Emmi and arrange for her service and burial. We can use the preacher at my father's church."

While she knew I was Jewish, Emily and I never discussed her religious affiliation or theological beliefs, though I suspected she leaned toward humanistic. She often repeated, "Help others, and whatever happens in the end should be a positive."

"Where does he attend?"

Delaney places her cup in the sink. "The AME Zion in the Hill District. I need to go home."

"I'm happy to drive you."

"That's unnecessary. I'll order a rideshare."

Her response is quick and pointed as if she had it keyed up. She fumbles inside her overnight and removes her phone. Her lips part, and I think she's about to speak, but nothing comes out.

"Is there something you want to say?" I ask.

"I googled you a bit."

There's nothing accusatory or judgmental in her tone, not that it matters. The onslaught of hatred has hardened me over the last two years.

"Emily never gave you the *Reader's Digest* version on my past? I assumed, being housemates, you knew everything."

"She said you were in recovery like her but very little about your history."

I'm relieved Emily didn't speak out of school about me. That's another thing I loved about her. She respected boundaries.

"Emily was aware of my legal troubles from the start. We attended the same AA home group, where I often shared details."

"Is it what the detective referenced?"

"Yes, Keane was the lead investigator."

Delaney's phone pings. "The car is here."

This was a start, but fifteen rushed minutes in the kitchen wasn't nearly enough to dismantle the wall of suspicion around me.

"Can we talk later today?" I ask. "I'd like to explain. Despite the salacious headlines, I'm not a monster."

"It's almost impossible to steal a free moment in the ER, but if a lull happens, I'll text you."

I follow Delaney to the Uber where she inspects the license plate and says, "Who are you here for?"

The driver recites her name, and she gets in. Before closing the door, she says, "There's a lot about you I didn't know. It doesn't make you a bad person, but I need more time to digest the last twelve hours."

The car drives away while I wonder how the hell I'll make it through the workday. Delaney's spunk in that regard is impressive. It might be how she copes. I'll try to do the same.

Chapter 4

*B*ack in the day, it wasn't unusual for me to arrive at work after being out all night and reeking of alcohol. This morning doesn't feel different as I fight through a sleep-deprivation hangover. Despite a scalding shower, I can't shake the lingering odor of chlorine given off by the paramedic's nitrile gloves.

After changing into a fresh pair of jeans and a blue sports jacket, I slide my handcuffs in my back pocket—the standard issue of Waggaman's Department Store loss-prevention personnel.

Emily-memory snippets consume the twenty-minute drive downtown. Our first public karaoke attempt was an off-key rendition of "Dancing Queen." I missed every high note. Emily, who'd been in high school choir, stayed on pitch while I croaked and rasped. When it was over, we laughed about how far we'd come in recovery, being able to risk embarrassment sober.

I'm jerked back to the road by a text alert from Maz:

Where the hell are you? People are stealing.

He's been on my ass since I landed the job as senior store detective.

When I interviewed for the position, Old Man Waggaman said, "Son, somewhere in this hallowed and historic department store, someone is planning or executing a theft of our merchandise. It's your job to ensure they don't get away with it."

At the time it sounded fantastic. After losing my law license and being internet-canceled, I was thrilled to have work, even if it didn't involve arguing to juries.

We average between five to six shoplifting detentions a week. Someone walks into the store with an old Waggaman's bag and stuffs in

26

a six-pack of men's briefs or dress socks. Thieves tend to focus on items without the RF 8.2 Mhz sensors that set off the front door alarms if not removed at checkout. Once they're out of the store, we have a no-chase policy, but inside, anything goes. Two weeks ago, Maz handcuffed a perp to a mannequin while he chased his accomplice all over the store.

Unexpected pangs of nostalgia grab at me as I walk through the Waggaman's lobby. With my license reinstatement on the horizon, it's almost time to move on. My stint arresting underwear, perfume, and purse thieves hasn't always been awful. His continual harangues aside, I also have measured respect for Maz, a beer-bellied, retired cop. Decades ago, he was a Pittsburgh Golden Gloves light heavyweight champion and ranked contender. He regales anyone who will listen with boxing war stories and reminds me at least once a week of his 25-0 record, twenty-four of them knockouts.

When I asked why he stopped, he said, "My last fight, the kid hit me so hard, for the next three days, I thought I was in Jersey."

I'm walking into the restroom when there's a familiar bellow from the escalator. "Grab her, Feldman!"

A woman sprints toward the exit, a young girl draped over her right shoulder as if she's rescuing a wounded war buddy in the middle of a combat firefight. In her left hand is a bulging suit bag, undoubtedly stuffed with merchandise she didn't pay for.

She barrels past me, wild-eyed and desperate, as the child wails, "Put me down, Mommy."

As her right hand touches the revolving door, I crane my neck around toward an out-of-breath Maz winding up like a major league pitcher and heaving his two-way radio in her direction.

The fast-moving blur is off course, rocketing straight for Irina, a Ukrainian import who's working the perfume counter. She started here two months after I did. With her impressive knowledge of clothing fashion, fragrances, and cosmetics, she's been an asset behind the counter. Now, she shrieks and covers her face as I flail my hand to stop the projectile's forward progress. It passes inches from my fingertips, wipes out a silver tray of testers, and then ricochets on a collision course with a street-facing display window. The glass shatters with a sharp crack, like the sound of a gun discharging, decapitating a female mannequin dressed in a summer-sale two-piece swimsuit.

Screams from the sidewalk echo through the lobby.

"What the fuck!"

"Was someone shot?"

"Why didn't you trip her? They got away."

I recognize the last voice, turning to face a heaving Maz, hands on his knees.

"Got away? You almost took my head off with that stunt."

Maz steps over broken glass, kicking the scattered plastic and metal fragments of his two-way radio. "You'll back me up on this, right? We need to line up our stories."

I tuck the mannequin head under my arm. "You want me to lie to the boss so he doesn't fire your ass."

"What happened here?" I didn't notice Old Man Waggaman coming up behind us.

I flick my head toward Maz. "Ask him."

He crosses his arms, glaring. "Well?"

"It's like this, Boss. I was chasing a shoplifter, slipped on spilled perfume, and lost my balance. As I fell forward, my two-way radio went airborne, shattering the display window. It was an accident."

Waggaman turns to me as the crowd disperses. "Do you have anything to add?"

I dart my eyes from Maz to Irina, who is on her knees picking up the shards of a shattered Lancôme testing bottle. "It's like he said."

"Did you witness this, young lady?"

Irina's hands tremble as she guides a small broom over the floor, pushing the remaining glass remnants into a dustpan. "No. I was assisting a customer."

Waggaman snatches the severed head from me. "Maz, I want to see you in my office. Feldman, help Irina take care of this mess."

With everything else going on, now I'm a janitor. My bar reinstatement can't come soon enough.

I gather rags from behind the perfume counter and join Irina soaking up puddles. For the rest of the day, I'll reek of rose blossoms.

"Please leave me out of this," she says. "I didn't see anything."

I flash her a reassuring smile. "Don't worry about Maz. I'll make sure he doesn't bother you."

She squeezes my arm. "You've been a good friend since I started here. Maz makes me nervous. He asks who I date and for photos."

The pictures she's referring to are on her 200,000-follower Instagram account. When Maz found out she had one, he hounded me to show him some of the more revealing shots. I said, "Dude, I'm not your voyeur pimp."

We finish our clean-up and I begin patrolling the store. The daily tedium leaves a lot of time for daydreaming. Today will consist of nothing but reliving attempts to revive Emily. If it really was a relapse, how did I miss the signs? I'm on my fifth rotation through men's suits when my two-way radio crackles. "A PPD detective is here. What's it about?"

It has to be Keane. "Have her meet me in the suspect pit."

I open the door of the room where we question shoplifters. It doubles as the corporate break room with a mini-fridge and coffee maker. There's also a portable video camera and tripod to record the interrogations.

Maz and Keane are drinking coffee and engaged in an animated conversation when I walk in.

"Remember the skell we chased on foot across the Fort Duquesne Bridge?" Maz says.

Keane pounds the table. "I never laughed so hard. He jumped over the railing and fell into the middle of a nudist cruise."

"Phew." Maz pinches his nose. "A bunch of naked pervs copulating on a nasty Pittsburgh River with mosquitoes, fireflies, and stinking of catfish. It was fifteen years ago, and I still gag thinking about it."

"You two obviously have history," I say, interrupting their crude banter.

"Glad you could join us," Keane says. "Eons ago, Maz and I were partners on the force. I was a baby junior detective, and he was my training senior."

How is it Maz and I have worked together for two years, and he never brought up that detail? I'm surprised they weren't telling jokes about my past. I don't think Keane would pour salt in the wound, but Maz wouldn't pass up an opportunity to talk shit.

"Jeanette filled me in on what happened last night," Maz says. "I'm sorry. Try not to take too long. Remember, people are stealing."

After he exits, Keane shuts the door and says, "He can be a real asshole sometimes." She flicks open her notebook with a backward wrist snap. "I've been unable to reach Dr. Martin, but I have some follow-up questions."

Answering her questions didn't bode well for me two years ago, but if she's going to make an arrest for Emily's death, I have to cooperate, but only up to a point.

"Is there anything you can think of that might help us determine where the fentanyl came from?" Keane asks. "For instance, was she hanging out with unfamiliar people?"

I shake my head. "To my knowledge, she was either with me, at work, or home. Nothing out of the ordinary."

Keane gets up and pours a refill. "Outside of that, have you noticed anything unusual in your life? Something that doesn't jibe with your daily routine?"

This is a good time as any to bring up crew cut man. "Something did happen early this morning. I couldn't sleep and walked to The Squirrel about five o'clock."

"Go on."

"A guy in a black Lexus stopped me and asked about the food. His car was still there when I left, but he was gone."

She snaps her notebook shut. "You think he's tailing you? Sounds more like someone had the early morning munchies like you and wanted a recommendation."

Keane may be right, but she also knows I'm no stranger to being followed. Two years ago, she was on my tail, along with bad guys, news-hounds, and crime bloggers. Being accused of murder will tend to do that. My instincts are better honed than the average citizen.

"Any chance you could run the license plate and tell me who owns the car?" I take out my cell and show her the photo.

Keane studies it for a few seconds. "Why would I do that for you?" She pushes the phone back across the table. "Are you under the mistaken impression we're pals?"

The air hangs heavy with her incredulity, along with my embarrassment and regret. "I thought—"

"That because you beat the rap on one of my cases we're BFFs? You're someone I arrested, Jason. One of many in my career. Tragic circumstances have brought us together again. That's not a friendship. It's my job."

The sting of her rejection and chiding morphs into a somber self-realization. She'd arrest me in a microsecond if there were evidence I supplied Emily with the fentanyl.

"You're absolutely right, Detective. My only ask is that you figure out what happened to Emily. *That's* your job."

"On that topic, let's revisit the missing electronics," she says. "Since you've had time to reflect, any thoughts on their whereabouts?"

I know what Keane's up to—repeating the same question, looking for differences in the response. It's how they catch people in lies. I'm still a person of interest, and she thinks I may have the items.

"Like I told you yesterday, Emily texted me earlier in the day, so she had her phone at that time. I have no idea what happened to her laptop and have to get back to work."

Keane stands. "They will turn up sooner or later, but before I leave, let's clear the air. You obstructed a homicide investigation with lies and misdirection. Is history going to repeat itself?"

Her dredging up old business pisses me off. "You're conflating different situations. One has nothing to do with the other."

"Be that as it may, if you find her laptop or phone, I expect a call."

Does she think I'd conceal that from her? Keane enters the elevator while I seethe at her insinuation that I'd obstruct the investigation into Emily's death.

The trudge to the coffin for my shift feels like the last walk to the electric chair.

It's cramped and hot. All Maz would have to do is hire extra staff to monitor real-time cameras around the store, and we could dismantle those relics. Sure, it would require an expenditure to upgrade, but in the long run, it would help the bottom line. My guess is that Maz views high-tech as a threat to his job.

As I wipe down the mirror, Delaney texts: *Some time freed up. Can you meet?*

I text back: *Under the Kaufmann's clock in twenty?*
See you then.

I scan the immediate area for Maz and bolt outside.

Chapter 5

I'm halfway to the rendezvous spot when my phone rings, followed by a text from Maz: *Did you leave the building during your coffin shift?* I text back: *Taking afternoon for personal matter.*

He'll throw a fit when I return, but also knows that I can tell The Old Man what really happened to the display window. It would be a firing offense.

I hustle to the old Kaufmann's Department Store and arrive a few minutes early. The remaining remnant of the iconic retailer at Fifth and Smithfield Streets is an ornate bronze timekeeper dating back to the early 1900s. Over the years, that clock was a once-a-month Friday meeting spot for me and my ex-wife, Sonya, when she was the Allegheny County District Attorney. We'd then have dinner and spend the night across the street at the William Penn Hotel. With her hectic schedule and long hours, we stole moments in lieu of longer vacations. We'd get a room as close to the top floor as possible and put out the Do Not Disturb sign. For two days, we existed on champagne, strawberries, and charcuterie boards. I haven't been able to walk into that hotel since she left me. I may never stay there again.

A light tap on my shoulder interrupts my reminiscence. Delaney is in her scrubs, the chest piece of her stethoscope hanging from the right pocket. The corners of her lips curl into a shallow smile. For the first time, I take note of her features. The blemish-free skin and rectangular facial structure are a cross between Halle Berry and Rosario Dawson.

"Sorry I'm late," she says. "Things got crazy after I texted. Where should we go?"

"Hemingway's Boat. It's close to here. A bookstore and café."

During the ten-minute walk, we pass a couple kissing. They lock arms and turn into a jewelry store known for engagement rings. Would Emily and I have tied the knot? After we made love two nights ago, she straddled me, the tips of her wavy brown hair tickling my chest, and said, "I'm not positive, still mulling it, but I might love you."

When I opened my mouth to respond, she leaned closer, touched a finger to my lips, and said sternly but affectionately, "Don't you dare say it back because you think it's what I want to hear. I prefer honesty over placation."

She was right. I was about to go full Pavlov's dog and repeat the words, unready on either a mental or emotional level. Instead, I pecked her lips. "There's a freight train's worth of baggage in my life."

Emily lay on me, chest to chest, her pelvis in a circular grind over my dick. "Your past was on blast, and I stayed. Unless you're married, it won't change how I feel."

The M-word got me thinking. She knew I was divorced and had a grown son but never once asked about my marriage to Sonya. It's possible she thought that six months was too soon to address such things. I don't know who she dated before me.

"Didn't we pass the place?"

Delaney's warning reminds me I need to focus on why we're here, or at least on my agenda—a frank conversation on neutral ground.

The front door is propped open with a chair, allowing dark roast aroma to greet us before entering. A sign tacked to the wall reads, "Air conditioning on the fritz. Apologies for the inconvenience."

Despite the stifling interior, a patron occupies every chair in the café area.

"Do you want to go somewhere else?" I ask.

"We're here, and I don't have much time," she says. "Look, a table opened up." She hurries to the spot, pushing past a guy holding a large Styrofoam coffee cup.

"Hey honey, I was here first," he says, maneuvering to cut her off and yanking the chair out of her grip.

I roll my eyes to the familiar, fake-tanned face with black, slicked-back hair. His sharkskin sports coat is so shiny I could use it as a mirror to brush my teeth. The outbreast pocket reveals orange fabric edges and a protruding lump of handkerchief. It's Colin Langdon, a fixture at the courthouse.

I tap the glass counter, eyeing the encounter, while the barista prepares our order.

"Excuse me?" Delaney says. "I'm not your honey, and this is my table."

"Are you inviting me to sit? Don't mind if I do."

With unexpected strength, she torques the seat out of Colin's grip, causing him to stumble backward.

Capitalizing on the opportunity, I snatch the drinks and maneuver around him, planting myself in the other seat. "It's been a long time, Colin."

"Feldman?"

"Yeah, this is our table."

He regains his composure and eyes Delaney like she's a slab of prime porterhouse.

"Is this your girlfriend? I hope she's a lawyer. We need fresh eye candy in the halls of justice."

His sleazy line is typical Colin, but he said it to the wrong person.

Delaney takes hold of her chair with two hands and raises the legs off the floor. "I'm a physician, and unless you want an ambulance ride to the ER, leave."

I tense in case I have to prevent her from being charged with aggravated assault.

Colin raises both hands and says, "No offense intended, Doc."

Delaney sets the chair on the floor.

"You can go now," she says.

"See you at the courthouse," I tell him.

"Weren't you disbarred?" The mention of my ban draws the eyes of patrons. Every profession has its share of jackasses, and Colin never misses a chance to bray. I grind my teeth, struggling to maintain composure in Delaney's presence.

"Only suspended. I'm reinstated soon."

"Lucky us. Are you still hitting the bottle and snorting whiff in the courthouse bathroom? What's the old saying? Once an addict, always one."

His condescension lies heavy in the air, amplifying the ghosts of past insults and shaming. I bolt out of my seat, pick up his coffee cup, and slam it on the table. The plastic sippy lid pops off, and hot coffee erupts over the rim, spraying the crotch of his pants. Delaney's mocking giggles draw attention from other customers, who also snicker.

"Don't be ashamed," she tells Colin. "Incontinence is not uncommon in a man your age."

Colin's orange, spray-on complexion changes to Mars red as he scurries to the counter, grabs paper towels, and then bolts out the door.

"I don't usually lose it like that, but the guy and I have a history." I pick the lid off the floor.

She sits and says, "You have a bit of a temper, don't you?"

Her accusation irritates me, given she's the one who chair-wrestled the guy, starting the whole thing. "I suspect we're both a bit on edge."

She checks her watch. "What did you want to discuss?"

"At my house, you said something that hit home."

"We both said a lot of things. Can you refresh me?"

Her impatient delivery signals that she's not here to play twenty questions. I need to be direct.

"We're strangers," I tell her. "And as such, especially given what you've read about me, it would be natural to fill in gaps with the worst. The only way you'll know me is to ask, so here we are."

She rotates her coffee cup and sips. Then does it again. "Fair enough. Did you give Emily the fentanyl?"

How many times do I have to deny it before she believes me? Then again, as I learned in jail: Everyone is innocent.

"No, and like you, I'm at a loss for why she would, out of nowhere, use again. There was nothing in our daily conversations or her behavior that would be a tip-off. Something isn't right."

Delaney picks pieces of Styrofoam off the rim of her cup. She catches herself and shakes her head. "I'm sorry. Nervous tic. What did that slick-haired jerk mean by you still being a civilian?"

"As you might have read googling my past, the Pennsylvania attorney-licensing authority suspended me for two years. The good news is, I can soon practice law again."

"I'm happy for you. I'd be lost without my work. None of the stories I skimmed were clear on why it happened, although I got through only a few before I dozed off."

I can't begin to convey how lost I've been. After fumbling with a packet of Equal for about thirty seconds, I reflect on what my AA sponsor hammered into me about rigorous honesty. More lies will only start another cycle of bullshit.

"Two years ago, I made false statements to law enforcement."

"You lied to the police?"

I'm now hyper-aware of the stifling atmosphere in the café. The stale, overheated air makes my face feel flushed. The back of my shirt is drenched like a used bath towel. "The FBI."

She sets her cup down, and folds her hands on the table. "Why?"

A question I've asked myself every day since it happened.

"It's complicated, but lying was a terrible decision for what I thought was the right reason. They gave me a year's probation. I'm grateful it wasn't worse. I could have gone to prison."

Delaney fastens the lid to her coffee cup like she's ready to leave. "While I don't condone what you did, it must be hard to relive."

It can't be harder than the tragedy we are both living right now. Grateful for a subject-changing event, I point over her shoulder at the television behind the coffee bar. "Isn't that King Fox, Emily's boss? They're talking about his new addiction treatment facility and sober house going up in McKees Rocks."

The chyron scrolling across the bottom of the screen reads: *After Neighborhood Battle, Addiction Rehab Center and Recovery Residence Set to Open.*

A reporter with red hair, a perfect nose, and skin so flawless it appears photoshopped faces the camera while protesters scuffle behind her, maneuvering to have their signs seen. One reads, "No Crackheads Allowed." Another, "Keep Our Community Safe."

"After a lengthy zoning battle and strong neighborhood opposition, a ceremonial groundbreaking will take place today for a ten-million-dollar addiction treatment center, including transitional housing for struggling addicts."

King's hand sweeps across the construction site. "Our state-of-the-art facility will rise, like the phoenix from the ashes of this once thriving neighborhood. We will never turn away someone in need."

"Who is funding this ambitious project?" the reporter asks.

"Generous, grassroots donations made through my nonprofit, The Sunny Awakenings Foundation, as well as other private sources are the sole mechanism."

I use a napkin to wipe the table free of Colin's coffee spillage. "King used to play professional baseball, lost his career to cocaine, and is now one of those online recovery gurus. His moniker is 'The King of Clean.'"

"Emily spoke about him, and I've seen his addiction commercials," she says. "Talk about cheesy."

"He's more successful now than he was as a ballplayer." I tap my Facebook app and navigate to his profile. "Check this out. He has close to a half million followers."

She takes my phone, scrolls a bit, and says, "I limit my connections to friends and family. I'm too busy to invest time in social media."

Emily felt pretty much the same. Before we started dating, I asked if I could send her a Facebook friend request. She replied that she valued her privacy and had made the decision to live without social media. I was impressed. It was such an integral part of my social and work life that I experienced anxiety after shutting my accounts down.

"I deactivated my social media for a while when my life fell apart," I tell her. "There were daily death threats and antisemitic attacks."

Delaney pushes away from the table. "I have to go."

Although the meeting didn't last as long as I'd have liked, we did make progress. Colin may have even helped with his antics. He confirmed that Delaney is no one to be messed with. She'll punch back without hesitation. I need to be the same way if we're going to see this through and get to the truth.

The rideshare pulls up to the curb. Delaney goes through the identification protocols and gets in. Before closing the car door she says, voice cracking, "After my shift ended yesterday, I went to the bank, then stopped for gas on my way home. My tank wasn't even close to empty." She then reaches into her handbag and takes out a box of Narcan. "I always have it with me."

I nod, but there's nothing to add. Guilt is eating me alive.

The moment her car is in motion, I beeline back to what I'm sure will be an irate Maz, waiting to chew me out. I catch sight of him through the repaired display window. He's leaning over the fragrance counter, elbows propped on the glass, conversing with Irina while she adjusts perfume samplers. He hits on her at least once a day and has as much chance of scoring as I do tossing a touchdown for the Steelers.

As I approach, her face contorts into a desperate smile, pleading for rescue. "How was your lunch?"

Maz wheels around, his eyes narrowing into angry slits. "Where the hell have you been?"

"Emily's roommate texted and needed to see me right away. Given what happened, I thought it best to go and that you'd agree."

"You could have warned me. People are stealing."

I bow my head, hiding my pained expression. If he repeats the phrase one more time, I might puke.

Irina, eavesdropping on the discussion, says, "Did something bad happen?"

"Someone close to me died. My girlfriend."

She gasps and covers her mouth. "Oh my. What happened?"

The two people sniffing their wrists at the other end of the counter dissuade me from elaborating. I'd rather not get into the weeds about this with customers milling about.

"We're not sure yet. The police are investigating."

Maz's derisive grunt is one of a bull about to gore his prey. "What are you talking about? It was an overdose."

A woman with a perfume gift box in her hand looks our way. My fists clench at my sides, fingernails digging into the skin. I glare at him and say, "Mind your business."

"So terrible," Irina says. "Drugs are a big problem in Ukraine. I stay away."

"Can we talk about this later? I whisper. "There are people around."

Maz ignores my plea. "It's no different from when I was a cop. Jeanette and I worked at least one junkie stiff a night."

The hairs on the back of my neck bristle, and my body temperature skyrockets. My inner voice is screaming, *Don't do it. Leave this job on your terms, not his.* I wiggle my fingers and step backward.

"She wasn't a junkie, and this isn't the time or place to talk about it."

He shrugs. "Whatever you say."

Screw the job and the customers. My fist arcs toward his right cheek. A guided-missile direct hit and he will drop like a sack of wet cement.

Maz, however, executes an almost imperceptible shift of his head, and my roundhouse misses, the torque twisting me 360 degrees. Unable to stem the rotation, my arm sweeps over the top of the counter and topples a bottle of Portrait of a Lady parfum. I reach for the spray nozzle with spastic imprecision as it somersaults to the tile floor. The glass explodes across the aisle.

Maz bends over and picks up the spray pump head. "Do I need to say the words?"

I spin around to Irina. "You saw it. He provoked me."

Her terrified eyes dart from Maz to me and back. "I prefer not to be involved."

After unhooking the handcuffs from my belt loop, I lay them on the glass counter. The metallic clink against the surface, a preamble to the inevitable.

"I quit."

"You can't. I already fired you."

Irina reaches over the counter, locking onto my wrist. "Please don't leave. You are my only friend here."

Maz picks up the cuffs. "I'm going to the head. Don't be here when I return."

When he's out of earshot, I write my phone number and email on a white perfume test-strip.

"We'll stay in touch," I tell her. "Get yourself some coffee and take a breather. You'll be fine."

She flashes an uncertain smile. "What about Maz and the customers?"

"Excuse my French, but fuck 'em."

She scans the area, then mutters to herself a phrase that, despite my grasp of Ukrainian and Russian, I don't recognize.

"What did you say?"

She leans in, inches from my ear, and whispers, "Same thing as you."

Chapter 6

*R*ather than go home, I stroll through Point State Park to clear my head. The drama with Maz will blow over, and only The Old Man can fire me. Regardless, how can I go back to my job when the only person I see through the two-way mirror is Emily, dead on Delaney's living room floor?

I take a seat on the concrete riverbank next to the massive fountain where the Monongahela, Allegheny, and Ohio rivers converge; it is a landmark of fond memories. My favorite pastime as a first-year law student was studying on the fountain steps with Sonya. Breeze-blown droplets from the 150-foot waterspout spattered our backs as we compared class outlines and quizzed each other on civil procedure, constitutional law, and my favorite subject, torts.

Downriver, two teenagers sit, fishing lines in the water. The taller one has his arm around the other. *Brothers bonding the old-school Yinzer way*, I think. For a moment, it's Sam and me. I'm teaching him how to cast his Zebco reel and hook the worms we brought in a cooler, along with peanut butter sandwiches and ginger ale.

"Daddy, if I catch a fishy, will we eat it?"

"No, Sam, we'll throw it back with its friends."

Now, he's even blocked me on social media. Sonya says he just needs time, but I know it's more than that. What child wants to watch his dad kill himself with alcohol and cocaine? I'd give anything for one more visit here. But not having spoken to him since my last relapse, I'm terrified to press his baby photo icon in my phone favorites. What if he hangs up on me or demands I never call him again? Not that I would blame him. My lies put him through hell. His last words to me were, "You broke your promise to stay sober." His only text in response to mine asking how he is doing was: *I'm fine*. Every so often, Sonya updates me, but it's the same abbreviated crap. He's doing well, with no detail. Alienation ferments isolation. All I can do is pray he's happy.

After removing my shoes and socks, I dangle my feet above the brownish water. A motorboat passing by creates a gentle wake, sending rhythmic wavelets against the concrete, nipping my toes.

I lean back and take in the sun, thinking about how I got from those early memories with my child to this mess. Before I can power down my phone, Maz is back in my texts:

Need you at the store. The boss wants a word.

I text back: *You fired me. I'm done.*

Please.

That's a word he had never uttered in my presence. He must be in trouble. My visceral reaction is that I don't give a damn. But should I disappear without explaining why I'm leaving to The Old Man? I don't want to burn that bridge, especially not now. I text: *It won't be for a while. Will message you when I'm in the building.*

"Such a beautiful view, isn't it?" The sudden and unexpected Scarlett O'Hara drawl from behind causes me to bobble my phone, almost losing it to the river.

A distinguished woman in a black jacket and matching slacks stands a few feet from me. Her hooded blue eyes dissect me with unsettling intensity.

"Yes, it is," I say, and wonder if I'm being hit on.

She points at the two kids. "What kind of fish do they catch? Any croakers?"

"A lot of catfish and carp. I'm not familiar with, what did you call it?"

"Croakers." She squats next to me. "My brother and I took Grandaddy's skiff and caught them in bunches on Lake Pontchartrain. On Sundays, Daddy would scale and fry them up in a skillet, then invite the entire neighborhood."

I nod and contemplate whether this is an entrée to some kind of grift. I'm also in no mood for conversations with strangers. "Is there something I can help you with?"

Ignoring my question, she watches the kids cast their lines and says, "Did you know a boat can sail from here to the Mississippi and onto New Orleans?"

"It would be faster to fly. I don't want to sound rude, but I'd prefer to be left alone."

A motorboat, with a water-skier in tow, speeds past, causing water to splash over the embankment. She hops backward as I pick up my shoes and stand before the growing puddle soaks my pants.

Maz is a 9 a.m.-to-close jerk, on my ass every minute of my shift. Keane was bothering me at work, and now, this stranger is interrupting the only quiet time I've had to reflect on Emily. I can't catch a break.

She digs into her handbag and hands me a business card. "There's an urgent matter we need to discuss."

I glance at the information. Mary Lou Dubois, President, Bayou Intelligence and Analytics. What could she want that involves me?

"My company is on retainer to Sunny Awakenings Treatment Center to retrieve electronic data devices entrusted to your late girl-friend, Emily Francine Wilson, their employee."

I feel as if she's slugged me. "I beg your pardon?"

She squints at her phone, tapping the screen. "Yes, here we are. Emily possessed two pieces of company equipment: a laptop and cell phone. I'm contacting everyone who might assist in their return."

My irritation escalates to anger. "How did you track me here? Couldn't this wait? She's not even in the ground yet."

"You exited the department store as I entered. Rather than stop you on a crowded sidewalk, I waited for a measure of privacy."

Screw this, I think. This was supposed to be a private moment, and she's stalking me.

"I don't know where you learned your trade, but this isn't the way to do things." After putting on my socks and shoes, I start toward the park exit.

"Jason, please stay. I'm only doing my job. Wouldn't you do the same in my position? It's not much different from ensuring shoplifters don't leave the store with stolen items."

Is she joking? It's not the same. I can replace stolen merchandise, but Emily is dead.

"Let's start over," she continues. "It's lunchtime. We'll hash this out over a pleasant meal. Then, you'll never see me again."

"I'm due back at work," I say.

"You don't eat lunch? I'm a stranger to this city. Pick a place."

One thing is clear. She's not going away. If she wants to waste her time, I might as well have a conversation and put it behind me.

"There's an Original Oyster House near here. I'm not in the mood for company, but if it will cross me off your list, let's go."

Mary Lou arrives at the restaurant entrance a few steps ahead of me and stops. I'm at the door when I realize she's waiting for me to open it for her. Emily viewed such old-fashioned protocols as anachronistic. She chided me on our first date: "I appreciate the thought, but you're enabling the patriarchy."

At the time, it was confusing. My father taught me to open doors for women. Now, the recollection stabs me in the heart. A reminder of how Emily challenged my comfort zones and the positive impact she had on my life. I open the door and follow Mary Lou inside.

A girl in her early twenties with a gold loop nose ring and a hurried, lunch-rush grit to her smile shows us to our table. Mary Lou stands behind her chair, again waiting. I'd let her stand there all day as a reaffirmation of her unwanted intrusion, but the server slides it out.

We order; the server collects our menus and then scurries to the bar. Mary Lou's head rotates left to right, and back, inches at a time, with a slight pause between each movement. It's as if she's breaking the room into grids, sizing up the crowd.

I decide to fire the first salvo and see where it leads. "I don't know where Emily's company electronics are. The cops searched her roommate's house and Emily's car. Are you sure she didn't leave them at work?"

The server sets our drinks on the table. "Your food will be out in a jiffy."

Mary Lou swirls the wine and sips. "We are positive her employer does not have them. I hope you won't think it's snooping, but part of my job requires background investigation on anyone Emily may have entrusted with company property. You've experienced some misfortune."

The notion of this stranger prying into my life when I know nothing about her has me even more on the defensive. This meeting wasn't a smart move.

"That's none of your business. Why would you think she gave them to me?" I ask. "She was my girlfriend, not a coworker."

"I know that." Mary Lou unrolls her napkin and lays it across her lap. "You were about to celebrate your six-month anniversary."

Her intimate knowledge of our private moment embroils me in a mixture of anger and confusion. I want to get up and leave but can't pry myself from the chair.

"How could you possibly know that?"

"Can I get either of you anything else?" I didn't see the server hovering over my right shoulder. Without breaking eye contact with Mary Lou, I hold up my right hand. "We're both fine."

Mary Lou nods in agreement and the server moves on to another table.

"I asked you a question," I say, my voice rising.

"This is what I do for a living, Jason." She makes it clear she's studying me. "Do I make you nervous?"

I am suddenly aware I'm tapping the tablecloth with my knife as if I'm sending a Morse-code SOS.

"First of all, you rudely accosted me, asking for something I don't have. Now, you're prying into my private life. I'm out of here."

"Perfectly understandable." She scrutinizes her fork, twisting it back and forth. Apparently satisfied with its cleanliness, she sets it on the table. "But before you go, it wasn't my intent to ambush you. I'm on a tight schedule and must capitalize on opportunities as they occur. Surely you understand that."

"I didn't come here for small talk. I've told you what I know."

She checks her phone. "My brother is texting. We work together. Would it be okay if you gave your home another once-over for my client's property? It's easy to miss something. We'd appreciate Dr. Martin doing the same."

For fuck's sake. That's the ask? We could have disposed of this in thirty seconds at the fountain. I'd have told her we both went through our homes multiple times.

"Why didn't you ask me this at the park?"

"I would have missed out on the pleasure of your company."

Her glib response doesn't obscure the truth. She wanted to size me up, but if it crosses me off her list, I might as well agree. It will also stop her from continuing to pry into my personal affairs.

"Okay," I say. "I'll speak with Dr. Martin. Are we done here?"

"Don't you want to eat?" she asks.

I'm not spending another second with her. "I've lost my appetite. Your time is up with me."

Mary Lou stands and smooths her pants legs. "I understand you're upset. I'll get a to-go box. One last thing. My client will pay a substantial cash finder's fee for information leading to the return of the electronics."

Why are they this eager to retrieve a phone and computer? What kind of work was Emily involved with?

"Substantial?" I ask. "Why?"

"All you need to know is that my client will pay $200,000 for the return of either or both items," she says. "I suspect you could use that, considering how much it's costing you to care for your father. That memory-care facility doesn't come cheap."

It's one thing to scan the internet, but accessing my financials is beyond the pale. She's right, though. The $100,000 deposit and twelve-grand-a-month rent depleted the safety cushion built up from my law practice. A store detective's salary doesn't come close to narrowing the gap.

"You contacted the nursing home?" I demand. "Who the fuck gave you authority?"

"Oh, Jason. In my line of work, there isn't one data byte out of reach. Please think about the offer. You have my card. I'll take your call day or night."

The moment she's out the door, I pay, take an empty stool at the bar, and type *Mary Lou Dubois New Orleans* into Google. To my surprise, there's only a single blurb mentioning her in the *New Orleans Business Daily*.

Armstrong Dubois, the President and CEO of Bayou Analytics and Intelligence, announced he is stepping down, and his daughter Mary Lou, along with her brother Phillip, will take the reins. A Metairie native, he enjoyed a long and distinguished career in Naval Intelligence. After retirement, he founded Bayou, growing it into a multimillion-dollar strategic consulting organization with clients in defense, intelligence, and commercial sectors. An MIT graduate, Mary Lou spent time at the National Security Agency before moving on to data gathering and internal polling for various political campaigns.

I enter Phillip Dubois into the search bar. The top hits are two separate mugshots. One for cocaine possession, the other, aggravated assault. His military haircut rings familiar. He could be the Lexus asshole, but I need that license plate run to be sure.

Chapter 7

The only reason Maz would ask me back to the store is if The Old Man demanded he rehire me. At the moment, I'm more concerned about Mary Lou and Phillip. If he's the guy outside The Squirrel, the last thing I need is a violent lunatic following me. Their involvement, however, doesn't bring me closer to the truth about Emily's overdose. Why did she decide to use again? What happened in that living room? The walk to Waggaman's is one of starts and stops. Every twenty feet or so, I glance over my shoulder for any sign of Mary Lou. Even in the store, I wouldn't put it past her to hide behind a clothes rack.

I text Maz: *In the elevator, coming up.*

A litany of possible responses to the expected reconciliation attempt run through my mind as I ascend to the fifth-floor corporate offices.

While I appreciate the offer and everything you've done for me, it's best to move on.

I'd rather pull my toenails out with my teeth than return and work with that clown.

And if things get really ugly:

When I'm a lawyer again, I'll bury you in slip-and-fall lawsuits.

The route to The Old Man's office takes me past Maz's cubicle. He's on the phone, holding a framed photo of his grandson Brian. "Grandpa won't be late tonight. Yes, tell the sitter it's okay to order pizza."

Maz never talks about how he came to be Brian's legal guardian, but it's common knowledge around the store, a tragic story embedded in the other photo on the desk: a Police Academy graduation portrait of his son Sean, killed answering a domestic violence call.

47

I head toward Waggaman's office door, tugging at the back of my collar, which is closing in around my neck. It's open, and the dim lighting makes it difficult to focus on The Old Man seated at his ancient steel desk. The room resembles a garment factory more than the office of a wealthy department-store tycoon. The smell of fabric combines with his store-brand aftershave. Wheeled racks of clothes are stacked two deep along the back wall. Naked male and female mannequins cluster in the corner, waiting to be dressed.

Waggaman's silhouette takes on defined features as I close the distance. A deeply receding hairline leaves his head bald to mid-scalp. He's wearing a Waggaman's label white dress shirt. The sleeves are rolled up to his elbows. On his desk, an assortment of retail items includes men's cologne samples, jewelry, and a book.

I squint to read the title, and as if reading my mind, he says, "*The Gospel of Wealth*. It's a first edition, signed by Andrew Carnegie to my grandad."

"Do you mind?" I ask.

"Help yourself," he tells me.

After skimming through a few yellowed pages, I return it and say, "An incredible keepsake, sir. Your grandfather must have been a great man."

"He was an asshole, but I learned everything about the business from him and my father. Here we sit in their creation, outlasting Kaufmann's, Joseph Horne's, Rosenbaum's, and every other department store in downtown Pittsburgh."

Maz enters the room and sits. The arm of my chair is almost touching him, so I stand and slide it to the right, giving myself more breathing room. The last thing I should have done was take a swing at a former professional boxer. I hoped my younger age and his sagging body would compensate for my lack of skill. He'll never let me live it down—and worse, he'll tell Keane.

"Are you afraid I'll humiliate you again?" Maz adjusts his chair farther away. "My grandmother has a faster right hook."

"Enough." The Old Man's tone is that of a father scolding his children. "Jason, I'm aware of this morning's kerfuffle, as well as the recent passing of your girlfriend. I speak for all employees in sending condolences. If I can do anything for you, my door is always open."

"I appreciate your concern, sir, but we handled everything."

He rises from his chair, circles behind me, and places his hand on my shoulder. "Considering what you've gone through, let's forget about this morning's unfortunate incident. You're an exceptional employee, and I don't want to lose you."

I point at Maz. "He fired me."

"We discussed the situation and agreed his decision was hasty."

"I appreciate the grace but—"

"It's settled." He slaps my back. "Take all the time you need to deal with this. "We'll be here when you're ready to come back."

Maz thuds my shoulder with a boxing jab. "Jason's a trouper. He's ready to return to the front lines right now."

Fat chance, I think. The Old Man opened the door with his offer of personal time. I'm walking through it.

"Thank you, Mr. Waggaman," I say. "It's been rough. If you don't mind, I'm taking two weeks off. Emily had no family. I'm slammed with funeral arrangements and winding up her affairs."

I stand to emphasize that my decision is nonnegotiable. If he says no, I'm gone regardless of my depleted bank account.

"Perfectly fine, son. We'll handle things here."

Maz grimaces and says, "No problem, sir. I'll mind the store."

You're damn right you will, I think. The Old Man is in my corner, not yours.

"I'm glad we reached an understanding," Waggaman says, shaking my hand. "Please let me know where we can send flowers."

In the elevator, Maz and I stare at the steel doors as if there will be a race to see who gets off first when it hits bottom. I sneak a glance at the scowling contradiction. A loving grandpa determined to be a cop-show stereotype, though I haven't made any effort to ease the long-standing tension, escalated by my failed roundhouse punch. It's time to start. Some self-deprecation may cut through his crusty shell.

"That was a lame swing I took at you. I'm embarrassed."

He chuckles. "You should be."

"I overheard you on the phone with your grandson. We've never talked about it, but I can't imagine the pain of losing a child. I'm sorry."

He turns to face me, and I wonder if I'm about to suffer a broken nose for not minding my business.

"Thank you."

The elevator hits bottom with a thud and shudder. "I gotta hit the head," he says. "I'm sorry about your girl and my big mouth earlier."

The doors slide apart as my text alert pings. It's from Delaney. My shoulders slump.

I heard from Detective Keane. The toxicology report is back. Fentanyl overdose.

Only three weeks before, Emily bubbled with pride at her one-year chip ceremony. She hugged her sponsor and said, "My life was once unmanageable, but today, I have a wonderful job, sober friends, and a supportive partner."

I understand relapse. My last one was a doozy, and there were several before that. But I never thought it would happen to Emily. If anyone had their act together, it was her.

I'm beset with a mixture of relief and fatigue during the walk to my car. My time off should be enough to piece together the truth. Then, I can engineer a graceful exit from Waggaman's and reenter practicing law.

The vibration of my phone rattles the plastic cup holder of my Accord as the caller ID flashes Delaney's number.

"Did you receive my text?" she says, her voice trembling.

"Yeah, I'm still processing and in a bit of denial."

The only sound is Billy Joel belting the lyrics to "Big Shot" on my satellite radio. The unspoken truth is that we both knew this was coming.

"You there?" I ask after another stanza passes. "We'll write an obituary, and as soon as the medical examiner releases her body, we'll make funeral arrangements. I'm exhausted and heading home."

Through muffled sobs, Delaney says, "Three days ago, Emmi and I ate breakfast together before my shift. Now she's laid out naked on a slab."

So much more happened from their meal to Emily's death. I've racked my brain and can't recall one sign of something being off. Yet, it had to be. What am I missing? Keane might be right about Emily's phone and computer. They may hold the key to filling in the missing pieces. Even if it was a simple relapse, I won't rest until we figure out who gave her the fentanyl. I owe her that.

Chapter 8

I turn onto my street, wondering if Mary Lou is still following me. It would be silly to assume she doesn't know where I live. However, I have no idea what she hopes to gain through continued surveillance.

A nap proves a fruitless endeavor. I'm unable to erase the vision of Emily laid out in a morgue with a tag hanging from her big toe. I want to call her but can't. There will be no text letting me know she's on her way over to spend the night. None of it will ever happen again, and why? Because she used, knowing I was on my way to pick her up? Delaney might have also come home at any moment. It borders on absurd. After another hour tossing and turning, I turn on the late afternoon news. Ten minutes in is another segment on King Fox.

"This is Courtney Capps. Up next, a controversial rehab begins construction in McKees Rocks. After a year of court skirmishes, the Sunny Awakenings addiction treatment facility broke ground this afternoon."

King is wearing a polo shirt bearing a logo of a sun rising over a mountain top. He stares into the camera, spreads a wide grin, and upends the shovel, dropping the ceremonial dirt on the target.

Capps continues, "According to owner King Fox, the facility will accept patients within six months. At capacity, it will house fifty residents with an attached adjacent recovery home providing continuity of care."

She cranes her head toward a small group holding signs and chanting: "Not in our neighborhood."

Mic outstretched, Capps approaches a protester who is pumping a cardboard poster up and down. It bears the caricature of a male sticking a syringe into his forearm with a caption beneath in blood red: JUNKIES = CRIME, BLIGHT, AND REAL ESTATE DEVALUATION.

"Why are you opposed to this facility?" Capps asks. "Isn't people getting addiction treatment a good thing?"

"Addicts smoke fentanyl on the park benches," he says. "It's also an open-air drug market."

The camera pans back to King. "We are, and will be, responsible neighbors, with safety a top priority. I operate many programs around the state with an unheard-of 90 percent success rate. Wouldn't the community rather have these poor souls in treatment than shooting up in the park across the street?"

The segment ends as my app alerts me that my pizza is at the door. I'm halfway through the Mineo's pie when the delivery service number appears on my caller ID.

"Are you enjoying your pizza, pal?"

"It's excellent. Did I forget a tip?"

An evil laugh is the response. "I'm not your fucking delivery guy. We want the video your girlfriend recorded."

I rush to the front door and swing it open. Instead of a peeper or any sign of trouble, there's the humid, eerie kind of calm that hangs in the air before a thunderstorm.

"Who is this?" I demand.

"Did you know your girl was banging King? She was a backboard-slamming slut. Why protect her?"

That derogatory reference has me wondering if he has the wrong person.

"Excuse me?"

"You heard me, Feldman. King Fox was boning your girlfriend, Emily."

I peer around the side of the house, then through the gate into my backyard. Where is this guy? "That's a lie. What the hell do you want?"

"Are you hard of hearing? It only gets worse for you from here."

My chest tightens. What does that mean? Mary Lou said nothing about a recording.

After another circle of the house perimeter, I check the lock on every window and vow to purchase a slew of home-security cameras. Telling Keane about this is pointless. She'll claim I'm making up drama to generate sympathy. What would I say to Delaney, short of asking her if it's true? *You'll never believe this, but the information came via a phony phone call from a fake pizza guy.* There must be a more subtle approach.

After checking the locks twice more, then staring out the living room window for an hour, I calm down and go through photos of Emily on my phone. She's clowning with the Pirate Parrot at a baseball game. Next is an intimate bedroom shot. She has her hand down her panties, inviting me to enter. Did she take the same photo with King? In every mental image of us together, my face is now his. My only escape from jealous projection and speculation is sleep.

I remember reading that, for a full night's rest, the phone should be on silent or powered off. As a personal injury lawyer, I soon learned that type of night peace was a luxury. Accidents happen twenty-four-seven. My finger hovers over the power button when a text containing a jpeg file pops up. My brain screams not to open it. It might be a virus. Only idiots click on attachments texted from unknown numbers and people they don't know. I can't help myself.

Fiber internet downloads it in seconds. Acetic bile jettisons up my throat. I rush to the sink, turn on the faucet, and slurp tap water from my palm. He wasn't lying about Emily.

There she sits, across the table from King at the LeMont Restaurant on Mount Washington, where Sonya and I celebrated our first wedding anniversary. The unmistakable window view of the city leaves no doubt as to the location. She's dressed in an unfamiliar, elegant evening dress. I obsess over every detail. I'm no fashionista, but it's significantly more upscale than the best Waggaman's has to offer. And that necklace she's wearing. Emily always said she hated jewelry. There's something off here. It's Emily, but it's not.

Another photo comes through. This one is Emily walking out the door of what appears to be a lavish mansion. She's carrying an overnight bag. Is that King's house? Whoever sent this wants me to think so.

I'm a boiling cauldron of jealousy and betrayal. The Emily I knew was unpretentious, frugal, and had modest financial resources. She wasn't a gold digger, either. My thoughts are racing full speed ahead like a freight train with no brakes. I'm confronting King tomorrow. I have to hear it from his lips.

Chapter 9

"Alexa, what time is it?"

"The current time is 8 a.m."

I wonder if I'll ever have an uninterrupted night's sleep again. Today, of all days, I need to be on top of my game. As soon as King shows up to work, I'm going down there.

Emily and I were chatting about her job two weeks ago, and she mentioned King's daily routine. He arrives at his office around ten o'clock, returns calls, then takes meetings. I kill the next two hours with a walk around the block, then three cups of coffee while staring at the photo of them. It's finally zero hour.

"Sunny Awakenings Foundation. How may I direct your call?"

"I'd like to speak with King Fox." Just saying his name causes my throat to constrict.

"He walked in the office a few minutes ago. I'll put you on hold while I see if he's available. Who's calling?"

"Tell him it's Jason Feldman."

I resist the nervous urge to hang up. Why would King take my call if he was sleeping with my girlfriend? Doubt and suspicion are filling my gut like quicksand. If Emily kept the affair from me, what else was I wrong about?

The wait on hold is spent listening to the same Sunny Awakenings commercial that was on the television. I'm not sure how many times it repeats before King picks up.

"Jason Feldman. I've heard a lot about you."

King's voice has a smarmy, snake-oil coating on it, as if he and I have been buds all our lives. What does he know about me?

"Mr. Fox. I'd like to see you."

"Call me King. I was devastated to learn of Emily's passing. The entire company mourns her loss."

I want to reach through the phone and strangle his fake ass. "Would today work?"

"Of course. When would you like to come down? We're in PPG Place downtown."

"I'll be there within the hour."

Delaney needs to know about this meeting, but I can't imagine her being enamored with my mission to confront King and kick his ass. It would only reinforce what she said at the café about my temper. It's better to see how it goes and then fill her in.

The drive downtown is consumed with thoughts about what I'll do when I'm face-to-face with King. With each red light, the plan changes. Punching him in the nose seems reasonable at one intersection. The next brings a calmer perspective. I'll listen to what he has to say and stay cool.

As I step into the opulent office space on the fortieth floor of PPG Place, I find it hard to fathom King as a filthy-rich addiction guru after a career as a mediocre ball player who became hooked on cocaine and then went broke.

After rehab and bankruptcy, he kept a low profile until appearing on the television show *Addicted Athletes*. It was the first time he referred to himself as The King of Clean. A best-selling memoir followed, and then the recovery and motivational speaking circuit. He was also the keynote at a Las Vegas recovery conference I attended with Emily. Were they hooking up under my nose at the hotel? I'm not leaving without the truth, even if it rips my heart out.

I have second thoughts as I approach the woman at the front desk. Last night, the plan was perfect. Now, it feels like a jealousy-driven behavioral outburst.

"Jason Feldman," I tell her. "Here to see King."

"He's expecting you. Please have a seat."

Nervous energy surges like an electric current from my heart down through my legs and feet. Instead of sitting, I stare out a floor-to-ceiling glass window. At any other time, over four hundred feet above the ground, the view alone would be worth the trip. Today, it agitates me. Across the Monongahela River, the Duquesne Incline gondola glides up the side of Mount Washington. At the crest, a few miles away on Grandview Avenue, is the LeMont, the same restaurant in the photo. I turn away to keep my mind from running wild. Time ticks away in slow motion. I'll bet he's in his office drinking coffee while making me wait because he can. I glance at the wall clock, and then the receptionist. She must notice my impatience and says, "It shouldn't be much longer."

Next to the lobby couch is a drawing on an easel. It's an architectural rendering of King's new addiction treatment center in McKees Rocks. It resembles a small college campus more than a rehab facility. A building for detox, separate men's and women's living facilities, and a stand-alone fitness center are a few of the labels.

The receptionist walks into the lobby. "King will see you now." I follow her to his office, reminding myself to remain composed regardless of what he says. I'm on his home field. King rises from behind his desk, and while the years and four-star restaurant scene have expanded the stomach and chipmunked his cheeks, his imposing six foot-three, wide-shouldered build looks like it could still jack a few balls out of PNC Park. His hand wraps around mine and constricts like it's squeezing coal into a diamond.

Behind him, a slew of framed pictures line the walls. I expected photos from his baseball career, in his private jet, and with the countless celebrities he bumps fists with. Instead, there is a cluster of baby photos alongside an oak-framed, twelve-by-eighteen-inch photo of King kneeling next to a group of children, one of whom is being given a shot by a woman in a white coat.

He must have noticed me leaning forward to get a closer look.

"This photo is from a mission to Sudan," he tells me by way of greeting. "It was a global vaccination initiative. Last month, my foundation pledged up to five million dollars to help drill wells that will bring clean water to areas lacking it."

Now, I'm conflicted. A cheating cad and a philanthropist. Something my father said to me echoes forward in time from childhood: *No person is one thing.*

King motions to my chair. "Please sit. Again, my deepest sympathies. We're all still grieving this awful tragedy. I wish Emily would have come to me. This is what we do."

His tone is one of confidence mixed with compassion. The ability to intertwine the two must be something you're born with. There's an authoritative authenticity to his condolence. Is that what Emily saw? Is it something I lack?

"Thank you for seeing me."

"Of course. How are you holding up? Sunny Awakenings is here for you during this difficult time."

"I'm hanging in there." Manufactured empathy and crocodile tears are common on the witness stand. I've prided myself on being a student of human emotion, but he's good. I can't tell if his compassion is genuine.

"I saw you checking out the rendering of our new facility. What do you think?"

"It's impressive."

"The total tab will exceed $10 million, all paid for by The Sunny Awakenings Foundation. It's a blessing to give back to the community that did so much for me."

Now he sounds like a mixture of a television evangelist and Dale Carnegie. I refuse to be manipulated like Emily was. Enough of this. I enlarge the photo and push the phone across his desk.

King's brows raise as he stares at it. I force myself to keep eye contact as he contemplates the phone as if it's infected with a virus.

"This was after a charity function Emily accompanied me to. My date bailed at the last minute, so I had an extra ticket. How did you come by this photo?"

King's delivery is calm, but his avoidance of eye contact gives him away. I saw it countless times cross-examining witnesses. He's lying.

I reach across and pick up the phone.

"That's not important. What event was that, and when?"

The mutual stare-down begins. I focus on the pictures behind him and wait. I'm not flinching first in this game of chicken.

He finally says, "I'll have my assistant get the information from my calendar. I attend so many of those galas. Raising money for my foundation is a nonstop string of extra-inning ball games."

"You also mentioned a date who backed out." Courtroom cross-examination skills dormant for two years kick in as if I never left the practice of law. "What was her name?"

"None of your business." King springs from his chair, face red and chest heaving. "If you think I was having an affair with Emily, you're mistaken."

He's on the defense and emotional, the perfect time to lean into a hostile witness. I show him the next picture.

"Photos don't lie. That is Emily leaving your house."

I'm taking a chance by assuming he lives there, but why would the person send it to me otherwise?

He runs his hands down the front of his polo shirt and sits. There's an interminable silence as we again each wait for the other to say something. Finally, he says, "Yes. But these pictures capture a millisecond in time without context. May I provide it?"

My rookie mistake slices me down to size. I let my own feelings get the best of me and shouldn't have confronted him with the photos until he locked himself into a story.

"Go ahead."

"When did you start seeing her?" he asks.

"Six months ago."

He hunches forward, taps the keys on his computer, and studies the screen. His smirk indicates I'm about to get sucker punched.

"I ended our relationship about a week before yours began," he tells me. "I felt awful about the whole thing, her being an employee and all. When she transitioned from marketing rep to my PA, we were together all the time. She also had a key to my house. It was more a fling than a relationship, and didn't last long."

I'm deflated. Emily never mentioned the job title change, and there's no hint of deceit in King's voice or eyes. And then there's the time frame. If he's telling the truth, our first date was right after they broke up. Was I a rebound? Emily said she hadn't dated anyone for a long while, and it was my only serious relationship since my divorce two years before. An uncomfortable surge of mixed emotions wash over me. I need to get out of my own head and on track. I'm here for a reason.

"When did she become your assistant?"

King reclines in his chair and rubs his chin. "I'll have my assistant check her file, but if memory serves, it was a month before we split up."

I don't need a calendar to process the truth. Emily lied to me. The other possibility kicks hard at the inside of my skull. King's also full of shit. She was unfaithful. Did Delaney know?

"Why did it end?" I manage to ask.

"Because she was an employee. It was wrong. To be honest, it got worse from there."

Now, I only want to leave but can't help myself.

"What do you mean?"

"She quit two weeks ago and took confidential company information with her. We'd been contemplating a lawsuit to recover it when I learned she passed away."

I press my lips together to stop my jaw from dropping to my chest. All those mornings we woke up together and she left for work. Where did she go? If I ask, he'll know she didn't tell me. I tug at my collar, unable to breathe.

"Thank you for your time. I should be going."

He stands and says, "I'm glad we resolved this unfortunate misunderstanding. Sunny Awakenings will cover all funeral expenses."

We shake hands, and he says, "One more thing."

"What's that?" At this point, I only want out of here.

"We hired a firm to recover Emily's phone and laptop. They both belong to us. If a Mary Lou Dubois contacts you, that's what it's about."

"We spoke," I say. "I don't know where they are."

I struggle to push the exit door open. Is this what running a marathon feels like? Every ounce of strength drained during that thirty minutes with King. The electronics are their problem, not mine. Are Delaney and I digging for answers that aren't there? The search for an alternative truth feels more like a windmill-tilting quest. I still want to know if Delaney was aware of the relationship. Isn't that what roomies who are also best friends gab about? How could she not know?

Chapter 10

*B*efore going home, I decide to upgrade my almost nonexistent security. It will provide some peace of mind with threatening phone calls coming in and Mary Lou lurking about. On the way, I text Delaney: *Met with King Fox this morning. Lots to discuss.*

You did? Why? I'll call as soon as possible.

Part of me is relieved she's otherwise occupied. It allows me time to disperse the anticipatory irritation of hearing her admit she knew about Emily and King. The worst thing for our budding but tenuous trust is for me to castigate her when she did nothing wrong.

After purchasing the store-recommended cameras, I arrive home and unbox my new toy. For $500 plus tax, the CATCHEM CAM security system comes equipped with four motion-activated tilt-and-pan 1080p cameras, each no bigger than my hand.

As I scour the house for the best surveillance vantage points, a text from Delaney comes through with a link to a *Pittsburgh Tribune* obituary. In the top left corner is a photo of Emily I've never seen. She's standing on her front porch, smiling, and wearing a shirt stenciled with *The Only Thing Narcan Enables is Breathing*.

"On July 5, Emily Wilson passed away. Emily was an avid advocate for drug overdose awareness and worked tireless hours, ensuring those struggling had the resources to stay alive. She is survived by her loving roommate and best friend, Dr. Delaney Martin, and her partner, Jason Feldman. Arrangements are pending. In lieu of flowers, please donate to the Greater Pittsburgh Harm Reduction Coalition."

Each printed word is a shot glass full of rotgut dread burning my throat. I'm also irritated. I hoped the obit would be a joint project.

While I could allow my annoyance to cloud Delaney's touching tribute, every piece of closure matters, and this is one. She did the right thing. One omission that stands out in the notice is the lack of parental recognition or any kind of lineage. It hits me that Emily's only mention of her parents was that they were both deceased. We had long conversations about my father and growing up in Pittsburgh, but she never once spoke of her childhood or upbringing beyond sparse generalities. How could I not have asked such fundamental questions about her past? It might have been an instinctive aversion to what would come next. More questions about my history. Or maybe this was a fresh start, and I wanted to take it slowly.

The doorbell, followed by several thumps on the wood, interrupts my camera setup. The peephole confirms that it's Detective Keane. She has her notebook out, so I suspect it will be another interrogation. I open the door and hope she doesn't stay long. Those cameras won't install themselves, and there's nothing else I can tell her.

"Good afternoon, Detective. I'm busy right now. Can you call in advance next time?"

Keane chuckles. "You know I don't do that. There's been a development in Emily's case. May I come in? This won't take long."

"You discovered who gave her the fentanyl?" I step aside, allowing her into the living room.

"We're running down leads. As part of the investigation, we also ran her prints through AFIS, the FBI's national fingerprint database."

"Yes, I'm familiar. And?"

"The report came back this morning. Did you know Emily had a record?"

I return a blank stare to hide my surprise. "Some people in recovery have law enforcement encounters. So what?"

"The Philadelphia PD busted her for possession of a controlled substance a decade ago. She gave a home address in the city."

She lived in Philly? How many more surprises are there?

"The bizarre part is, the prints come back to a different name," Keane says. "Emily Williams."

"What are you saying?"

"Emily Wilson isn't her name."

I turn my head away to process the revelation.

"Bullshit."

She hands the report to me. "I can interpret it for you, but it's correct."

I study the perfect 12-point match while shaking my head in disbelief. It's her. Who was this woman who professed her love for me?

"You didn't know about her arrest?" Keane studies my face, waiting for an answer.

I don't care about a possession bust, but why didn't Emily tell me about Philadelphia and the name change? "Did you find out anything else?" I hand her back the paper and swallow to keep my voice from cracking.

"Philly PD should respond to my inquiry soon with additional background. The investigation into who sold her the narcotics is ongoing. In the meantime, live your life. Aren't you about to practice law again?"

That's the last thing I want to discuss, and it's none of her business.

"If you must know, my suspension ends in two days."

"What are your plans?" she asks.

Does she genuinely care, or is this part of her interrogation schtick? One thing I learned from our shared past is that Keane is laser-like with questions. There's always a reason.

"I'm mulling options."

"You spent all that money and time becoming a lawyer. If they are letting you back in the fraternity, it makes sense to take advantage, doesn't it?"

I want to ask if she's going to scrape the internet clean of the bad press and accusations that flowed from arresting me. I can hang out that shingle, but clients will be hard to come by.

"We'll see. I'm taking it one day at a time."

"Makes sense," she says. "We've subpoenaed Emily's cell phone records to reconstruct her last day, but that will take a while. Have you given any more thought to what could have happened to her phone?"

Keane has gone from beyond redundant to annoying. I want that phone found as much as anyone, but it's her job, and she's not moving fast enough for me.

"If I knew where it was, you would as well. Don't you have connections at the cell carrier to speed things up?"

Keane pockets her notebook. "You watch too many of those CSI shows. I served the warrant this morning, but the cell provider has thirty days to provide the data."

Fair enough, I think. At least she's not dragging her feet. "Please let me know what the cell records show."

Keane turns and heads for her car. "I'll do that, and likewise, I expect an immediate text or call if you learn anything about the phone's whereabouts."

When she's gone, I go online and navigate to the Philadelphia county website to review the requirements for a legal name change. It's not a simple process. In addition to fingerprinting, a birth certificate and social security card are required. It doesn't end there. The request must be published in two newspapers, either print or online. The court also must be made aware of all litigation judgments. This is not something done on a whim.

Now, I have to break the fingerprint bombshell to Delaney. The person she regarded as a de facto sister, and who confessed her love for me, wasn't who either of us thought. What's more, if Delaney knew Emily's true identity, she withheld vital information from the police and from me.

After several more failed online attempts at tracing the Lexus license plate, I resign myself to a stomach-churning reality. I stare at my phone for fifteen minutes and then peck out the painful text to Maz. He's bragged about his pals on the force doing favors for him and can probably get this done with one phone call.

Can you run a license plate for me?

Against department policy. What's in it for me?

I'll owe you huge.

Not good enough.

What can I offer him? A personal style consultation, new clothes included? There's no point to a back-and-forth without something of value to him. At this moment, I have no clue what that might be. In the meantime, the news I have to break to Delaney won't get any easier by stalling. My throat is bone dry, waiting for her to pick up.

"Hi, Jason. I'm walking into my classroom, so can we keep this quick?"

"Emily's fingerprints came back. The police ran them as part of the investigation."

"And?"

"The fingerprints aren't hers."

"They printed the wrong person?"

I struggle to get the words out. I saw the report and still only half believe it.

"Jason?"

"No. Emily Wilson isn't her real name."

Jumbled background conversations dominate the phone line as I wait for her response.

"Utter nonsense," she finally sputters. "They've made a mistake."

"That was my initial reaction, but Keane showed me the report. Her real name was Emily Williams."

Again, I'm listening to extraneous sounds, this time more defined.

"Dr. Martin, will today's lecture about the molecular structure of fentanyl analogs be available online?"

"Yes, Chris. Take your seat. I'll be a few more minutes."

She returns her attention to me and says, "I have to teach my class, but I'm meeting a lawyer at nine tomorrow morning. She saw the obit and reached out. Apparently, Emmi had a will. I'm the executor."

Why the hell would Emily need estate planning? To my knowledge, her only possessions were her clothes, a fifteen-year-old silver BMW, and her bedroom furniture.

"Where's the meeting? I'll join you. We can discuss the prints, and I still need to fill you in on what happened with King."

"Andi Coffey and Associates, downtown. You don't need to come."

The coolness of her response drives home what I've already suspected—that she's still not comfortable with me. It doesn't matter. I need to know why Emily hired a lawyer as much as Delaney does.

"I want to go with you."

An exasperated huff is her only response.

"Why don't you want me there?" I ask. Multiple, overlapping voices become louder, as if she's walking through a crowd.

"Everyone, please take your seats," she says, and then whispers, "I don't know this lawyer and would prefer to not have my private affairs broadcast to a stranger."

"It's exactly why you need me with you. Andi is a high-profile personal injury lawyer. To my knowledge, she doesn't practice probate law. Who knows what else this is about."

"Fine. I have to go," Delaney says, disconnecting.

Her tone is reminiscent of Sonya scolding me as our marriage imploded. I'd phone that I was having a drink with the guys after work, and she'd say, "Fine!" and slam the phone down. The subtext, however, was, *I'm not okay with it but don't want to argue.*

I navigate to the law firm website, also known on her billboards across the city as "GetCoffey." Andi is front and center on the homepage, sitting on the edge of her desk, dressed in a dark-blue courtroom suit, holding an oversized, law firm-branded white coffee mug. To the right, it reads in white lettering:

"In a whiplash auto accident? I can't help you. Slip and fall? Take it somewhere else. We only handle tough state and federal cases that make or break lives and reputations: Wrongful death, mass tort, complex litigation. Tell us about your case. If you're lucky, you'll GetCoffey!"

Chapter 11

The fingerprint news combined with the fake pizza guy threat unnerves me into insomnia. I spend much of the night unable to sleep. After breakfast, I inventory the meager lineup of clean business attire for the meeting. One black pinstripe and two blue courtroom suits hang unused since my suspension. As a store detective, I only need a sports jacket to hide the handcuffs and two-way radio, which I need to return. Regardless of what my future offers, I'm done sweating in the coffin.

I text Delaney that I'm on my way and punch Andi's address into Google Maps.

A mental list of questions scrolls through my head as I park and exit the parking garage across the street from Andi's office. Does she know Emily's true identity? Why is there a will? Does it mention electronics or a video? Why did Emily choose her? This city boasts an abundance of lawyers with expertise in drafting estate documents.

I spot Delaney pacing in front of the main entrance. She's clad in red slacks and a white, buttoned-up blouse. Her jet-black hair is pulled into a neat ponytail.

"You look spiffy," I say.

"Thanks." She lowers her head. "I spend 90 percent of my existence in scrubs and the rest in pajamas." Then she points to the street sign, Coffey Way. "She has her own thoroughfare. Impressive."

I chuckle. "Nah, this road has been around a long time. She's business savvy, though, locating her office here."

"Do you know much about her?" Delaney asks.

"Duquesne Law grad. She has a reputation as a smart, aggressive trial lawyer who loves media attention. You ready to head upstairs?"

Delaney grasps the entrance door handle, pauses, and says, "My stomach is swimming."

"Mine too," I tell her. "Let's get some questions answered."

Why would Emily need a high-powered lawyer like Andi Coffey? I'm afraid we're in for an unpleasant surprise.

The client waiting area is what I'd expect at a major law firm. A plush, brown leather couch is one of several designer furniture pieces. Two waist-high bronze statues of Themis and her scales of justice guard the engraved, double wooden doors behind the receptionist.

Signed paintings and watercolors depicting Pittsburgh landmarks decorate the walls. The largest is a panorama of the city from the vantage point of Mount Washington. The view never ceases to tingle my gut with awe. It's the Pittsburgh version of looking over the Grand Canyon.

Prior to the forced hiatus, my office furnishings resembled something out of an AA meeting room: bulk-purchase plastic chairs along with a mandatory television bolted to the wall, tuned to game shows or playing a loop of my latest commercial. Why invest in sprucing the place when the client's sole concern is the size of the settlement check?

"May I help you?" Coffey's legal receptionist matches the high-powered feel of the office. His ivory-colored lightweight summer sweater and tie are understated but drive home Coffey's attention to image and detail.

"I have an appointment to see Ms. Coffey. My name is Delaney Martin."

"She's expecting you, but on another call," he says. "Please make yourselves comfortable, and I'll let her know you're here. There's a coffee and espresso station behind you. I can also fetch a soft drink or water if you prefer."

"I'm fine," I say, taking a spot at the end of the brown leather sofa.

"Nothing for me, thank you," Delaney says and positions herself on the opposite side.

The *Action News* late-morning segment on the big screen draws my attention. The caption at the top of the screen, in particular.

Two bodies discovered in abandoned McKees Rocks row house.

Erin Campanara, the reporter on the scene, is standing in front of the same dilapidated buildings being demolished to make way for King Fox's rehab facility.

"Police were called to vacant structures behind me when a worker prepping them for demolition discovered the decomposed remains of two bodies in the basement. They also found needles and other addict paraphernalia. Neighbors allege these long-abandoned row houses have long been a magnet for squatting and drug use.

Delaney picks up a magazine and says, "The area has been blighted for a while. It's no surprise the unhoused are using the buildings for a roof over their heads and protection from the elements. Where are they supposed to go?"

The double doors swing open. Andi Coffey strides into the waiting room, hand extended. "Delaney, a pleasure to meet you. I'm sorry it's under these circumstances."

Andi's matching black blazer and skirt are classic high-powered, courtroom-ready attire. I want to once again put on my armor and stand before a jury.

"Me too," Delaney says. "I brought a friend. This is—"

"Jason Feldman," Andi says, pivoting the handshake. "It's been a while."

"It has," I say, with no clue where we met.

She gestures toward her office. "Why don't you both come back."

Her desk resembles the trash aftermath of the annual Fourth of July concerts at Point State Park. They take days to clean up. Depositions, empty water bottles, files, and loose documents are strewn about. Banker's boxes line the credenza, each with magic marker hieroglyphics I suspect only her paralegal understands.

"Please excuse the mess. I'm preparing for a major trial set for next week." She pushes aside a stack of papers and opens a manilla legal folder. Her eyes crinkle, and she shakes her head in frustration.

"It's here somewhere. Again, I apologize. It's been crazy." She picks up her phone. "Jonathan, is the Emily Wilson file on my desk? I can't locate it."

I tap Delaney's ankle with my foot and shoot her a *Should we tell Andi about the fingerprints?* eyebrow raise.

"How did you know Emily died?" Delaney asks.

"It's morbid, but I scan the obits. It seems like someone I know passes away daily. It wasn't hard to put two and two together with the name and photo."

But it wasn't her real name, I think. How could the identity math add up unless she already knows about the alias?

Jonathan enters the room and digs under a pile of depositions, extracts a file folder, and hands it to Andi.

"Right under my nose," Andi says, laughing. "I wish I could say this is the first time it's happened. I don't know what I'd do without him."

Andi opens the folder and takes out what appears to be the will, along with a sealed letter. She hands them to Delaney and says, "Take your time reading. I have plenty of work to keep me occupied."

Delaney's lips tighten, and I can tell she's fighting tears as she reads. The lull gives me an opportunity to check a question off my list.

"Why did Emily retain you instead of an estate lawyer?"

Andi picks up a Mont Blanc pen and rolls it back and forth between her fingers. "How did you know each other?"

"We were in a relationship."

"I didn't know. My deepest sympathies. I'm sure you're aware that attorney-client privilege survives Emily's passing, and the presence of a third party can destroy it. It's best you wait in the lobby while I speak with Delaney."

Andi is nuts if she thinks I came here to stand on the sidelines while details of my girlfriend's life are bandied about.

"I'm a lawyer, so privilege remains intact," I counter.

"My mistake." Andi flashes an uncomfortable gaze at Delaney. "Was your law license restored?"

Being caught in an ill-advised fib shrinks me into a miniature doll in my seat. "I'm back in the saddle at midnight."

Andi, being the consummate professional, doesn't pile on. "I don't think it's a big deal, but as a precaution, give us a few minutes alone."

The opportunity for a graceful exit triggers a deep breath, and I vow to never bullshit her again.

"I'll be in the waiting room if you need me."

Andi stands and circles to the front of the desk. "It was a pleasure, though I wish it wasn't under such sad conditions. Emily was a sweetheart."

We shake hands, and I say, "Earlier you referenced seeing me again. I've racked my brain but can't place a prior connection."

"You and Sonya sat next to my ex and me at the Allegheny Bar Association Annual Gala three years ago. I was sorry to see her step down as district attorney. She was what this county needed, a real reform DA."

Ah, I think. She doesn't need to know that I was drunk as a skunk at that event. Sonya and I had a huge fight about it. One of my many nights on the couch. I wonder if she's aware Sonya's now in Washington DC, engaged to a lobbyist.

"I'll be outside," I say, not interested in rehashing my failed marriage.

"You don't need to stay," Delaney says. "When I'm finished here, it's running errands all day, and I start a double shift in the morning. I'll call and fill you in."

I'm not leaving. Despite Delaney's misgivings, Emily would want me by her side.

After grabbing an espresso, I sort through periodicals. Some options include *Pittsburgh Magazine*, *Whirl*, and *Western Pennsylvania History*. A markedly different selection from the usual fare of my law office, *People*, *Us Weekly*, and the *National Enquirer*.

The home and condo listings in the *Pittsburgh Real Estate Guide* remind me how much the city has changed since I graduated from law school. Expensive condominiums now line the North Shore along the Allegheny River where the old Heinz plant used to be. Halfway through the magazine is a story about King Fox. The guy is everywhere. He must have a top-notch publicist.

"A Point Breeze mansion is the new home of former ballplayer and Pittsburgh addiction recovery royalty, King Fox. Situated in the same neighborhood as the former residences of Pittsburgh industrial titans Clay Frick and Andrew Carnegie, the seven-bedroom, eight-bath behemoth of a home also boasts an indoor batting cage, Olympic-size swimming pool, and pickleball court."

The photo of his home confirms what I suspected, given that King didn't deny it when I confronted him. Emily was leaving his house.

The two-page article goes into further detail, including another picture of King sitting at what they describe as an early twentieth-century mahogany roll-top desk costing $15,000.

The rich get richer, I think, and toss the publication on the table. Then, I call Maz to prod him into checking the license plate number.

He answers in a hushed tone. "In the coffin, can't talk."

"This will only take a second. You've mentioned friends in the department who do you favors. I really need your help with that plate."

Chapter 12

*A*s we exit to the street, I say, "Thank you for not belaboring my past in front of Delaney."

"That's not my concern right now." Andi pushes the button to the stoplight. "How much does she know?"

"She's aware, like the entire city."

We round the corner to the club entrance. The doorman, attired in a walnut-brown uniform and gold-trimmed Pershing cap, pulls the door open.

"It's superb to see you again, Ms. Coffey. Will you be joining us for breakfast?"

"Thank you, no, Adam. Are the billiards tables in use?"

"No, Ma'am. Not at the moment."

Did I hear her right? We can't be playing pool.

Greeting us in the lobby is an oversized oil-on-canvas portrait of General John Forbes with a gold plaque underneath. The inscription outlines his service in the French and Indian War and occupation of the French outpost, Fort Duquesne, in what is now Point State Park.

Andi's heels clack on the marble floor as I follow her down a hallway to etched-glass swinging doors. We enter an expansive room of dark oak furnishings. Paintings of famous Pittsburgh historical figures line the walls like White House portraits of former presidents. Two Persian rugs cover the hardwood floors. On top of each is a pool table unlike the beer-and-a-shot bowling-alley felt slabs I've played on. These are carved mahogany with ivory inlays.

An attendant in a monogrammed red jacket hurries to us from the far end of the room where he was wiping down the bar.

"Ms. Coffey, wonderful to see you again. Will you be playing with us today?"

"Yes, Albert. I'd be grateful if you would uncase my stick and rack us for a game of nine-ball."

She has her own pool cue? I want to ask, "How is humiliating me in a skill game going to advance our dialogue?"

Albert opens a glass case with cues aligned and a brass plate under each. I peer over his shoulder as he selects the one above Andi's name. With intricate, multicolored inlays and ivory rings in the handles, it looks like it's on loan from the Carnegie Museum of Art. He then opens a separate cabinet and hands me a plain, house stick.

"Do you play?" Andi asks.

The last time anyone asked me that question was in law school. After an evening studying for the bar exam, Sonya and I went to Bowling City in the South Hills and hit the pool room. When I asked her the same question, she sipped her beer and then kissed the tip of the pool cue. "I'm the Asian, female Minnesota Fats." She wasn't kidding and kicked my ass three straight games.

"Jason?"

"Sorry, it's been a few years. I appreciate the innovative approach to business discussion, but I'd rather sit in one of those comfortable over-stuffed chairs and relax."

"This is how I find my inner balance," she says. "A difficult but well-executed shot is an exercise in cause and effect. Each angle is calculated in advance. If you are wrong, no ball rolls the way you want, and the shot goes to shit."

I chalk my cue and wonder if she's taken a subtle dig at my life. "Let's skip the break shot. You go ahead."

She leans over the table, draws back the cue, and says, "Tell me about your relationship with Emily."

Before I can answer, her right arm pistons forward, striking the cue ball. It explodes against the triangle-shaped rack, scattering the numbered billiard balls. I gawk in awe as the eight rolls toward the corner pocket. If it goes in, she wins.

"We dated for six months," I say, as it comes to rest less than an inch away.

"Damn, thought I had it," she says. "How did you meet?"

I'm unsure if death extinguishes the moral obligation to not out others in the program, but in this case, necessity demands it.

"We were in the same Alcoholics Anonymous group."

She chalks her cue and says, "Emily mentioned being in recovery but not a boyfriend, which brings me to this impromptu meeting. I felt it best to speak with you separate from Delaney."

I survey the table for the best shot. How can I concentrate on this when my girlfriend is dead? Then again, that might be the point. Focus under stress. No effective trial lawyer can function without mastering that quality.

Andi must sense my shot selection indecision. "I'd try for the five ball in the side pocket," she tells me. "There's little angle and an unobstructed line to the hole. For a beginner, it's best to go for simple solutions with high probabilities. It builds confidence."

Is this pool or Andi Coffey life-coach lessons, I think, lining up the shot.

"Why did Emily hire you?" I ask. "It wasn't for you to draft her will."

"You're right. A colleague took care of it for me. Emily retained me to file a wrongful death lawsuit against Sunny Awakenings Treatment Center and its owner, King Fox. I'm sure you've heard of him."

My heart skips as I thrust the cue forward. The five ball tracks wide, missing the target. King didn't say a word, but why would he?

"I'm sorry," Andi says. "Background noise helps hone my concentration, but I'll keep quiet if you like." She bends over the table and lines up her next shot. "Four in the side pocket."

The cue ball impacts the purple sphere and stops dead while the four spins on a silent track to its target and drops.

"I know who King is. What do you know about Emily's name change?"

She chalks her cue. "Everything. It's all legal and on file with the Philadelphia County Prothonotary."

Before I can ask why Emily changed it, Andi says, "If you want to know more about that, you'll have to ask Delaney."

I wonder how deep this rabbit hole goes. "Who would Emily sue on behalf of?" I ask.

"Her son."

I drop my cue onto the table, causing several balls to career in different directions. The eight ball skips over the table edge and drops to the floor. It bounces, then rolls toward Albert. He picks it up and says, "It happens all the time, sir."

"Her what?" I ask.

"You didn't know she had a child? His name was Patrick. He died of an overdose in Philadelphia." She motions to Albert, who takes her stick and returns mine to the case. "The news caught you by surprise. I didn't mean to upset you."

"Surprise" is the understatement of the century. I'm floored. Maybe Emily needed more time, but if you tell someone you love them, wouldn't you also mention that you had a child? I told her about Sam on our first date. For the first time, it dawns on me that Emily always skirted the nitty-gritty of her past, even in AA sharing. Alcoholics opened up about incarceration, addict parents, and even losing their kids to overdoses. Emily rarely raised her hand, and when she did, gave only her sobriety date and said that she was happy to be there. I didn't think much about her reluctance at the time. Not everyone's talkative in the meetings; they're just trying to stay sober. Many times, I've sat for an hour without saying a word.

"Does Delaney know?" I manage to ask Andi.

"Of course." She takes a towel from Albert.

"For how long? Before we came to see you?"

Andi cleans the chalk off her hands. "You should discuss that with her."

Her evasive answer pisses me off. It reminds me of my last car accident mediation. After three hours of back and forth, the defense lawyer made an insulting low-ball offer, and we didn't settle the case. As we all left the building, I overheard him saying to the claims adjuster, "Good job. We didn't tell them anything new or pay the claim." I thought, why the hell did you bring me here and waste my time if you had no intention of acting in good faith? I wonder if that's Andi's strategy. Divulge little and, in the process, get as much information as she can. I'm not falling for it.

"How old was Patrick?" I ask.

"Seventeen."

My god, so young. I fight to stay analytical and on a steady emotional keel. "Then King is aware of the lawsuit."

"The county sheriff served him last week. We also sued the Philadelphia recovery home Patrick lived at when he overdosed."

Facts King conveniently neglected to mention in his office.

"I'd like a copy of the lawsuit," I tell her.

She takes a step back and studies me. "I'll have Jonathan email it to you. I'm guessing you've had enough pool."

She's right. What I need instead is a drink or an AA meeting.

"Did you bring me here to tell me about Patrick?"

"I'm interested in anything Emily may have said regarding King Fox or Sunny Awakenings," she says.

That's the point. She didn't tell me a damn thing, including her real name. She must not have thought she could confide in me, and that tears at my heart. Was our relationship real?

"Are you and your guest finished playing?" Albert takes our hand towels, and Andi hands him a twenty.

"Before we leave, let's sit and finish this conversation." She points to the overstuffed chairs by the bar. I follow, annoyed that we didn't do this in the first place while also taking note of the top-shelf offerings of whiskey sipped as privileged power brokers plot the downfall of modern civilization—an alcoholic's dream or nightmare.

"What else do you know about Emily's past?" I ask.

"She told me about her name change the first meeting but was not what I would consider a trusting person," she says. "You shouldn't take it personally that she didn't tell you about that or about Patrick. There were good reasons, and six months is a lifetime in some relationships, only a blip in others."

I get the point. Emily and I revealed ourselves in bits and spurts. In active addiction, I'd snort a line, down shots of Jack, and vomit a fabricated story in a bar. But in sobriety, the truth is raw and painful.

"Can you tell me why she changed it?" I ask.

Andi shakes her head. "Again, my concern is privilege. Nothing is stopping Delaney from filling you in. She is not bound by lawyer confidentiality and knows everything."

No wonder Delaney was upset, I think.

"Do the cops have any leads?" Andi asks.

"Not to my knowledge. Jeanette Keane—she's the lead detective— promised to make the case a top priority. Sunny Awakenings also hired a company to retrieve the laptop and cell phone. They claim both belong to them. Do you have them?"

Andi shakes her head. "Emily didn't entrust any property to me. Who did they retain?"

That's strike three. On my way here, I held out hope that Andi had one or both of the items. I can't think of another logical choice that hasn't already been ruled out. I slide Mary Lou's card to her.

"Bayou Intelligence and Analytics out of New Orleans," I tell her.

She picks up the card. "An investigation firm? The police didn't find the items?"

"No, but the president of the intelligence firm, Mary Lou Dubois, offered me a big reward for the return of the phone and laptop."

Andi rubs her fingers together. "I can never get the cue chalk residue off. Did she make the same offer to Delaney?"

The question knocks me off center. Wouldn't Delaney have told her if they did? Maybe this is a test of how forthcoming I am.

"If they have, she hasn't said a word to me, and I haven't asked yet. I also met with King Fox at his office yesterday."

Andi cocks her head. "Is that so? For what reason?"

My inclination is not to admit that I flew into a jealous rage and made a stupid decision to confront King. Even worse, that he handed my ass to me. I unfortunately don't see any other choice. That he admitted dating Emily will be important to Andi's case.

"Someone sent me a photo of him and Emily together," I say. "It led me to believe they were having an affair. I blew my stack and confronted him." Without waiting for the ask, I open the snapshot on my phone and slide it across the table.

She studies it. "Glamorous outfit. This only proves they were together at this moment. Where does the romantic relationship come from?"

"His lips. He admitted it but claims it was before Emily and I began our relationship."

I brief Andi on everything King revealed in the meeting. What I leave out is the fake pizza guy. Maybe Andi already knows about the video he demanded? If so, she's not going to tell me because of privilege. Until I'm sure it exists, and know what's on it, there's no point in broaching the topic with her, or anyone else.

Andi taps the crystal on her watch. "We'll pick this up later. A witness is coming to the office for trial prep. I'll fill Delaney in on this discussion."

My self-inflicted wound stings. I should have briefed Delaney about the meeting with King. She'll think I'm holding back information. I need tell her before Andi does.

Chapter 13

Ten minutes later I push through the Waggaman's revolving door and text Maz: *I'm in the lobby.*

Irina isn't at her station, which is disappointing. I wanted to say goodbye, but I can send her an Instagram DM, which she checks about as often as I do texts or voicemails.

"Feldman!" Maz's voice booms from the top of the escalator, reverberating off the glass fragrance counter. He descends to the bottom, and I close the distance until we are nose to nose.

He thrusts his index finger into my face as shoppers pass, oblivious to our drama. "Don't bother lying. I know you're not coming back."

My instinct is to swat his hand away, but I need that favor and keep my arms plastered to my sides. "I don't know where you're getting that from," I tell him. "The Old Man okayed two weeks off, and this is only day one."

"I didn't just fall off a turnip truck," Maz says. "Jeanette told me you're getting your law license back this week, and now you want me to help you?"

It might have been an innocent disclosure, but I don't appreciate Keane putting my personal business out there. I need Maz to run that plate, and she may have screwed me.

"What do you want? Cash? I don't have much on me, but I'll hit an ATM. Name your price, within reason."

"I don't need your money."

In unison, we wave at Irina, who is walking into the building holding a venti Starbucks cup. She smiles, wiggles her pinky, and enters the restroom.

Maz swings around with a wide grin, highlighting three chipped upper teeth, no doubt the result of his boxing days.

"You and Irina have gotten close the last year. Anything I should know?"

Where the hell is this going? "We're friends, nothing more."

"Good. Here's what I want in exchange for the license plate number."

"How about you do it because we're long-time coworkers?"

"Yeah." Maz snickers. "We meet weekly for tea and crumpets at the William Penn."

He jerks his head toward Irina, who is now at her station, spraying the wrist of a woman who sniffs and puckers her lips.

"I want you to set us up."

"Irina? You're joking."

"You think she's out of my league?" Maz expands his chest and plants his hands on his hips.

I inspect his rotund stomach bulging over the belt of his Waggaman's expandable waistline, "Easy Stretch" slacks. "Irina's in her early thirties. How old are you?"

"I'm fifty-two, and age is only a number. Do you want the plate? That's my price."

I've seen worse age differences, but it's more than that. Her Instagram account is replete with hot-guy-date photos. My gaze bounces from Maz to Irina and back as I dig for another solution. In the old days, a line of white powder courage would give me the confidence to make this happen. With a sigh, I resign myself.

"I'll do my best."

"I'm not interested in your best. If you want my help, make it happen."

"Don't you want to know why I need this?" I ask him.

"Nope, and I don't want the plate number until you deliver on your end. I'm headed up to the office. Let me know when you close the deal."

I can't remember the last time I set a guy up on a date. Not to mention, Maz already has two strikes against him. Both are that Irina can't stand him. A direct approach will best serve this situation. When she slaps me, I'll cross Maz off my list of potential allies and move on to Plan B, which I haven't yet devised.

I approach Irina. A litany of opening lines run through my head.

I have this friend...

Doesn't Maz exude an understated lumberjack masculinity?

Don't you agree, looks aren't everything?

She's ringing up a customer as I tap her shoulder. "Hey, Irina, you have a second to chat?"

Before she can answer, my phone vibrates with a text from Delaney: *I'm livid! Can you talk?*

Sure, what's wrong?

Seconds later, she calls. I step away and answer it. Irina is busy taking a selfie for her side hustle as an Instagram influencer. She holds up a $400 perfume bottle and smiles into her phone camera.

"Is everything okay?" I ask.

"No. The medical examiner won't release Emmi's body for burial. I purchased a plot at Allegheny Cemetery and wanted to discuss the service with you. There's no point now."

Delaney's usual calm and confident tone is rushed and an octave higher. Her stress is palpable, and the guilt of not doing enough to help her stabs into my stomach lining. She's working double shifts, saving lives, while I just took two weeks off to devote all of my time to this.

"I know it's frustrating, but there's a positive aspect," I tell her. "They wouldn't hold on to Emily's body unless the investigation is ongoing. That's a good thing."

"You wanted to speak with me?" Irina hovers over my shoulder.

I cover the mouthpiece. "Yes, one second." Part of me hopes that Irina tires of waiting and leaves. It would postpone the inevitable humiliation of her laughing in my face.

"Delaney, are you still there?"

"I'm here. Would you be interested in an early dinner at my place? I've got a late call at the hospital, so I'd need you to be punctual."

Given her distrust to date, I'm taken aback. I want to close the gap but would rather not walk past where Emily's body lay and I failed to save her. I also can't shake the EMT's last words and Emily's half-open eyes. It was our anniversary. I should have taken the afternoon off. We could have done so many other things that would have brought us together earlier in the day. Kennywood park. A romantic walk along the top of Mount Washington. We had talked about driving out to Idlewild Park.

"There's a lot to discuss, but can we meet somewhere else? I'm not ready to return."

"Imagine how it upsets me being here every day." Delaney's breaths are deep and quick. "If I have to walk through that door, you can manage two hours."

She's right, and I feel like a heel for pushing back. I've been focused on my own grief without considering hers. "What time should I be there?"

"I leave for the hospital at nine, so six will do. Does sushi work for you? I can pick some up."

This will be the perfect opportunity for both of us to lay all of our cards on the table. I'm not leaving there without knowing everything she does about Emily, and I won't hold back either. I'm tired of our piecemeal approach to trust.

Irina taps me on the shoulder. "I'm leaving soon."

"Sushi's fine," I say to Delaney. "See you then. I'll be on time."

Irina sprays Windex across the countertop and wipes it down with a glass polishing cloth. The perfect time to ask her about Maz, though it might as well be a rhetorical question. There's no way she'll agree, and I'll be back where I started with the license plate.

"Sorry about the interruption. Can I ask a favor?"

"What kind?"

There's a nervous hitch in her voice. I get it. She knows me at work, but outside these walls, we're strangers. I could be asking her for anything. In the spectrum of possibilities running through her head, I'm sure that what I'm about to pitch her isn't on the list.

Here we go, I think. *Swing away.*

"What do you think of Maz?"

She wrinkles her nose. "I don't like him. Crude and vulgar man. He's not a gentleman like you."

It's the expected response, but hearing it from her lips triggers a low-grade nausea.

"I understand, and I wouldn't ask if I had a choice."

"What is the favor?" Her tone isn't enthusiastic.

"Would you have dinner with him? Nothing else, only a meal. He can do me a massive favor. This is the only way he'll agree."

She touches a gold crucifix hanging around her neck. "I'm sorry, Jason. I'd prefer not to."

How can I bring her around? Maz isn't the most polished guy in Pittsburgh, but how many old-school cops are? On the rare occasion he lets his guard down, there's a funny subtle softness underneath. Also, if I lost my son as he did...I'll bet she doesn't know.

"Have you been in Maz's office?" I ask

"Yes, I had to sign statement about the window he broke with his radio."

"Then you saw the two framed photos on his desk, a young police officer and a child."

She noodles the cross between her fingers, and then allows it to fall back against her neck. "I think so. Why?"

"They are his son, Sean, and grandson, Brian. Sean died in the line of duty. Maz has custody of Brian. He can be abrasive, but he has a good heart."

"That is sad," she says. "Where is the mother?"

That's a great question. In all the time I've worked here, Maz hasn't mentioned her. She could be dead for all I know. If it was a divorce, I'd expect a guy with his demeanor to bitch about child support or some other aspect of their broken relationship. Yet, not one word.

"I don't know. He's never spoken of her. It's only dinner, Irina. I'll even park outside the restaurant if it will make you feel safer."

She twirls at a strand of hair until it envelops her index finger. "Perhaps you can do something for me? I'm in legal trouble and need help."

Irina is aware I went to law school, but we've never discussed why I'm a store detective and not a practicing lawyer. I guess she didn't want to pry. How bad can her predicament be? A minor car accident? Maybe a traffic ticket? She could be my first post-license-reinstatement client.

"What's the problem?"

"You know ICE?"

I nod and kiss my first case goodbye. Her ask will be way above my pay grade. "Yes, Immigration and Customs Enforcement. Why?"

"Two men come to my apartment and tell me I must go back to Ukraine, or they will arrest me. I need a lawyer to stay in America."

"Did you overstay your visa?"

"It does not matter. I need your help. You are a lawyer." She looks left and right as if worried that someone is overhearing her. She clearly doesn't want to say more here. How can I assist her if I don't know what the specific issue is?

"Immigration law is tricky. You need an attorney who specializes in it."

"Help me stay, and I will have dinner with him."

That was a sharp reversal. At least I know upfront what the quid pro quo is.

"I'll do what I can."

Irina rushes around the counter and hugs me.

"Thank you, Jason, my friend."

We walk to a more private area where she confides that it's a visa issue. The problem is, I've been out of the game for two years and don't know any lawyers who handle that type of case. Maybe Andi can help. Now, it's time to break the good news to Maz. He's hovering by the store entrance, watching us like a teenager checking out his high school crush.

"She'll have dinner with you." I hand him a yellow sticky with Irina's number on it. "It's not a hookup. Keep your hands to yourself."

Maz raises a fist for a bro-bump, but I'm in no mood.

"You da man," he says and drops his arm. "Did she say anything else? Where do you think I should take her?"

Three scalding showers won't wash this stink off, I think and hand him a slip of paper with the plate number written on it.

"That's up to you. I need the plate owner today."

"Not how it works, sonny boy. I'll do it, but delivery on receipt of goods. The date comes first."

Now I'm worried. Will Irina attach the same condition to her part of the deal and demand I help her first? The tangled web of favors stops here.

"No, I'm altering the deal terms. You have a yes from her. Give me what I want today, or it will change to a no. I'll hire a private investigator instead."

Maz steals a quick glance at Irina, then nods to himself.

"It's about time you grew some balls," he says, laughing. "Fine, I'll have your plate number in an hour or two. Fast enough?"

"By the way," I tell him, "You can't reach out to Keane."

"Mum's the word. Running plates outside of an official investigation is against department policy. But I have a pal who will do it on the down-low."

I'm about to exit the store for my dinner with Delaney when I pause and scrutinize the outdated, brown plaid sports jacket he's worn since his days on the force. He's also wearing a dress shirt that accentuates his beach ball stomach.

"Can I make one tiny suggestion for your date?" I ask. "Use your employee discount on some Spanx."

As I push through the revolving door to the sidewalk, he yells, "I have a dad bod. Women love it."

Chapter 14

*P*arking in front of Delaney's condo, I imagine knocking and Emily answering the door. She'll kiss me and say, "Early as always. I need a few more minutes." Why wasn't I early that evening? I still can't shake the vibe that something is off. At a minimum, I want to hit the pillow tonight knowing everything Andi told Delaney and vice versa.

The curtain edges aside. Seconds later, the front door opens to Delaney wearing a baggy Pitt Medical School sweatshirt and jeans. With one foot inside, I hesitate and catch my breath, unable to look at the spot where Emily died. Delaney was right. It can't compare to walking through this door into emptiness every day.

"It must be painful back here for the first time," she says. "Have a seat, and I'll set the table."

I know this condo. I've eaten, slept, and made love here. The furniture is in the same place. Yet, I'm a stranger, as if this is my first time here. Emily's familiar smell is gone, replaced by Delaney's antiseptic skin soap and steam vac detergent. For me, this place is now a receptacle of grief and painful memories.

Delaney transfers the sushi from a plastic container to a serving dish. I'm drawn to Emily's room, where her belongings are piled on the bed. Whenever Delaney worked an overnight shift, we'd order out and binge on Netflix. I'd be gone the next morning before Delaney got home. We weren't embarrassed, but Emily understood the stress Delaney was under with her increased workload. She didn't want to be the roommate from hell.

"What are you planning on doing with her things?" I ask.

Delaney comes out of the kitchen. Rolls and sashimi are arranged in a perfect circle, with ginger and wasabi in the center of the sushi plate.

"I'm donating it all to charity."

That's what Emily would want, I think. Whether it was addiction, the environment, or animal rescue, she was continually giving small amounts of money to various nonprofits.

"Any luck finding her phone and computer?" I ask.

"No. They're for sure not here."

It's like they vaporized into thin air. I tick off the events leading up to her death. When we went to bed the night before, she placed the phone on my nightstand. Then we made love. After using the bathroom, she checked her email and texts. The next morning, I kissed her on the cheek and said, "Happy anniversary, sweetie." Her skin smelled of lavender body lotion. The last thing on my mind was her phone. I don't remember seeing it again, but she texted me later that day. What happened in those hours before I showed up at her place?

Delaney snaps me out of it. "Let's eat. These are your Philadelphia and rainbow rolls. The sashimi is my favorite, but help yourself. Here we have maguro, and next to it is ika."

My phone vibrates.

"Would you consider it rude if I check texts? I'm expecting something important."

She pinches a piece of squid. "No insult taken. If I were on call, mine would be next to my soy sauce."

Three Rivers Luxury Leasing. 50 Stanwix Street. 412-279-2371.

Maz came through. Now I have to devise a plan to get the name of the Lexus driver. I can't just show up and ask them to hand over confidential client data.

I text back: *Thanks!*

He responds: *Dinner with Irina is tonight. You didn't mention she had a daughter.*

I had no idea Irina had a child. The three of us saw each other practically every day but only revealed our filtered selves. As it turns out, Emily and I were no different.

I text back: *Remember what I said, best behavior.*

"Is everything okay?" Delaney asks.

I turn my phone face down. "All good. Let's eat."

During dinner, I talk about my life while she tells me about being an emergency room doctor and a med school professor. We don't cover any new ground, and there's a growing undercurrent of tension like the buzz of an electricity transformer about to explode. Isn't she going to brief me on what Andi told her? Every unanswered question raises my blood pressure. I can't stomach another redundant platitude from either of us.

"You were beside yourself getting in that elevator at Andi's office," I say. "You also promised to fill me in on the meeting but all we've done is gab. What the hell is going on, Delaney?"

Her body stiffens the way it did in response to Officer Sunseri's insults. "I was going to tell you but wanted to eat first."

I bow my head and take a breath. The fact that I'm here demonstrates how far we've come in the trust department. A tantrum risks undoing it.

"I know about Emily's son," I tell her. "Andi filled me in after you left."

Delaney's lips purse and she lets loose a long exhale of air as if she's relieved. She stands and puts the sushi plate on the breakfast bar. "I'm glad you know and was going to tell you after we ate. I might as well have been living with a stranger. Who was Emily?"

"That's what I want us to figure out. We were tethered to the same lie."

I help Delaney clear the table. Is this the right moment to ask if she knew about Emily's romantic relationship with King? If she thinks I'm accusing her of concealing it, she might kick me out, and I'd be on my own.

"Would you like some coffee?" she asks.

"Sure. May I read the will?"

"It's on the sofa side table."

I pick up the document and underline each word with my finger so nothing gets missed.

The Last Will and Testament of Emily Wilson.

It contains mostly boilerplate clauses. Section 4.1 reads: *I appoint my friend, Delaney Martin, executor,* followed by Delaney's social security number and birthdate.

Section 4.2 gives Delaney authority to initiate or continue litigation on behalf of the estate, but it's the supplemental request that adds another piece to the puzzle:

> *If still pending at the time of my death, I request that Delaney Martin, executor, continue my legal action against Sunny Awakenings Treatment Center and King Fox, or their successors in interest. I've explained as much as possible in the attached letter.*

Delaney sets the coffee mug on the side table next to my chair. She's holding an envelope in her hand.

"Unless it's too personal, may I also read the letter the will refers to?" I ask.

"Of course you can." Delaney slides the letter out. "It's written as much to you as it is to me."

The only sounds for the next ten minutes are our occasional sips as I digest Emily's hidden truth and swallow down both coffee and relief. Delaney didn't know about Patrick until we met with Andi. No wonder she was upset leaving the office.

> *Dearest Delaney:*
>
> *I arrived in Pittsburgh from Philly scared and alone. You took me in and were the best friend I ever had. You made me laugh and held me when I cried. I did that a lot. You will learn I have not been candid about my past, including my name, which was Emily Williams. I went through the legal process of changing it to Emily Wilson before moving to Pittsburgh.*
>
> *I'm not a criminal or wanted by the police, but I had good reasons. The primary being justice for my son, Patrick. Shocked? Yes, I had a son. He was the light of my life and the sweetest boy you would ever meet. No parent's journey is without challenges, however. He also struggled with addiction.*
>
> *I spent every penny I had to help him, ending with his stint at the Sunny Awakenings Treatment Center, then the Safe Harbor sober home in Kensington. He lived in deplorable conditions, and drug use was rampant. One night, Patrick overdosed and died. I tried to get the police to investigate, but they wrote it off as accidental. It was clear I was on my own.*

After changing my name, I moved to Pittsburgh and took a job with Sunny Awakenings as a marketing representative. The goal was to prove they not only murdered my son but are body brokers, sending many other parents and addicts down the same tragic path for their own profit. That is why I hired Andi to pursue a wrongful death case and expose them. It turned my stomach, but I also did what was necessary to get close to King so the truth could come out.

You're the only person I trust to see this through. Patrick's father died when he was a child. Of course, it's your choice, but I hope you'll bring these horrible people to account. I'm sure they've followed me and hacked into my computer and phone. Hence, this will and letter.

My son and the many victims of King Fox had the right to find their light and change their lives. I hope you will agree.

Love always,

Emmi

Emily and I lived six months of lies. Maybe she was afraid I'd tell someone? I would have helped her. And what the hell is body brokering?

Memories of my childhood summers at Emma Kaufmann Camp bring to mind the eerie tales the counselors shared about waking up in the bathtub and missing a kidney.

"What's the connection between a rehab center and selling body parts?"

"She's referring to a different type," Delaney says. "Have you played the stock market?"

"I'm no Mark Cuban, but I've dabbled."

"Do you understand the practice of churning?"

I think back to my Securities Law class. "A broker buys and sells stocks to generate commissions without regard for the needs of the investor."

"Correct. It also goes on in the treatment industry," Delaney says. "An addiction treatment center or recovery house fills beds while disregarding the patient's specific needs. As soon as the insurance runs out or the family goes bankrupt, they release the patient back to the street. Marketers then scour the streets for more bodies."

When my last stay in treatment ended, I returned home to a bank account and roof over my head. Health insurance took care of all of it. I had no concept of this practice. Emily never once mentioned it. Maybe she thought that straying into any casual discussion of body brokering might risk blowing her cover.

"Sounds shady and unethical. Aren't there laws?"

"There are, but they are difficult to enforce. For every facility the authorities shut down, another takes its place like whack-a-mole," she says.

For every action, there's a reaction. Was it Emily's mission to get justice for Patrick that triggered King to hire Mary Lou? Whatever is on that phone may be the key to figuring out the truth of what happened in this living room.

"There's more to this you're unaware of." I set my now-empty mug on the table and brace myself, unsure if she'll be upset that I didn't tell her sooner.

"Such as?"

"The other day, a woman named Mary Lou Dubois approached me at the Point. She claimed to work for a company called Bayou Intelligence and Analytics."

"What did she want?"

The same thing the cops are searching for, Emily's phone and laptop." I hand her the card Mary Lou gave me.

She studies it and says, "What's her interest in this?"

"She claims the items belong to Sunny Awakenings. They hired her to retrieve them."

Delaney's unblinking eyelids signal her full attention with a trace of anxiety.

"It doesn't end there. I'm certain someone is following me."

Delaney inches the living room curtain aside and peers out the window. Maybe I shouldn't have sprung that on her without a plan to deal with it. All I've done is up her stress level. Neither of us needs that.

"Do you think someone is watching us right now?" She asks.

I join her at the window but don't see any sign of the Lexus, though I have no idea what kind of car Mary Lou drives.

"If they are, so what? We don't have what they want. Sooner or later, they will move on. Have you received any strange calls or texts?"

Delaney lets the curtain fall back. "Not that I'm aware of, but I have an app that filters out and blocks spam callers and text messages."

It makes no sense that Mary Lou wouldn't initiate contact with Delaney. As Emily's roommate, it's logical she'd be number one on the target list. Though I'm happy they haven't bothered her, why me first?

"Does it keep a log of those calls?" I ask.

Delaney shrugs. "I've never bothered to look."

She retrieves her phone from the bedroom and brings up the spam caller application.

"Found it," she says, showing me a list of date- and time-stamped spam from area codes all over the world. Telemarketers and political robocalls dominate the list. Of particular interest is a call from a 412 area code the morning after Emily died.

I point it out. "Do you recognize this number?"

"That's my employer, University Hospital," she says. "Odd it would go to spam."

"Dial it back," I say.

"Right now?"

"Put it on speaker. Let's see if it's actually from the hospital."

I'm betting it's spoofed and probably the same fake pizza guy who called me.

"We're sorry. You have reached a number that has been disconnected or is no longer in service. If you feel you have reached this recording in error, please check the number and try your call again."

"It's him," I mutter under my breath. "Are you positive, at a minimum, the phone isn't here? The cops don't always find everything." Now I sound like Keane, the difference being I'm sure Delaney didn't provide the fentanyl that killed Emily.

"I dug through every nook and cranny of this place. The police did overlook a small notebook in the back of her undergarments drawer. It contained three Philadelphia area code phone numbers."

"When did you find it?" I ask.

"Yesterday, when I was packing up her belongings." I fight off minor annoyance. I know she's busy, but I'd like to know about these discoveries in a more punctual fashion.

"Did you inform Detective Keane?"

"Not yet. I wanted to discuss it with you first."

That's a relief, I think. I'd rather be a step ahead. We can fill Keane in once we understand how the phone numbers impact Emily's case. I'm convinced that someone in Philly knows why Emily died with a large supply of fentanyl and counterfeit pills in her pocket. She wasn't a dealer. There must be another explanation.

Delaney disappears into Emily's room, returns, and hands me a three-by-five pink notebook.

"This first number, labeled DOC, could be company initials or someone's name abbreviated," I tell her.

"Are you going to call it?" Delaney asks.

"Yep, we might as well find out what these numbers can tell us."

"What will you say if someone picks up?"

That's a great question. Without knowing who will answer, I can't prepare a script.

"I'll wing it. Maybe we can save them $500 on their auto insurance."

Delaney sighs, and I immediately regret the attempt at low-level humor. This isn't the time.

I put the phone on speaker and dial the number next to DOC. "We're sorry. You have reached a number that has been disconnected or is no longer in service. If you feel you have reached this recording in error, please check the number and try your call again."

"Let's move on to this next one—Clyde."

I'm about to press the last digit when Delaney says, "Won't your number come up on the other phone's caller ID?"

My finger freezes in place. "Thanks for the warning. I'll dial star-six-seven to hide the caller ID."

A gruff voice answers. "Safe Harbor Recovery Residences. This is Clyde."

I might as well mine for information. "I have a friend struggling with addiction. Your treatment center comes highly recommended."

"We're not a rehab but make referrals," he says. "Does your friend live in the greater Philly area?"

His subtle sarcastic enunciation of *friend* doesn't escape me. How many times did I make that call, claiming it was for someone else? "He's in the Centre City area."

"We're in Kensington. Tell him to stop by Sunny Awakenings Treatment Center on Castor Ave. It's not far from us. He should tell them it's a Clyde referral. They'll take it from there."

"You've been more than helpful," I say. "Thank you."

"What's your name?" he asks.

I disconnect and say to Delaney, "I don't want to volunteer information until we know what we're dealing with."

I'm about to dial the third number when I realize that the internet is a safer route than flying blind with only a phone number.

"Get your computer. We'll search for the last number online."

Delaney retrieves her laptop from her bedroom, and I enter the phone number. The first hit is Sunny Awakenings Addiction Treatment Center in Kensington. Everything we've learned so far confirms that I'm in the wrong city. I'll have to go to Philly.

"Should I worry about the spoofed call?" Delaney asks.

We both should. Sitting here, I sense that the danger to our safety may escalate, but I don't yet have a solid feel for how bad things will get.

"Better to err on the side of safety. Lock this place down. Check every window as well." As I follow her to the door; a gold-framed, black-and-white photo under a lamp catches my eye. An unsmiling young man in a suit and tie, a stethoscope draped around his neck.

"Is this your dad?" I ask.

"It is." She picks up the photo. "His first day as a family practitioner with his own office. I wasn't born yet."

"You followed in his footsteps. He must be proud."

"He's my hero. A Black doctor in my father's day fought every inch of the way to establish himself, and it's still a challenge."

As I start down the front steps to my car, she says, "Jason, wait. I need to get something off my chest."

The last time I heard that phrase was when Sonya told me she had decided to file for divorce. We were separated but trying to work things out. I invited her to dinner at an upscale restaurant and planned on asking her to move back in with me. Little did I know she had her own announcement. In the middle of my tiramisu, she said, "I need to get this off my chest and have been trying to find the right time to tell you." She reached into her purse and handed me a divorce petition. There was someone else in her life. Our marriage was over. I can't imagine Delaney saying anything that devastating, but I tense for some kind of bomb.

"Go ahead," I tell her.

"I'll speak my mind and never bring it up again," she says. "It's true my first impression was to proceed cautiously with you on the trust front. I also won't deny suspecting you had a hand in Emmi's overdose."

"And now?" I ask.

"I wouldn't have invited you over if I still believed you did anything to her. That said, you've used horrific judgment in your past, and many suffered as a result. But it can't be undone, and how you conduct yourself moving forward is what matters. People change, and I hope you have."

Change doesn't come from secrets. Delaney needs to know everything King told me.

"Did you know Emily quit her job two weeks ago?"

Her shocked stare answers the question.

"I had no idea. How did you find out? Where was she going every morning?"

Truth be told, I was ready to jump all over Delaney for keeping it from me. How do you not tell your best friend or significant other that you left your job? Emily was running scared.

"King Fox told me. I don't know what Emily was doing, but there's one thing I'm sure of. Her death wasn't an accidental overdose or a suicide. Out of the blue, she decided to use when you might come home any minute, and I'm on my way over? And after celebrating a year sober? Does that make sense to you?"

Delaney motions with her hand for me to lower my voice. I forget that we're standing on her stairs, drawing the attention of passersby. "It doesn't," she says. "But nothing has since she died."

I nod in agreement while internally battling with what might be our last secret. I can't drive away without knowing, not because Emily didn't have a right to see who she wanted, but because of one question. If her death wasn't accidental, who had motive? I can think of at least one potential suspect, and I can't allow the system to engulf Emily's memory.

I wait for a lull in pedestrian and auto traffic and say, "King was seeing Emily before we dated."

Delaney doesn't flinch or look away as a hot wind gust off the river sways the thin branches of a red maple tree, disturbing a flock of chirping robins. We both glance up as they ruffle through the leaves and take flight across the street.

"They were having an affair?" she asks.

"Not according to King. Unless he's lying about the timeline, Emily and I hadn't begun dating yet."

"I swear I didn't know, Jason. Work and teaching have dominated my life. I regret not asking her how she was doing. Our friendship demanded more from me."

If that's true for her, then I was the worst boyfriend in the world.

"Believe me, I have my share of regrets," I tell her. "We are the only two people who truly loved Emily. From here on out, I promise, no secrets. We'll figure out what happened to her and, in the process, put an end to King's body brokering operation, agreed?"

Delaney stares into my eyes and pauses. Then, she says, "I agree."

Chapter 15

*W*aking up to no text messages or missed calls is a luxury I haven't enjoyed in a while. It's like the world stops. Nothing bad happens if no one is bothering me. It's also resurrection day, back to life from the bowels of the state bar roster of disbarred and suspended attorneys.

I power up my laptop and navigate to The Disciplinary Board of the Supreme Court of Pennsylvania website. My heart pounds, and my fingertips are superheated as I type my first and last name into the search fields.

Attorney ID 05201250 Jason Feldman

Status: Active. Reinstatement from two-year suspension.

I fist pump and shout, "Yeah, baby!" to the empty kitchen.

With the licensure obstacle navigated, my focus shifts to reconstructing Emily's life in Philadelphia. Now that I know her real name, something useful should turn up online. I enter her name and city into the search bar.

The first-page hit is a wedding registry. The header is a picture of Emily and her groom-to-be mugging for the camera on the Atlantic City Boardwalk. She appears in her early twenties, innocent, and baby-faced. Her entire life ahead. Emblazoned on her T-shirt is a hand pointing to the side, and below it reads, "He Thinks I'm Special."

He's wearing a shirt with "She Thinks I'm a Goof" printed on the front. The smiles are ear to ear. Jealousy jolts me as I zoom in on every aspect of her features. Missing are the solemn eyes I attributed to the stress of working in the addiction field.

The next match is an obituary.

"Richard Williams: Beloved husband to Emily, and father to Patrick. Behind a smile that would light up a room, he fought addiction, beginning with a sports injury and ending with a fentanyl-tainted painkiller. Those who knew him will miss his infectious grin and sharp wit. The opioid epidemic is catastrophic and is killing an entire generation. See the signs. Intervene. Save a life. One more grieving family is one too many."

The memorial photo in the upper left corner is a professional headshot. Even with the retouch, he looks decades older and far more worn than in the registry snapshot.

As I mentally process the new information, a Gmail notification pops up on my phone. It's the lawsuit Andi promised. I take my laptop into the kitchen and open the PDF file.

Emily Francine Williams vs. King Tiberius Fox, et al. is in my wheelhouse, having filed numerous wrongful death actions. The lawsuit alleges that King, Sunny Awakenings, and Safe Harbor Recovery Home were negligent in failing to take care of Patrick, resulting in his fatal overdose.

There are no bombshell revelations, but Andi is too savvy to give away intimate details of her case off the bat. Overzealous, fresh-out-of-law-school lawyers often make that mistake, believing it will scare the other side into paying big money. Their lawsuits have more pages than a novel, with paragraph after paragraph of unsupported and melodramatic allegations. The tactic never works. Keep it short and simple. If you're overpromising in the lawsuit, the client will almost certainly have unrealistic settlement expectations.

The next order of business is running down the renter of the Lexus at Luxury Leasing. It caters to celebrity VIP types in addition to weddings and other special events.

I hate that my head is on a swivel during the short walk from my front door to my car. I'm supposed to feel secure in my home. I merge onto the Parkway East and contemplate the possible futility of this endeavor. Luxury Leasing's reputation depends on discretion, which translates to zealous protection of client confidentiality. Phillip's mugshot provides a low level of confidence he was the asshole driver in front of The Squirrel. But it was dark, and I was tired. I need to be positive.

Whoa! I slam the brake and spin the steering wheel as the rear lights of the car in front illuminate. My body thrusts forward against the seatbelt while my knees smash the dashboard. Lost in thought, I hadn't noticed that traffic was at a standstill. As my heart rate slows, it occurs that an auto accident might be the perfect pretext to get the information I need.

The rental building exterior is nondescript red brick with a barb-wire fence securing the rear lot. A silver box at the gate requires a code for entry and exit. A sign reads "DO NOT BACK UP. SEVERE TIRE DAMAGE." I count three surveillance cameras zeroed in on the vehicles inside the perimeter. Limos and multiple makes of luxury vehicles, including Lexus, dominate the inventory.

A buzzer goes off as I push through the front door and limp up to a mop-haired, zit-faced kid behind a plexiglass barrier. He's wearing a Carnegie Mellon T-shirt with some kind of engineering textbook by his elbow. My guess is this is a part-time gig for tuition and beer money. He'll wilt at the slightest hint of confrontation. This will be easy.

He stops messing with his phone and says, "How may I help you, sir?"

"One of your vehicles hit-and-ran me last night. I need the driver's information to track him down."

"How do you know it was one of ours?"

I pull out a slip of paper and slap it, along with my Pennsylvania Bar card, flush against the plexiglass. "Here is the license plate number. It comes back to your company."

He leans forward, studies it, and says, "I only work here part-time. The owner will be back soon. You're welcome to wait and ask him."

All I need to do is pressure him a bit, and he will fold.

"This is an urgent matter, son." I slide the card back into my wallet. "A drunk driver operating one of your vehicles injured me." I step backward, grab my knee, and grimace. It wasn't for effect. They both ache from the impact.

"Oh wow, sounds bad. But I can't, my boss—"

"What's your name?"

He responds in a quiet, anxious tone. "Michael."

"Michael, I'm not here to cause trouble, but this is your chance to be a hero. Give me the name, and I'll make sure the cops nail this dude. Otherwise, I have to file a lawsuit against you and your boss for negligent leasing. If you help me out, however, I'll settle with the driver and his personal insurance carrier, and this will go away."

He swivels his head east to west and then twists at the hips, checking behind him. "Give me the plate number."

I push the paper through the slot. He taps the computer keys.

"It was a black Lexus. I remember him. A big dude with a buzz cut. Phillip—" He stops, jumps back from the desk, and says, "Sir, we have a strict policy and don't release information about our renters."

Behind me is a guy with a head like a sixteen-pound bowling ball, tattooed tree-trunk arms, and a gorilla chest.

"May I help you? I'm the owner."

"I was in an accident with one of your renters and need his name."

He eyes me and then glares at Michael. I know before he says a word. This won't go my way.

"We don't hand out customer data," he says. "Give me your contact information and details of the accident. We'll verify with the driver and turn your claim over to our insurance carrier."

Courtroom bravado is my next tactic. "I'm a lawyer, and this is time-sensitive. Give me the name."

"Get the wax out of your ears, jagoff. I don't care if you're fucking Mario Lemieux. We protect our clients' privacy."

I've gotten all I'm going to out of this place. Time to retreat.

"There's no need for the hostility," I say.

He rolls his eyes. "Can I assist you with anything else, counselor?"

"No, and thanks for your incredible hospitality." I brush past him, yanking the door open and limp away from the building. I don't need the last name. The Carnegie Mellon kid gave me enough. The guy in front of the restaurant was Phillip Dubois.

The next destination is Waggaman's. I text Maz: *Need to see you. Headed your way.*

Before entering the store, a peek through the display window allows me the surreal sight of Maz leaning across the display counter, smooching Irina. I never bothered to ask either of them how the date went, but that's a good sign.

Their lips disengage as I come up behind Maz. "You two make a cute couple. I guess dinner was a hit."

Irina wipes her lips and flashes an embarrassed smile. "You were right. Maz is a good man. We are taking our kids to Kennywood park tomorrow."

Dinner, and now she's meeting his grandson. That was fast, considering her previous disdain for Maz. With Sonya, I knew she was the one on our first day of law school, though it was a year before I worked up the nerve to ask her out. Emily and I had shared so much in AA that our trajectory was different. We were both damaged. That brought us together. There were also fewer secrets, so I thought.

"I love Kennywood. Make sure you take Maz on the roller coasters."

He rolls his eyes. "Shows how much you know. Sean is eight years old and a coaster fanatic. Who do you think sits with him?"

We've worked together two years, and not once did Maz mention his grandson in casual conversation until today. I hope it works out for them. Did she tell Maz about her legal problem? It would be great if I were off the hook.

"Are we copacetic on the plate I ran?"

"Yeah. I got a name."

"Good. We're even-steven. I gotta run. I'm late. Bought a new house, and the furniture movers arrive today."

"One more question," I say, as he starts toward the store exit.

"Make it quick."

"If someone put a GPS tracker in my car, where would be the best place to conceal it?"

Maz scratches his nose. "Why do you want to know that?"

"There was a story in the paper the other day. A woman's ex hid one in her glove compartment. I was just curious." If I tell him my suspicion, he'll think I've gone full conspiracy nut.

"My buddies in auto theft tell me the latest scam is those AirTag gadgets. They conceal them behind license plates, wheel wells, and bumpers. The skells can then monitor the car until they find the right spot to boost it. The downside is they're easy to detect if you have an iPhone."

As he heads to the exit, I shout, "Mine's an Android."

"You're a lawyer. Figure it out."

The moment I'm home, I google "Locating AirTag with an Android phone." The search result explains the tracker is incompatible with the Linux operating system but directs me to an app capable of zeroing in on the device: Tracker Detect. Then, I navigate to the app and begin the download. As I wait for it to finish, out of the corner of my eye, I notice my laptop isn't on the kitchen table where I left it.

An upstairs bang follows the familiar squeal of my bedroom window grinding against rusted frame rails. Someone opened it. I hit the 911 autodial on my phone and sprint out the back door. Running footsteps squashing sun-burnt grass echo from the side of the house.

"Nine-one-one. What is the nature of your emergency?"

My heart is beating so fast that I palm my chest to regulate breathing. "An intruder was in my house."

"Try to calm down, sir. Is anyone still inside?"

"He jumped out a window and ran. I came outside, but he was gone.

"Don't go back in your home until officers arrive."

After providing the address, I'm about to disconnect when, without thinking, I say, "Can you please locate Detective Jeanette Keane and ask her to come here?"

"I will try, sir. A car is on the way."

Thirty minutes later a squad car rolls up, and a uniformed PPD cop about my age gets out. "I'm Officer Cranston. Did you call in a burglary in progress?"

"Yes. He escaped through an upstairs window."

"Is there anyone else in the house?"

The question sends a chill down my spine. Was he alone?

"I'm not sure."

"Wait outside while we sweep the house," he tells me.

Cranston and his partner slide 9mm handguns out of their holsters and enter the house. I scan the street for Keane's arrival. I don't know how much time passes before they exit, their weapons no longer drawn.

"It looks like he was alone," Cranston says. "Did you get a look at him?"

"No."

"Then how can you be sure it was a male?"

Cranston won't know anything about Emily or my past forty-eight hours. I'll wait for Keane.

"You're right. I'm assuming and don't know if it was a man or woman."

"Have you inventoried your belongings?" he asks. "We can do a walk-through with you."

We proceed through every room in the house, confirm the intruder didn't steal anything else, then go back to the living room.

Cranston scribbles on a form. "It could have been an addict looking for quick cash, something pawnable. We'll need the make, model, and serial number of the laptop."

His speculation is erroneous, but what's the point of trying to explain?

"It was a Dell," I tell him. "I didn't record the serial number but may have the receipt and warranty information."

"Stay downstairs until Crime Scene arrives." He hands me a form and points out the report number. "Please reference this in any communications with the department. A Burglary Unit detective will follow up in a few days."

In my experience, that means at least a week, but the delay is not a bad thing. I need more time to consider an appropriate response. If Phillip broke into my house, should I confront Mary Lou on my own? My concern is that it would trigger an escalation. Once they are sure I don't have the file they're after, this may all end.

"Anyone home?" Keane enters the living room, her notebook in hand.

Took her long enough, I think. At least now I can speak with someone familiar with my situation.

"Since when do you respond to burglaries?" Cranston asks. "Is the captain pissed off at you again?"

Keane laughs. "That's a daily occurrence. I know Jason. What did they take?"

"His laptop. Mr. Feldman says that when he arrived home, the suspect was still in the house and jumped out the upstairs bedroom window."

"Did you see the perp?" Keane asks.

"Kind of. Can we speak in private?" I point at the front door, hoping she catches my drift.

Cranston frowns. "You told me different. Which is it?"

I flash wide eyes at Keane. "Detective, a word, please, outside."

We exit to the front porch, and Keane says, "Why am I here? Cat burglars are not my forte."

I want to tell her that she's here so I can make my case that this is more than an addict looking for score money. The problem is that I'd also have to fill her in on Mary Lou, Phillip, and my trip to Luxury Limos. Without hard evidence, she'll tell me it's a figment of my conspiratorial imagination.

"How is the investigation into Emily going?" I ask.

Keane's lower back cracks as she stretches. "My spine is killing me. I'm sitting in the damn office or on my feet twelve hours a day. I've faxed what we have to the Philly PD. You might have asked me this by text or phone instead of dragging me to a humdrum electronics burglary."

Should I tell Keane about the contents of Emily's will and the letter? Andi will jump my ass if I do it without first consulting her.

"Why did you give two different stories about getting a look at the perp?" Keane asks.

I check the front door to ensure Cranston isn't headed our way. "That's why I wanted to speak with you alone."

"You got your wish. We're alone."

"I don't think this is a random burglary."

She studies me while I watch the Crime Scene van pull up to the curb.

"Why do you think that?" Keane asks.

This may be my only shot to get Keane on my side. I point to my car. "Follow me."

When we get to the vehicle, Keane says, "What do you want to show me?"

This is it. If the AirTag isn't there, she won't believe another word that comes out of my mouth.

"I think there's a tracking device in my car, and the guy who broke in has been following me."

Keane exhales a sarcastic laugh. "Since when are you an expert on the subject?"

Rather than answer, I pray the Tracker Detect app does it for me. With no opportunity to test the application, my pulse is in overdrive.

"I think it's one of those AirTags people put in their luggage so they don't lose it. An app I installed is supposed to pinpoint the device."

"I have an iPhone." Keane reaches into her pocket and takes it out. "It's compatible with the tags. The locate function will tell me if it detects something."

She begins a revolution around the car, starting on the passenger side. Within seconds, there's a faint noise, like a metallic ping. The volume increases as she moves. Keane stops at the rear of the vehicle and crouches behind the license plate. "It's here. Do you have a Phillips-head?"

The surprise in her voice is worthy of an *I told you so*. Instead, I bolt into the house and return with the screwdriver. As Keane removes the top screws, I activate my TrackerDetect app. The alert confirms the AirTag.

Keane dons a pair of nitrile gloves. She then bends the top rim of the plate toward her and runs her hand along the other side. She grunts and says, "Got it."

The tag is partially covered with all-weather tape. She rips it off and hands me the device.

I rotate it between my fingers. "Do you believe me now?"

"Never said I didn't," she says. "Disbelief and distrust often intersect but are different concepts."

As far as our relationship, they've been one and the same since we first met.

"Do you have any thoughts on who might have put it there?" Keane asks. "Is your ex-wife pissed at you? Behind on your car payments?"

How much should I tell her? It has to be Mary Lou, but as things sit right now, I have only conjecture.

"It's nothing like that. A woman approached me the other day. She wants Emily's cell phone and computer. It might have been her."

"Who is she?"

"Her name is Mary Lou Dobbs, a private investigator out of New Orleans." I fill Keane in on how she ambushed me at Point State Park, our lunch, and the reward offer.

"Two hundred grand is a lot of cash," Keane says. "Your girlfriend must have pilfered highly sensitive information."

"So they say, but I haven't seen any proof."

"Speaking of, can you prove she planted the AirTag?"

Do I have to fucking draw her a treasure map? They obviously think I either have the electronics or know where they are. Of course, they'd follow me.

"Isn't sticking a tracking device on my car a crime?"

Keane proceeds to paraphrase the Pennsylvania surveillance statute and concludes that whoever put it there broke the law. My conundrum is whether to pursue it. If Keane takes the tag, Mary Lou will know I'm onto her. It might be to my advantage to have her think I don't know it's there.

"Well, are you pressing charges?" Keane is about solving homicides and annoyed at being here. I could tell she was ready to leave fifteen minutes ago.

"Let me think about it."

Just then, Keane's phone rings. She answers, and after sixty seconds of "*Uh huhs*," hangs up.

"A multiple overdose situation at Peabody High School. Three kids are dead. Five are in the hospital. I have to go."

I remember what Keane said about the possibility of a mass casualty event.

"That's awful. What happened?"

"They ingested counterfeit pills laced with fentanyl."

Keane said the pills Emily had were almost certainly counterfeit. Again I consider whether I'm searching for something that isn't there. Even worse, was Emily dealing? That baggie of pills didn't jump into her pocket on its own.

I follow Keane to her car. "A horrific situation. Will you please keep me apprised of any new developments on Emily?"

"Of course." Keane gets in and starts the engine. "If you decide to press charges on the AirTag, call the department. They'll route it to the appropriate detective." Her car rolls away from the curb, then stops. She lowers the driver's side window. "I warned you more people could die."

If she's trying to throw a guilt blanket over me, it worked. Even if it was an accidental overdose, I'm going to figure out how that fentanyl found its way to Emily's pocket.

Chapter 16

The chaos of the last few days has left little time to plan my new life chapter back into the practice of law. In my heart, I know that there's no future trying to latch on with another firm. I'm damaged goods. When my name appeared on the roster of suspended lawyers, it was the equivalent of a scarlet letter in the legal community. With my dwindling financial reserves, starting with a home office and rented conference space to meet clients is the most logical path forward. I can build from there. I've done it before.

I'm on my phone pricing out a new laptop and watching local news. A breaking live segment interrupts the ten-day weather forecast.

"This is Paige Turiano in Braddock, on the scene of what police are describing as a crippling blow to the Allegheny County fentanyl trade. Early this morning, a joint task force raided the home of Franklin Sobotka, a reputed drug dealer with alleged ties to the cartels and believed to have supplied the counterfeit pills that resulted in three deaths at Peabody High School."

"Next to me is Jeanette Keane with the Violent Crimes Unit, who accompanied Pittsburgh SWAT and the DEA. What did you find, Detective?"

Keane's sunken eyes, mussed hair, and bulletproof vest take me back to her appearance when she slapped her handcuffs on me after a cross-country chase. My combative reaction then was in stark contrast to the relief I feel at this moment. Good for her, busting those scumbags.

"Thanks, Paige. We located a substantial amount of pure fentanyl and multiple quart-sized bags of counterfeit pills. There was also a cache of automatic weapons, as well as bundles of cash."

Paige inches the mic closer to Keane. "What could we have expected if this poison made it to the streets?"

"An important question," Keane says. "Fentanyl is fifty times more potent than heroin. While many factors come into play, only two milligrams, barely enough to obscure the date on a penny, can cause a fatal overdose."

Emily had to be well-versed in the unpredictability of how much fentanyl can kill someone. The notion that she carried a large amount along with counterfeit pills becomes more ludicrous with each passing day. Only drug dealers have that much product on them. I can't wrap my head around such an absurd thought, but what was it she told me once? *Many people turn to dealing out of necessity to support their own habits. That doesn't make them bad people.* The parents of those dead high school kids might disagree.

Paige turns to the camera. "An epidemic of death with no cure on the horizon. This is Paige Turiano—"

Keane interrupts, "One more thing. Just the other night, fentanyl took the life of a young woman named Emily Wilson, who devoted her time to helping those struggling with addiction. This plague does not discriminate."

I hurl the remote toward the front door. It strikes the wood, causing the battery cover to come off. Two AA Duracells scatter across the floor. Why would Keane make this public without first alerting Delaney and me? What's gained by releasing Emily's full name?

I shut off the television and press the wrong person's contact twice in anger before hitting the correct one.

"This is Keane. What do you want, Jason? I'm busy."

What the hell does she think I want? Didn't it occur to her that her disclosure would piss me off?

"I watched your interview about the Braddock raid. Why didn't you tell me the bust was going down? You agreed to keep me updated. What's worse, you never mentioned outing Emily as a potential customer. Was it necessary?"

An official-sounding voice in the background admonishes reporters to stay behind the barricade. The distinct whoosh of rotating helicopter blades tells me that the crime scene is still active.

"My promise didn't include jeopardizing an ongoing investigation," Keane says. "You should be thrilled I solved her case. We'll charge the perps with drug distribution resulting in death, conspiracy, possession, the kitchen sink. They're looking at hard time."

I hesitate, processing mixed feelings of relief, disbelief, and sadness. Accidental overdoses happen all the time, but I was ready to bet the mortgage there was something more nefarious at play. "Of course, I'm happy you made an arrest. But why out her?"

"Take a breath, and then I'll explain."

I lower the phone away from my mouth, shut my eyes, and run through a silent ten-count. "I'm calm. Why did you do it?"

"It's fresh. People with knowledge may come forward. Who knows what we'll learn? By your own admission, this is a woman with secrets."

I realize I'm nodding. Keane's right. After all, Emily changed her name and never mentioned her time in Philadelphia, much less her dead son and previous marriage.

"I have to go," Keane says and disconnects.

Exhausted, I collapse on the sofa, drifting in and out as my body calms. Emily calls out from the dream fog, her fingers tracing along my lips.

"Wake up, asshole."

My eyes snap open, and my brain struggles to focus on a cool metal pressure on the tip of my nose. A latex-gloved hand wraps around a 9mm automatic.

He hovers over me, biceps bulging, the barrel of his gun pressed into my upper lip. His crew cut buzzed down almost to the scalp. It's Phillip.

"How the hell did you get in here?" I say, still orienting myself.

He waves his pistol toward the front of the house. "You should upgrade your ancient lock. I picked it in thirty seconds."

As my head clears, the gravity of the moment takes hold. "Delaney." Has Phillip harmed her?

"I haven't visited the Doc, yet. The niceties and games, however, are over. I want the fucking video. One of you is going to tell me."

"I have no idea what you're talking about."

The barrel moves its way up to my forehead. "You're lying," he says. "This is your last chance to tell me where it is."

My mind muddles through escape scenarios. The twenty feet to my front door might as well be a mile with a gun pointed at me. For a split second, I contemplate making a grab for it, but he's massive. If I fail, he'll kill me on the spot. My only option is to buy time.

"I swear that I don't know. Is this about Emily's laptop? If I knew where it was, I'd give it up so you and Mary Lou would stop harassing me."

"We'll soon know for sure. He digs inside a leather shoulder bag, and out comes a rectangular plastic device. Two stainless steel prongs on either end protrude from a concave top, like the teeth on a radiation-enlarged anthropoid. It's a Taser.

I push myself away from the muzzle, but the couch armrest halts my backward progress. There's nowhere to go.

"I'll locate what you want. Give me a little more time."

"That ship sailed." He presses his thumb into one of the pointed, steel lightning rods. "When I pull the trigger, over one hundred million volts will pass between these electrodes. Unless you want this so far up your ass you spit lightning bolts, sit in that chair next to the couch."

My pulse throbs through my carotid artery as if I'm on the verge of stroking out. "If I had the file, don't you think I'd hand it over so you and your sister would stop harassing me?"

He depresses the trigger. I gasp as a white thunderbolt arcs between the prongs, the noise resembling the rat-a-tat of a Thompson submachine gun in a 1930s gangster movie. Needing no further encouragement, I move to the chair. Seconds later, he zip-ties my wrists, one to each armrest.

"I love my sis, but she's soft with these types of command decisions. The Navy shrink at Fort Belvoir said I had sadistic tendencies before they dishonorably discharged me. Can't disagree with him."

My entire body stiffens like a wood plank. "Please don't do this. Get your sister on the phone."

He ignores my plea, walks to the front door, and turns the deadbolt to the locked position.

"When our dad ran the company, he was more like me—do what needs to be done. Complete the mission."

He returns and jerks on the zip ties, ensuring my hands are secure. "I'm not going to BS you. This is going to hurt like hell. You'll wish you were dead."

As the Taser prongs depress the skin on the side of my neck, I shout, "Emily sent me the file you want. It's stored in my cloud."

The pressure eases, and I gasp, chest heaving, "You can access it from my phone on the kitchen table."

He presses the device into my groin. "If you're lying..."

"I'm not. Get the phone."

I strain against the restraints as Phillip disappears into the kitchen. The plastic edges cut into my wrist, causing me to wince in pain. For a brief second, I consider making a run to the front door with the chair on my back.

Phillip returns with the phone and says, "Tell me how to get in. Wait, a text popped up. It's from Jeanette Keane. She's stopping by in thirty minutes."

A fear-infused shiver migrates from my neck to my toes. I might be dead by then.

"Take my phone and leave. Your sister should have no problem hacking in."

"What does the cop want? Call and stop her from coming."

Keane made a point of telling me that she doesn't make appointments, and now she's texting me before coming over? Why did she pick this fucking moment to be courteous?

"My girlfriend died the other day. She's the detective handling the case. Untie me, and I'll get rid of her."

Phillip circles the room like a trapped wild animal, talking to himself. "I can handle this."

Cornered animals attack. Keane's text may have sealed my fate. He's going to cut his losses and kill me. Then he'll take the phone and figure out how to get into my cloud account. When they don't find anything, Delaney is next.

A smile spreads across his face. "If I text the cop, she'll think it's Feldman. He sends a farewell message that the pain of losing his girlfriend is unbearable. It will look like a suicide."

There's no way out of this. While Phillip continues talking to himself, I wonder who will attend my funeral. Delaney will have to write another obit. Who will take care of my dad? Unlike Emily, I don't have a will.

Phillip sets his gun on the coffee table and messes with my phone, uttering an expletive every few seconds. "What's your screen lock password?"

If I give it to him, he no longer needs me. He'll also have my contact list, which means he might text Sam and Sonya.

"It's your gun, not mine. They'll never buy suicide."

"This isn't my first Mardi Gras. The wound, prints, weapon, and body position will all make sense from a forensic standpoint. You're not saving yourself, but if you want the doctor to live, get me into your phone."

It makes no sense that he would leave Delaney alive. They have to assume we both watched the video they're looking for. If I don't figure a way out of this, we're both dead.

"Mary Lou won't harm her," I say.

"You're right. I will, and it won't be cinematic. She will suffer, and then her dad."

The mention of Delaney's father drops a suffocating blanket of terror over me. When I'm dead, there's no one to warn them.

"Going near her father would be a huge mistake. I found the AirTag behind my license plate. They are looking for you."

Phillip taps his finger against my forehead. "Nice try, pal. That tag is untraceable."

As if our shared history created a telepathic connection, Keane's name appears on my caller ID. Phillip's panicked eyes flit from the screen to me. "I'm going to answer and put it on speaker. You tell her you're not home, so don't bother coming over."

He picks up his gun and holds the phone to my mouth. "Think of the doctor and your family."

I wondered when Phillip would get around to that. If he's willing to take out Delaney and her dad, killing my son wouldn't bother him.

"Detective, I got your text, but I'm not home. Don't waste a trip."

"I'm not coming. Headed to a crime scene in East Liberty. The reason for the call is this morning, King Fox showed up at the Allegheny County District Attorney's office with a bunch of suits. The scuttlebutt is he accused your girlfriend of stealing trade secrets after ending their romantic relationship."

Phillip presses the tip of the muzzle into my forehead. The message is loud and clear. My next sentence could be my last.

"That's interesting, Detective. I'm at work and about to enter the coffin. Gotta go."

I pray that my voice didn't exude the high pitch of someone full of terror. If he thinks I'm signaling Keane, he'll pull the trigger.

Phillip presses the end-call button." You were prophetic. You're *close* to a wooden coat if I don't get what I want."

"Answer one thing first. Why me and not Dr. Martin? After all, she was the most logical person Emily would have entrusted with a secret."

"Targeting you first was my sister's idea. Whatever the doctor told you, we'd learn. And because of your penchant for booze and the white powder, it will be easier to stage your death. People like you either over-dose or off themselves all the time."

Why didn't I finish setting up those damn cameras after Keane left? It wouldn't save me, but in death, I'd still nail his ass.

"If you believe it's that easy, why not stage an overdose the way you did with Emily?"

"She's dead. You should be worried about your life." Phillip reaches into his shoulder bag and takes out a silencer. As he screws it onto his gun, a helpless realization floods my brain. I have nothing left to bargain with.

"Promise you'll leave Delaney and her father alone. I'll bypass the home screen lock, open my cloud account, and you'll have what you came for. What am I going to do? Your bullets are faster than my feet."

Phillip takes a serrated hunting knife out of the bag and says, "I don't make deals, but if you give us what we need, there's no reason to harm either of them. If your fingers do anything resembling a call, I'll zap your balls for fun and then kill you slow."

He slices through a restraint with a quick thrust, and the pressure on my wrist disappears. I rotate my shoulder and shake the numbness out. He hands me the phone and says, "Make this quick."

I struggle to remember the emergency call procedure. Depress the power button five times. One, two, three, four, five.

Less than a second after I press the power button for the last time, an AI-generated female voice enunciates a countdown as if a spaceship is about to self-destruct.

Five, four, three, two...

"Power it off," Phillip screams, grasping for the phone.

On the one count, I activate the external speaker, set the phone on the floor, and with my foot, shove it sliding toward the front door.

"Please state the nature of your emergency."

I suck in, release and scream, "1546 Hobart Street! This guy is going to kill me! Hurry!"

Phillip places the tip of the knife to my throat. "I ought to gut you here and now."

"Sir, are you okay? Units are on their way."

"You'll see me again, asshole." He stows the blade and gun in the satchel, scoops up the zip tie he cut, and sprints out the back door.

I drag the chair into the kitchen. With my free hand, I cut the remaining restraint with a steak knife. After snatching my phone off the floor, I bolt out of the house to the main commercial drag of Squirrel Hill, Murray Avenue. Sirens wail into earshot as I duck into the Smallman Street Deli. *God, please prod Delaney to answer*, I think, dialing the phone. Within seconds, three squad cars whiz by.

"This voice mailbox is full and unable to accept messages."

Fuck. You'd think a busy ER doctor would clear her voicemails.

Keane is next up on the panic dial list.

"Jason, units are at your home, and I'm on the way. Did you make an emergency call?"

I want to scream, "Who the hell do you think made it?"

"Yes. I hauled ass out of the house, but I'm okay. Delaney's in danger. Get to the University Medical Center emergency room. I'll meet you there."

"I'm not meeting you anywhere but your house. Get yourself back to the scene right now."

Is she out of her mind? I have no idea where that maniac, Phillip, is. For all I know, he's across the street waiting for me to step out the door.

"Unless you've caught the guy, that's not happening," I tell her. "He tied me up and threatened to kill me, Delaney, and my son. It's about a video he claims Emily recorded."

"Who?"

"The Phillip dude. Mary Lou's brother. They work together."

"What are you babbling about?" she demands. "No one is trying to hurt Delaney or your family. If you don't return home, I'll bust you for making a bogus emergency call."

She might not think it was bogus if Phillip pressed a gun to her head. The last thing I care about right now is her lame threat.

"Cuff me at attorney Andi Coffey's office. I'm picking Delaney up at the hospital, then heading that way."

"No, you're not. Didn't you hear me say that units are already at your house?"

I can incur Keane's wrath or risk Delaney's safety. The easiest choice ever.

Without my car, I have no choice but to Uber. The five-minute wait might as well be an hour. When the car pulls up to the curb, I don't bother checking the plate. I practically dive into the back seat and slide as low as possible. The driver glances at the rearview mirror and says, "Is everything okay, sir?"

"All good, thank you." The last thing I want is to get booted from the car. I straighten up in my seat and smile.

The ride to the hospital seems endless, hitting every intersection red light. On the way, I text Sam: *Where are you? Are you okay?*

Out of the country on business. Yes.

Right about on par for our level of discourse the last two years, but at least he's out of Phillip's reach.

Delaney is at the reception desk chatting with a nurse as I rush into the ER waiting room.

"Jason, what are you doing here? Are you hurt?"

"Thank God you're all right. You have to come with me."

Her pitch rises. "You're frightening me. What happened?"

There isn't time for an explanation. Phillip could be here already.

"I'll go into detail on the way, but I had a home visitor. These people are demented and dead serious about wanting the video. They may come here. We're going to Andi Coffey's office."

She turns to the astonished duty nurse. "I have to leave for a personal matter. Please call Dr. Stevenson and ask him to cover for me. He can reach me on my cell."

"Is everything okay, Dr. Martin?"

Delaney takes her hand. "It's fine, Jenna. A minor emergency. Please don't worry. I should be back soon."

"Let's go," I say, clasping her wrist. "You'll need to drive. I Ubered here."

"Why are we going to Andi's office?"

"She's fifteen floors up with lobby security. If we're being followed, they won't try anything."

A glance at my phone shows three missed calls from Keane. At the moment, I couldn't care less.

Chapter 17

The moment we're in the hospital parking garage, Delaney says, "Tell me what's happening."

"Mary Lou's brother Phillip broke into my place today, demanding a video he thinks I have. He was going to kill me, but I managed to get away."

"Oh my god. So that's what this is about." She reaches over and grabs my arm. "Jason, I accessed Emmi's cloud account this morning and found something."

I shoot her a wide-eyed, what-the-hell glare. "You waited until today to do that?"

"I have two jobs and run my butt ragged every day," she shoots back. "When I had a little downtime, I used passwords from Emmi's letter. God, I'm sorry. There's a transcript on the cloud, Jason, a conversation between King and some other person."

I wanted corroboration. This is it.

"That has to be a transcription of the video," I tell her. "Was that all you found?"

"Yes," she says. "But there are multiple mentions of fentanyl."

We are both silent for the rest of the drive. I want a dissertation from Delaney on every word of the transcript, but it will come soon enough in Andi's office. Rather than risk the garage where Phillip could block us in if he shows up, I tell her to pull into the alley behind Andi's office building.

"We'll be able to see behind and in front of us when we leave."

She nods, and we hurry into the building.

The elevator doors open, and we rush to Jonathan's desk.

"Dr. Martin, I don't think Andi has you on her schedule for today," he says.

"Tell her it's an emergency," I say.

"She's extremely busy prepping for a trial. I'm happy to help you instead."

Who does this guy think he is? I don't have time for gatekeeping protocol.

I march around him to the closed, double wooden doors. "No need, I'll help myself."

He bolts to his feet. "You can't go in. I told you—"

"Yeah, she's busy," I say, twisting the knob and yanking so hard the door edge almost takes my nose off.

Delaney and I enter the room. Andi is pulling a *West Reporter* off her shelf. Jonathan rushes in behind us. "I told him you were busy. Should I call building security?"

"Everyone, calm down." Andi lays the book on her desk. "Why don't you both sit down and tell me what's going on."

Delaney takes a seat, but I can't. My body prickles with nervous energy.

"Why did Emily hire you?" I ask. "The real reason."

Andi picks up her pen and spins it backward and forward like a propeller. "As I told Dr. Martin in this office and you at the club, to file a wrongful death suit for the fatal overdose of her son." The Mont Blanc continues its rotation. Is she bored or hiding something?

"But there was more going on, and you had to know it. Less than two hours ago, someone threatened my life."

"Who would do that and why?" For a minute, it's Keane sitting across from me. The same skeptical subtext.

"It's about a video file they claim Emily had in her possession. Delaney found what we think is a transcript of it in Emily's cloud account."

Andi leans back. "What's on it?"

Why didn't Emily tell Andi, her own lawyer? If she wasn't going to confide in someone, why take the risk of surreptitiously videoing King in the first place?

"Emily never told you?" At this point, I'm not sure of anything.

"She didn't, but I wish she would have, given the potential impact on her case. Are you going to keep me in suspense?"

"It's King Fox engaged in a conversation about selling drugs," I tell her. "I don't know what else, but that's what they're after. The guy who tried to kill me is Mary Lou DuBois's brother. He works for her company."

"What are you saying?" Andi asks. "Do you think King's involved?"

It all fits, doesn't it? Emily records something she shouldn't have and dies of an overdose a short time later.

"It sure seems that way," I tell Andi.

Her phone rings. She picks up and says, "Show her in. Why is a Pittsburgh PD detective here?"

"At my insistence." I crane my neck around. The doors swing open, and Keane enters. Her grim scowl portends an unpleasant conversation. Jonathan positions a third chair at Andi's desk.

Andi gestures to the empty chair. "Have a seat. I'm Andi Coffey."

"Jeanette Keane, PPD Violent Crimes Unit," she says, extending her hand. She shifts her focus to me. "You shouldn't have fled the scene after making an emergency call."

What did she expect me to do? Wait for Phillip to slit my throat? I touch the still-tender cut on my neck. "It was a matter of run for my life or die."

"Did you catch Phillip?"

"Your place was empty," she says. "Other than the open back door, there were no signs of anything unusual."

I struggle to make sense of her pronouncement through an already muddled thought process. How is that possible? "There was a zip tie in the kitchen. I cut it off before getting my ass out of there. You didn't find it?"

"I'm not aware of anything like that," she says. "The Crime Scene Unit will scour for prints and other forensics, but other than your 911 call, we have little to go on."

Part of me regrets not telling Keane about the video sooner, but now that we have a transcript, there's at least circumstantial proof it exists.

"I told you. Phillip said that Emily had a video. He apparently thought she gave it to me."

Keane throws up her hands. "What are you talking about? Your hysterical phone call to me was the first I've heard of this. What's on it?"

"We have a transcript," Delaney says.

"That doesn't answer my question." There's an impatient agitation in her tone that makes me want to scream, *How the hell would I know? I've been busy trying to stay alive.*

Andi holds up a hand. "Everyone relax. I haven't even reviewed it yet."

"How do you know it's authentic?" Keane asks.

Maybe because a violent psychopath broke into my home and would have killed me if I hadn't thought fast?

"I don't know for sure," I tell her. "But if Mary Lou and her brother believe it exists, that's good enough for me."

"I want a copy," Keane says.

Andi opens her laptop. "Nobody gets anything until I determine its impact on my client's case. I assume you have her login credentials, Delaney."

"No need for that," Delaney says. "It's downloaded to my phone. I'll email it to you."

She could have sent it to me as well, but it's moot at this point.

"I have to step out and take this call," Keane says. "It's from the response team at Jason's house."

"If you need privacy, the conference room is down the hall," Andi tells her.

I'm thankful for the lull. It's a chance to reconstruct a mental replay for evidence at the scene that supports my version of events. I have to convince Keane this is real.

Chapter 18

Keane reenters and takes her seat. She removes the cuffs from her belt with melodramatic flair and dangles them in front of me. "I spoke with the response team at your house. There's no sign of a struggle or other evidence supporting your version of events. A bunch of irate cops want me to arrest you. In case you're interested, a false 911 call is a third-degree misdemeanor punishable by up to a year in jail and a $2500 fine."

Delaney shifts in her chair and won't look at me. The notion that she might think I've concocted this bothers me more than Keane's implied threat.

Keane shakes her head. "They found no restraints. We'd also expect overturned or broken furniture or maybe displaced picture frames if there was a struggle. Nothing seemed out of place, though we'd know for sure if you had stuck around like you should have."

I shake my head, realizing what an idiot I am. In all the hubbub, I forgot that the zip tie I cut off is in my pocket.

"Will this help?" I present it to Keane.

Keane studies it and runs her thumb over the plastic edge. "Where's the other one?"

"I told you. He took it with him. I'm not crazy or trying to scam you."

Keane puts her cuffs away and pockets the tie. "It's not like you haven't lied before. You're coming downtown for a full statement."

She hasn't believed a word I've said since this started, and I'm tired of it.

"I just handed you evidence that I'm being truthful."

"For all I know, you found it on the sidewalk."

I can only imagine what's going through Delaney's mind. *How can I trust this looney toon? Did he give Emily that baggie of drugs? After all, he found her.* No doubt, Andi is pondering the same. They might even think I planted a concocted transcript to deflect suspicion to King.

As if on cue, Keane adds, "I want a detailed accounting of your whereabouts the day Emily died."

Queasy memories raise my body temperature as if I'm back in my sweltering jail cell. Once again, Keane is targeting me as a person of interest for a murder I didn't commit. My gut screams for me to shut my mouth and hire a lawyer. Such an aggressive response, however, might seal my fate with Delaney.

"Do you have anything to say?" Keane asks.

Jail cells are full of suckers who spoke to law enforcement types without counsel. That doesn't stop me from blurting, "I was at work all day. Talk to your ex-partner."

"We already spoke," Keane says. "Maz confirms you were at the store from that morning until you left for the day around 5 p.m. I also did the math. During evening rush hour, the drive to Emily's place in the Southside should have taken about twenty minutes. There's still an open window."

Delaney's head is bent toward her knees as if she's trying to avoid eye contact. Did Keane unravel our fragile thread of trust? I spring to my feet and explode. "An open window for what? I had nothing to do with her overdose."

Andi, who didn't utter a peep during the exchange, says, "Why don't you work out your differences later? Here, the focus is on my client's case. After reading the transcript, I have no objection to letting you and Jason read it with the understanding no copies leave this room."

Keane reaches into the breast pocket of her blazer and removes her badge holder. She snaps it open, exposing her gold detective's shield.

"You see this, counselor? I don't make deals for potential evidence."

"Neither do I," Andi says. "This isn't a negotiation. It's take it or leave it. I have no legal obligation to assist you in any way."

My first thought is that Keane will agree, then refuse to honor her promise. What's to stop her? Andi has to suspect the same.

Keane shakes her head and sighs. "Fine. Hand it over."

Andi has her paralegal print the necessary number of copies. She then reviews a deposition while Keane and I immerse ourselves in King's hidden life.

About five silent minutes later, Keane utters, "Jesus, King Fox is a drug dealer."

I fight back the desire to shout, *I told you so! This is what Mary Lou is after!*

"What happens next?" I ask.

Keane straightens up, rubs her forehead, and says, "This is hearsay. It might make a good screenplay, but as evidence, it's useless. King would laugh me out of his office."

"You can't arrest him?" Delaney says, her voice tinged with anxiety.

"I agree with Detective Keane," Andi tells her. " Even if Emily was alive and we had the video, it was almost certainly an illegal recording, and therefore inadmissible."

"That's crazy," Delaney says. "It proves he had a reason to kill Emily."

I learned a long time ago that the law and facts are often at odds, and nod in agreement with Andi's painful truth.

"Pennsylvania is a two-party consent state," I tell Delaney. "We should assume King didn't give anyone permission to record him engaged in illegal activities."

"Correct," Keane says. "And for all we know, it's a fabrication. I'm not throwing my career and pension to the wind, going off half-cocked and accusing a prominent public figure of being Pablo Escobar."

It now makes sense to me why King would lawyer up and accuse Emily of wrongdoing even though she's dead. Despite the efforts of Mary Lou and Phillip, he knew this would come out. That transcript is legitimate.

Delaney stands and paces around her chair. "Does this mean I have to live in fear, looking over my shoulder for the rest of my life?"

Her concerns are valid. I've lived that life, afraid for myself, my son, and my then-wife. I silently vow that Delaney won't go through what I did.

Keane locks her hand around Delaney's wrist. "Sit down. You're making me dizzy. We can protect you while this plays out."

Why offer that up if she doesn't believe me? Maybe she values Delaney's life more than mine.

I muster as much sarcasm as possible and say, "You've done a bang-up job so far. What about her work and her father?"

Keane ignores the jab and flips through her notebook. "With the help of my Philly PD colleagues, I dug up background on Emily. Her son Patrick had a history of heroin and fentanyl possession busts. He also spent time at a rehab facility in Philly and overdosed at seventeen years old."

"We're aware," I say, realizing she doesn't know about the letter.

Keane sets her notebook on Andi's desk and twists her body toward me, revealing an eviscerating stare. "What does that mean?"

I'm walking a tightrope between figuring out what happened to Emily and not giving Keane anything she may use to arrest me.

"It was in a letter she wrote Delaney," I say, bracing for a tirade.

"Why wasn't I told about this?" Keane says.

Andi comes to my rescue. "It's not his place to reveal the contents of a private communication between the deceased and my client, the estate executor. You come to me for those items, not Jason."

"I want to read it," Keane says.

Andi points to Delaney. "It's her call. If she doesn't mind, I'll print out a copy."

Delaney shrugs. "Sure. Why not?"

Keane reads the letter and hands it to Andi. "That's quite a story, but as I'm sure you know, counselor, it's pure hearsay."

"What about a dying declaration," I ask. "Isn't that a hearsay exception?"

"Nice thought but a nonstarter," Andi says. "I'd have to prove Emily wrote it knowing she was about to die."

She's right, and I decide not to speak again on matters of law to avoid being proven the fool. This misstatement and my thrashing in King's office confirm that getting back into the legal groove won't be as easy as riding a bike.

"Not to worry," Andi says. "I'll figure out a way to get it admitted in our civil lawsuit against King. If not, there's always TMZ."

I'm not sure if she's joking, but Andi has a reputation for using the media to advance her cases. If she thought it was beneficial, I'm certain a copy of the transcript and letter would end up with media outlets and gossip bloggers.

"When are you bringing King in for questioning?" I ask Keane.

"I told you he has legal counsel," she says.

So what? She can invite him downtown and lock him into a story. He thinks he's smarter than everyone. With his ego, his lawyers might not be able to shut him up.

"What about Phillip?" I ask. "He's still out there."

Keane takes out her notebook. "I'll put out a BOLO to pick him up for questioning as a person of interest."

Good luck with that, I think. He got into my house without any trouble. I suspect he can go off the grid with the same ease.

"BOLO?" Delaney asks.

"Be on the lookout," Keane tells her. "In the meantime, I'll do my best to strong-arm King Fox into coming in for a sit-down."

That's a step forward, but we have to get Delaney out of harm's way.

"How about posting someone outside Delaney's condo?" I ask. "And her dad's place as well."

"Why does my father need protection?" Delaney looks at me, her eyes filled with concern.

I clear my throat and swallow. She needs to know Phillip's threat, but I can't force the words out.

"I'm sure he's fine," Keane tells Delaney. "Let's take this one step at a time. What's the plan for your own safety? I strongly advise against going home until this is sorted out."

"You'll stay at my place," Andi says. "I have a spacious home in Fox Chapel with a state-of-the-art security system. Other than me, your housemates will be my two pit bulls, Atticus and Elle."

Delaney's eyes roll toward the ceiling as she appears to consider the offer. "If they come after me, won't my presence endanger you?"

Andi reaches into her desk and out comes the Magnum. She lays it on a stack of depositions. "There's one in my home as well. Mafia, the cartel, crooked politicians— they've all threatened me."

"Of course, you have a license to carry that," Keane says.

Andi sticks it back in her drawer. "I don't need one for this weapon. It never leaves my office, but I have a permit for the .357 in my glove compartment. Delaney, you can stay here with me until I finish for the day."

"What about your work?" I ask Delaney.

"I'll inform the hospital and med school that I'm taking personal time." In her blood-stained scrubs, Delaney projects a dead-on-her-feet state of exhaustion." Andi inserts the transcript and letter into the file. "It goes without saying, Detective, the documents you reviewed here are not to be discussed with third parties. You agreed as a condition of access."

"I keep my word, unlike some people," Keane says, side-eying me. "Jason, where will I be able to find you if needed?"

I struggle to remember any word she's kept other than her promise to arrest me two years ago. "No idea, but I'll let you know."

Keane stands and says, "What did you decide about the tracker? The sooner we get on it, the better chance we have of arresting whoever put it there."

I want to scream, *I told you who did*, but settle for, "I haven't decided."

"It's odd you don't want to press charges," Keane says. "If it were me, I'd bend over backward to figure out who did it."

I hear it in her voice. She thinks I may have put it on my own car, and that I'm stalling. "I never told you that I'm not pressing charges."

"What tracker?" Delaney asks.

I want to thump myself upside my head. Things popped off so fast I forgot to tell her. "We found an AirTag behind my license plate."

"I've read about people using them to stalk women, Delaney says. How do I know they didn't put one in my car?"

She's right. I should have used my TrackerDetect app on her vehicle. I'm making the kind of mistakes that can get us killed. It has to stop.

Keane opens her notebook. "Give me the location of your vehicle, plate number, and the make and model. I'll check it out for you."

After Delaney provides the information, Keane tells her, "If you don't hear from me, there is no AirTag. Unfortunately, it doesn't mean you're in the clear. There are many ways to remotely track a car."

"You mean I'll never be safe?" Delaney's facial muscles tighten.

I want to kick Keane for making things worse. Delaney's worried enough already.

"I'm out of here," Keane says. "Like I told you, if you don't hear back, the car is clean."

As soon as Keane is in the lobby, Andi rises from her desk. "Delaney, why don't you and I head to my club for a bite to eat and a glass of wine. We can talk, and no one will bother us. Then I'll take you to my house."

We're running for our lives, and Andi's taking her out for lunch? Didn't I impress on her the seriousness of our situation? Is she as skeptical of my story as Keane?

"Are you sure that's a good idea?" I ask. "I'd take her straight to your place."

Andi doesn't answer, and Delaney runs her fingers down her scrubs. "Will they let me in dressed this way?"

Andi winks. "I promise they'll make an exception."

"What about my car?"

"Give me the keys. If we don't hear anything from Keane in the next few minutes, I'll drive it to your place," I tell her. What's unsaid is that when they leave the Forbes Club, I'm following them to Andi's house to ensure they arrive safely.

We all leave the building together, and I circle to the alley. Keane is nowhere in sight. She didn't get back to Delaney, so I assume there's no tracker in the Audi. To be sure, I activate my app, but the only ping is from the AirTag in my pocket. Satisfied that no one is watching, I lay it on the pavement and pick up one of several bricks lying around. Then, I repeatedly slam it down on the Apple logo until the pieces separate. Keane might be pissed at me for destroying evidence, but Phillip said it was untraceable anyway. At least he won't be able to stay on me using that any longer.

I exit the alley and find a parking spot near the Forbes Club's underground garage. Andi's white Bentley will be easy to spot when they leave. I recline my seat and message Delaney: *Text me when you're on the road to Andi's.*

I spend the next ninety minutes mentally blackboarding our way out of this mess. Stay in motion. Now that he lawyered up, confronting King again is a nonstarter. Learning about the Emily who is unknown to me—the Philadelphia mother trying to save her son—is top priority.

My phone pings.

We're finished. Driving to Andi's house.

Fifteen minutes later, Andi's Bentley rolls up the garage ramp. Given the circumstances, she may pay more attention to her rearview, so I drop back and allow another vehicle to move between us. My hope is that Delaney is too distracted to recognize her own car. The drive to Fox Chapel, a high-end northern suburb, should take about thirty minutes.

As we approach the Andy Warhol bridgehead, connecting downtown Pittsburgh to the north side of the Allegheny River, I'm two cars behind Andi. Traffic slows to a crawl, then a complete stop, horns blaring. I raise myself to see over a line of stationary vehicles and spot a stalled auto blocking both lanes, hood up.

Throngs of people stroll the pedestrian walkway, some in Pirates gear, probably headed to one of the bars or restaurants in the stadium's vicinity for a pregame meal or drink. I remember walks Sonya and I took along the same route, even securing a love lock under the bright yellow handrails like we did at the Pont des Arts in Paris on our honeymoon.

Ten minutes later, the disabled vehicle hasn't budged, with no cops or tow truck in sight. If this had occurred an hour later, off-duty cops hired to direct game traffic would be on the scene within minutes.

The north and south traffic lanes are at a standstill. Between my Honda and Andi's vehicle is a black Impala. The driver maneuvers into the emergency lane and speeds up. Shit. Andi now has a direct line of sight to me in her rearview mirror. My hands tighten around the steering wheel, and I crunch down in my seat so that my forehead barely crests the dashboard.

Siren wails bounce off downtown buildings. The Impala is parallel to the Bentley when the heavily tinted driver's side window opens. A hand extends, holding what resembles a mini machine gun.

"Holy shit!" I scream as two distinct bursts from the weapon reverberate off the bridge's steel girders. Panic erupts with multiple screams of, "Shooter!" from the passersby.

The pedestrians on the walkway stampede away from the noise toward either side of the span. Milliseconds drag into eternity as the ski-masked driver exits his vehicle and rams his arm through the shattered Bentley passenger window. He then opens the door and drags Delaney out by the hair. With her hands clamped around his wrists, she screams and thrashes, kicking her legs outward.

A second masked person jumps out of the rear passenger door, machine gun in hand. Delaney continues to resist, kicking at the driver's arms as he tries to get her into the back seat of the Impala.

I open my door, crouch behind it for cover, and scream, "Delaney!"

The second gunman joins in trying to force Delaney into their vehicle. Now, all I see are her feet churning like pistons against his body as he struggles to get ahold of her.

"Delaney," I shout again and rush forward. Andi stumbles out of her vehicle and crouches behind the front right fender, both hands gripping a handgun.

I'm standing between the carjacker's vehicle and mine, defenseless and frozen as if a pair of hands reached up through the bridge deck and grabbed my ankles.

The driver fires a burst at Andi's car. He then turns and looks at me. I raise my hands toward the sky in a surrender position. He raises the barrel of his gun until it's chest high. I close my eyes.

Two sharp cracks from Andi's direction jolt me back to the moment. His gun is no longer pointed at me. He's on the concrete deck with blood seeping out of his ski mask.

The remaining carjacker releases Delaney and aims in Andi's direction. Her wrists jerk toward the sky, followed by another ear-splitting explosion from her .357. His head snaps backward, and he crumples to the ground.

I rush to the Impala and help Delaney out of the car. "Are you okay?"

"Jason?" She seems to look through me with glazed eyes. My first thought is that she's in shock.

"Yes. Can you walk? We have to get out of here."

"I think so," She takes my arm to steady herself.

"Get your butts out of here." Andi circles around the back of her car, gun hand moving left to right like a pendulum.

As I tug Delaney toward the bridge exit, she's heaving for air. "We should wait for the police and make sure Andi is okay," she says.

I scan both ends of the bridge. It resembles a scene from an apocalyptic asteroid movie. Between panic-induced fender benders, abandoned vehicles, and drivers trying to maneuver through the maze of steel, the only way the cops will get here is on foot.

The whishing of rotors slice through the air as we serpentine side streets toward PNC Park. I look up but can't see the helicopter. It could be either law enforcement or a news chopper circling the area.

A bang echoes down the street, followed by cement fragments exploding from a concrete streetlight pillar. I slap at a burning sensation in my neck. "Oh god. I've been shot."

Spinning around, I catch sight of a guy peeking around the corner of an office building. Is he a terrified bystander or the shooter?

Delaney rushes to my side and pries my blood-covered palm away from the wound. "There's something lodged in your neck; it's not a bullet."

The street, cars, and screaming pedestrians merry-go-round in my vision as I fight for balance and tamp down nausea. Delaney locks her arm with mine.

"The ER is less than a mile."

A mile might as well be ten with a gunman in hiding.

"No, to the river," I say, pointing in the general direction as blood oozes through the gaps between my fingers. "If we can get to Wagga-man's, I know someone there who can help us."

"Whatever's there is in deep," she says. "If it isn't removed, you could develop sepsis."

"Clear this area. Take cover. Active shooter." Pittsburgh SWAT officers rush in our direction, the barrels of their AR-15 rifles raised to firing positions.

"Let's go before they detain us as suspects," I say.

When we reach the river promenade, Delaney probes the gash again. "Take off your socks."

After I remove them, she uses one to wipe the blood. "This isn't sterile, but I need to stop the bleeding. Keep the pressure on."

"We need to find a way across the river over to Point State Park before they seal off the area." I glance back towards the bridge, The yellow girders intermittently turn blue and red from the lights of the multiple law enforcement and emergency vehicles now on the scene. Two police officers at the south end direct traffic away from the entrance while a crowd of onlookers hover close by. One seems to be arguing with one of the cops, pointing towards the mash-up of vehicles left on the span. My guess is he left his vehicle and now wants to get back to it. Fat chance of that. One of them might also belong to the person who fired at us.

"I don't know where the other gunman came from," I tell Delaney. "We need to keep moving."

I start toward the Robert Clemente Park pedestrian walkway with Delaney striding lockstep beside me.

The calm in front of us is surreal against the violent backdrop we left behind. Headphone-wearing joggers and couples pushing baby carriages pass each other and wave, looking as if they don't have a care in the world. Boats line the embankment. Occupants are laughing and drinking, oblivious to the chaos about to rain down upon them. I had forgotten about the pregame ritual of river tailgating. I was a fixture on this circuit before sobering up.

"Shouldn't we warn them?" Delaney says.

How are we supposed to do that? The line of boats stretches down past Heinz Field. "They'll get the message soon enough. Come on."

We weave through a cluster of partiers in front of a cabin cruiser with tables set up along the riverbank. They're stacked with hot dog buns, a portable grill, plastic cups, and margarita mix. I can't imagine the boat's owner would be amenable to shutting down the party to give us a lift.

"We have to tell them," Delaney insists.

I turn around to see approaching SWAT cops. They're about a quarter mile behind us, now attracting the attention of startled boaters and pedestrians. "There's no need. All hell is about to break loose," I say, and pull her past the gathering while fighting the chill of desperation. A mile of boats, yet we're no closer to the other side of the river.

"Feldman!" Perched on the bow of a houseboat, with his hairy gut protruding over a black Speedo, is Colin Langdon. Stenciled in red across the stern is *The Hard On*.

Delaney and I stop and gawk at the fake-suntanned captain of our possible escape.

"Are you jealous of my forty-footer?" he shouts down to us.

"I'll give you $100 to take us across the river to Point State Park."

He laughs. "A Benjamin won't buy you passage on this luxury liner, but if the doctor wants to come on board and party, it's ship's ahoy. She can operate on me any day."

Delaney says, "He's a misogynist ass. I'm not going anywhere with him."

"We're running out of options." I scan farther down river, where a docked thatched hut boat is loading passengers. "That must be one of those tiki cruises I've heard about."

We approach the floating bar as Delaney raises her right arm and flips Colin the bird.

I make an educated guess that the skipper is the guy at the helm draped in a loose-fitting floral shirt with "Hawaiian Dale Tiki" printed on the back.

The engine sputters and water churns as the boat drifts away from the embankment.

"Wait!" Delaney and I shout in unison, catching his attention. He stops the engine, cups his mouth, and says, "How many?"

I hold up two fingers, and the boat reverses, its rubber bumper squishing against the concrete.

"Good thing you got us close," he says, unhooking the entrance rope. "It's forty dollars each, cash or credit."

"We're in," I say, but my first rushed step misfires. Instead of finding its place on the deck, my foot drops into the open space between the boat and the embankment as pain and nausea from the neck wound continue their assault on my equilibrium. Delaney snatches a clump of my shirt below the collar and yanks me backward.

"Easy. Take it slowly, one step at a time."

I nod and compose myself before stepping safely onto the deck.

Hawaiian Dale runs my credit card through a point-of-sale device attached to his phone. "You're good. We're shoving off. It's a two-hour cruise, hitting all three rivers, with me, Hawaiian Dale, as your skipper and guide." He eyes my neck and says, "That looks painful. Did you fall or something?"

Before I can answer, a booming voice from inside the stadium announces, "Due to ongoing law enforcement activity in the immediate area, we regret to inform you tonight's game between the Pirates and Cardinals is postponed. Please shelter in place until authorities give the all-clear to exit the stadium."

Within seconds, a conga line of party boats churn away from shore.

"Yeah, I slipped on some glass and cut my neck. Do you have a first aid kit onboard?"

He nods. "Yessiree. I keep one in case someone loses balance and whacks their noggin on the railing. It happens more than you'd think."

"Evacuate the area. The ball game is canceled." The megaphone-enhanced commands reverberate off buildings and the water.

Dale glances toward the shore. "With those boats all departing at once, someone's going to get hurt. Something bad must have gone down. I should wait until they give us the all-clear."

We're not waiting around or staying on this floating bar for two hours. I tap him on the shoulder. "You can run a two hundred dollar tip on my card if you leave now. Take us straight across the river and drop us off."

The SWAT commands echo louder as two Pittsburgh River Patrol Boats do their best to bring order to the river chaos.

Dale glances at the couple seated at the bar. They are kissing, seemingly oblivious to the unfolding drama. "Sure, why not."

The boat shudders, and river water bubbles as we glide toward Point State Park. Dale runs my credit card again, then glances back toward the stadium. "That was a nice gratuity. Did you have something to do with that ruckus?"

"No," Delaney answers for me. "Would you be kind enough to get the first aid kit?" She pulls my hand and the bloodied sock off my neck. "The bleeding stopped, but whatever is in your neck needs to come out sooner than later."

I collapse onto a bar stool next to the kissing couple. He's drinking out of a plastic cup. The sweet scent of tropical margarita mix pulls at my nostrils. Admitting I want to get hammered is the easy part.

Dale drops the first aid kit on the bar. "Help yourself to anything useful."

Delaney sorts through the contents while I knock on hell's door. "Do you sell booze?"

"Strictly BYOB, but happy to comp you and your friend bottled waters. You look like you need them."

I wave him off, but Delaney says, "Yes, that would be wonderful. I need to clean this gash. Twist your neck away from me."

As I crane to give her better access, the guy leans toward me and says, "Gross. What did you get into, dude?" He reaches into a cooler, coming out with a cup and a jug labeled "Margaritas." "You want a slug? A few of these and you won't feel a thing."

It's only one time, I think. *After taking shrapnel from a bullet, I deserve a slip. Tomorrow, I'll get back on the wagon.* "Pour me—my god," I moan, jerking my head as Delaney wipes the gash with an alcohol swab.

"Hold still. I might have it," she says, manipulating tweezer tips deeper into the crevice.

I death squeeze Delaney's free hand as the pain intensifies.

"One sec. Almost there. Got it."

What feels like a pebble pops out onto the bar, rolling with the sway of the boat.

Delaney replaces the prongs with a gauze pad. "Lay your head down so I can clean this off." She tips the mouth of the water bottle toward my neck, allowing liquid to cascade into and fill the gash. I sigh with relief as the ache subsides.

"Thank you for allowing me use of your supplies," Delaney says and closes the kit.

As we chug toward the opposite shore, I continually look over my shoulder at the chaos we've barely avoided. Every second of the shootout plays back in my head like a slow-motion movie. Is Andi okay? And the guy who risked his life to help us? So many questions that, at the moment, only Andi can answer.

Chapter 19

Ten minutes later, the tiki boat bumps the embankment at the Point State Park. Dan unhooks the rope and says, "I checked online. It was an attempted carjacking on the Warhol Bridge. Watch your step."

I stumble off the boat, followed by Delaney as she answers her phone.

"Andi, are you okay? Yes, we're unharmed. Don't ask. I don't know. Hold on." She turns to me. "Where are we going? Andi will send a car for us."

"Let me speak with her." I reach for the cell and cover one ear as a fleeing cigar boat buzzes past. The tiki pitches like a low-magnitude earthquake hit.

"Are the carjackers dead?" I ask Andi.

"One creep I shot was DOA at the scene. The other was taken away by ambulance."

"What did you say about us?"

"Nothing. The cops think it was a couple of carjackers after my Bentley. They fucked around and found out."

My blood-soaked collar and bandaged neck draw the attention of curious pedestrians as we make our way to the department store. That aside, nothing stands out as odd on this side of the river with people going about their business.

When we reach the store entrance, I text Maz: *I'm downstairs. Need to see you.*

He texts back: *I'm heading your way.*

Maz steps onto the escalator, cradling a box. As he approaches, I make out pictures and boxing paraphernalia, including his Golden Gloves trophy.

Before I can ask, he blurts, "The Old Man terminated me over the broken display window. The skell I was chasing and you let get out the door sued. She's claiming permanent damage from glass fragments."

I actually feel bad for the guy, but it's his own fault. He'd still have a job if he hadn't used his walkie-talkie as a baseball.

"Did you hear about the incident on the Warhol Bridge?" I ask.

"Yeah, it was on the police scanner in my office. This city is getting worse by the day. What happened to your neck? You look like shit."

I pull my collar outward, and it's red with blood. "We need to speak in private."

"This is as good as it gets since I no longer have an office," Maz says. He glances at the elevator. "Screw it. Let's use the interrogation room one last time for kicks."

The moment Maz shuts the door, Delaney blurts, "I was on the bridge. They tried to kidnap me."

"And who are you?" Maz examines Delaney with the probing eyes of an ex-cop.

"This is Dr. Delaney Martin, Emily's roommate."

"A doctor, huh. I thought some skells were just trying to jack a Bentley." Maz sets his box on the floor and sits.

"They weren't after the car," I tell him. "Two masked guys with automatic weapons tried to drag her into their vehicle. Andi Coffey was driving Delaney to her house."

"Why would someone want to nab the doc? This is Pittsburgh, not Juarez, Mexico."

You could have fooled me, I think. With the ski masks and machine guns, the would-be kidnappers looked straight out of a Narcos episode.

Maz folds his arms and puts his feet up on the table. "I'm going to regret this, but start from the beginning."

For the next twenty minutes, I recount the last two days, beginning with Emily's overdose, the encounter at the Point, then the home invasion. Maz's stoic demeanor is a cop in investigative mode instead of a grouchy, sarcastic asshole, as if he's flipped a switch. That all changes when I get to the King of Clean. "You've heard of King Fox?"

"Of course. He bought suits from us until he upgraded to designer. Now he helps addicts get sober. Good guy. What about him?"

I had no idea that Maz was an admirer of King. No one loves a recovery success story more than me, but this isn't that. King Fox is crooked.

"You won't believe it," I say, trying to force the accusation out of my mouth.

"You got that right," Maz says.

"Your good guy is dealing fentanyl. There's a transcript of a video confirming it."

"Bullshit. Let me see it."

Keane and I promised Andi we wouldn't disclose the contents. I shouldn't have opened my mouth, but there's no going back.

"It's under lock and key with Delaney's lawyer."

"What exactly is on this supposed video?" Maz circles behind his metal desk, sits, and leans back in his chair. "This had better be good." His skepticism hangs on every word.

"The transcript describes King involved in illegal drug activity."

"With who?"

He's waiting for the other shoe, and all I have is a bare foot. "I don't know."

Maz jiggles his head as if trying to clear cobwebs. "It's malarkey. He lost his career to blow and booze but turned it around. The guy has more money than god, with rehab centers across the state."

How does he think King became so wealthy in such a short time period? Addiction treatment centers can be lucrative, but it takes time to build a legitimate business. And where did the ten million come from for the McKees Rocks facility? King said it was from his foundation, but who gave the foundation the money? Hero worship is blinding Maz to the truth. It's time for facts.

"I'll tell you what's not malarkey. Someone busted into my house and threatened to slit my throat with a serrated hunting knife if I didn't cough up the file. They want the recording bad enough to do what's necessary."

"Assuming this isn't a psychotic break on your part, why would anyone believe you have it?"

"All I can come up with is my relationship with Emily," I tell him.

"I don't believe a word of it." Maz crosses his arms over his chest. "I'll tell you what happened. It's an age-old story. Your girlfriend was boning King, got jilted, and this was her way of getting even, concocting a bogus document to frame him. She returned to the powder to console herself and OD'd."

Delaney bolts to her feet. "You have no idea how it happened. I'm tired of strangers mansplaining my best friend's life to me."

"I'm sorry, Doctor," he says, "but two decades with the Pittsburgh Police Department says otherwise. Two skells and a civilian are dead. Have you reached out to my old partner? I'll call her right now."

Three bodies. That answers what happened to the good Samaritan with the gun. He didn't make it. A guy minding his own business. Maybe heading home from work to his wife and kids. She worried and called when he didn't show up. It went to voicemail. It might have gone through her head that he was stuck in traffic. Then the phone rang. Every decision I've made since Emily died led to his death. I can't get the vision of him toppling into the river out of my head.

"Don't make that call," I tell Maz.

"Why not? Jeanette's a great cop. She'll figure this out."

The last thing I want at this moment is Keane knowing we were on that bridge. Right now, I need to keep us safe, Delaney especially. Maz mentioned buying a house. There's no way Mary Lou or Phillip could know that. I'm going to need another huge favor.

"You mentioned closing on a new home?"

"Yep, bought a place in Mt. Lebanon. Four bedrooms, three baths, in-ground pool, the works. I'm officially upper class."

Perfect, I think. He has more than enough room to put Delaney up for a few days.

Now I have to persuade her. If I can convince a jury to award one hundred thousand dollars to my barely-injured client when the insurance company surveilled him waterskiing a week after the accident, this is doable.

"I'll drop Delaney off at your place," I tell Maz. "She needs a place to hole up for a while."

"Why?"

"That's not important at the moment. Will you do it?"

Delaney's jaw drops. "You have to be joking. I'm not staying with him."

Maz shrugs. "Fine with me, Doc. For the record, I didn't agree to put you up. I'm still moving in, and the place is a mess." He checks his watch. "Speaking of which, I need to get home."

Delaney pulls me into the hallway. "I'm not staying with that man. What happened to Andi's place?"

"That ship sailed on the Warhol Bridge." It's clear Delaney's tenacity and independence will be an ongoing obstacle. "Whoever attempted to kidnap you is on to her. There may also be at least one shooter still out there, as evidenced by my wounded neck. We can't risk it."

Delaney continues her protest. "I'll go back to my place."

The hell she is. That's the first place they'll look. Not to mention, she has no car.

"There's something you need to know."

"Go ahead." Her staccato delivery tells me she's bracing for more bad news.

"Your Audi."

She goes still and I feel like a kid about to break it to his parents that he took their car without permission and wrecked it.

"You drove it to my house, right?"

"Not exactly. It's on the Warhol."

"You followed me in my own fucking car, and left it there?"

It's the first F-bomb I've heard from her since we met. What was I supposed to do?

"I wanted to make sure you got to Andi's safely."

She nibbles at her bottom lip, then somehow manages a half-smile. "You saved my life. The car is replaceable. What now?"

"Maz's place is our best option, and we're on the clock. Mary Lou and Phillip know I worked here. We have to leave. Now."

Delaney's voice chokes. "My entire life and autonomy have been ripped from me. I feel helpless."

She's not the only one. It wasn't long ago that my every decision was reactive, trying to stay alive. Nothing has changed.

"I've been there, and it sucks, but right now we have to think in steps. Maz is uncouth and sometimes indelicate, but there are things you don't know. He's a decent guy. Let's at least get far away from here."

Delaney sighs. "Tell me what I should know about him that I don't."

I hate to spill Maz's personal business again, but if Irina saw through his hard edge, Delaney surely will.

"I know trust has come hard, but take one more leap of faith and come with me to his place. I'll explain on the way."

"What about you? You're in as much danger as I am."

"I have a plan. We can discuss that on the road as well."

Delaney closes her eyes and appears to be in deep thought. Her analytical mind is undoubtedly dissecting each option. All of them carry risk. I peek into Maz's office. He's on the phone. From what I can decipher, he's talking to Irina.

Delaney taps me on the shoulder. "I'll try it for one night, but if it's a disaster, I'm leaving."

That's one obstacle overcome, albeit temporarily. Now we need wheels. My home may be under surveillance, so driving my car is out.

We reenter the room where Maz is now munching on an apple. "I spoke with Irina. The Doc is welcome to stay with us." He tosses the core into a garbage can. "I voted for the Holiday Inn, but for some reason, she thinks the world of you."

"Please thank Irina," I tell him.

Maz writes his address on a slip of paper and hands it to me. "Bring her by the house in two hours," he says, eyeing my blood-stained collar. "By the way, you both look and smell like skells on the run. Find yourself some clothes here before you come over."

The moment Maz exits the room and shuts the office door, Delaney says, "I've reconsidered. This is a mistake. I don't know him."

She didn't know me either, and here we are. "How about this? We'll check on your father first. Then we'll go to Maz's place. If you don't want to stay, we'll figure something else out."

Delaney shakes her head. "I guess that works. I hate all of this."

She's not alone in that regard. The immediate problem is that her car is on the bridge. That means the cops will assume she was there, though I can't be the only person who abandoned their vehicle. It will take them a while to confirm her presence. They'll have to run the license plates and obtain the bridge CCTV video, as well as review social media videos posted by onlookers.

"Great," I tell her. "We'll rent a car, then go see your dad. There's an Avis down the street."

We navigate through the men's and women's clothing departments, putting everything on my credit card. After changing in the restrooms, we pick up the rental car.

For most of the drive, Delaney is silent, with only the occasional movement of her lips, as if she's conversing with herself. She finally says, "You were going to tell me more about Maz and your plan."

I recount everything I know about Maz's life history, including the death of his son and custody of Brian. Aside from a few head nods, Delaney maintains a poker face as to what she's thinking.

"We're here." Delaney points out a modest, red brick, split-level Cape Cod-style home with a one-car garage. A sprinkler jet pulses water across a manicured lawn, the blades of grass aligned in height as if someone used a ruler.

"There he is on the porch swing. He loves to sit out front and read," Delaney says.

"Should I come with you?"

"No. He'll assume you're my boyfriend. Let me speak with him first."

"What are you going to say?"

Her lips curl inward, followed by a deep inhale. "I wouldn't know where to begin, and I've never lied to him. I won't stay long and risk putting a target on his back.

I sense my opportunity. "Mazansky's experience in protective details will be an immense help. We can keep you safe."

Delaney doesn't respond and exits the car. I adjust the rearview mirror and slide down in my seat as she climbs the wood stairs, kisses her dad on the cheek, and then sits next to him. As their lips move, the swing arcs out and back like gentle waves hitting shore, then receding.

She signals me to come up.

I twist around to the rear window and scan the tree-lined street. Two houses down, a man mows his yard. Across the street, a kid is hosing down a fire-red Ford Mustang in his driveway. A Norman Rockwell painting of middle-class suburban America. Nothing out of place. That's what worries me as I walk up to the wood-plank porch.

His handshake is precise and firm.

"It's an honor to meet you, Dr. Martin."

He motions to a blue wooden rocking chair facing the swing.

"The pleasure is mine, and please, call me Thaddeus, or Thad if you like. That is what my friends use, and any friend of Del's is one of mine."

He pinches and kneads his trimmed, silver beard. "Del says you're a lawyer. What's your specialty?"

"Litigation. Car accidents and such."

"I see. And how did you come to know my daughter?"

Not knowing what details she divulged, I glance at her and say, "From the hospital."

He sips his drink. "Del tells me you're accompanying her to a medical conference. Why does a lawyer go to one of those?"

Hoping he doesn't dive into the weeds about plenary topics at a made-up event, I explain, "The nature of my practice exposes me to some complicated injury scenarios. I try to stay abreast of the latest medical developments."

"An admirable endeavor," he says. "You appear to be an intelligent, fine young man. What did you say your last name was?"

The response should come in less than a second but sticks in my throat as I imagine everything he'll read about me if he as much as searches my name online. Or, he may recognize it immediately from the incessant news coverage two years ago. "I'm sorry, sir. What was the question?"

"Your surname."

"His last name is Feldman, Daddy." Delaney leans down and pecks his cheek. "We have to skedaddle."

I stand, grateful to be leaving. "It was nice to meet you, sir," I say, focusing on a confident grip as we shake hands.

Delaney rests her head against his. "I love you, Daddy."

"I love you too, baby girl. Drive carefully." She waves as we pull away, but her grim frown tells the story. Along with worry, the lie is tearing her up inside. If I hint at even a sliver of similar concern for Thad's safety, Delaney won't leave his side.

"There's nothing to worry about," I tell her with faux confidence.

The truth is, there very well may be.

Chapter 20

*G*oogle Maps directs us through the Fort Pitt Tunnel to the Virginia Manor section of Mt. Lebanon, a suburb nine miles south of Pittsburgh. A wrought-iron gate with a call box creates an imposing barrier between us and a row of massive homes along an oak-lined street. I'm relatively sure that once I get Delaney in the house, it will be easier to keep her there. When she knows where I'm headed, however, the whole thing may blow up.

I text Maz: *At the gate.*

Three beeps emanate from the box, and the gate swings inward. Three houses down the street, Irina stands in the doorway. I've never seen her this casual. She's makeup-free. Maz's Pittsburgh Police Department sweatshirt hangs below her waist over black leggings.

"Jason and Miss Delaney. It's wonderful to see you." Her voice carries the childlike excitement of unwrapping Christmas presents. "We are excited to have you in our home."

We follow her into a living room, where Maz is lounging on a sectional sofa facing an eighty-inch HDTV. He gets up, heads to the wet bar, and pours himself a glass of bourbon.

"What's your poison, Feldman? I know you don't drink, but I have soft drinks and bottled water."

"Nothing for me, thanks."

On the television, three talking heads debate the flow of fentanyl across the Texas-Mexico border. One pundit drones on about finishing the border wall. The other counters that the government's own data shows that the vast majority of illicit fentanyl flowing across the southern border is transported by US citizens through legal points of entry.

Maz raises his glass. "Here's to stringing up a few shitbag drug mules during halftime of a Steeler's game. Watch how fast fentanyl disappears from the streets.

I glance at Delaney, wondering if she's going to lose it over his comments. I remember Emily's annoyance when I spouted the same narrative about illegals bringing fentanyl across the border. She huffed in irritation and immediately pulled up the data on the DEA website proving I was mistaken. She followed with, "I'll also have you know that almost ninety percent of fentanyl trafficking convictions are of US citizens."

When I pushed back, she again showed me the statistics and said, "I thought lawyers were supposed to know this stuff." Her admonition shrunk me to six inches tall. Emily was passionate about her work.

Fortunately, Delaney is busy checking out framed photos of Maz and his late son on the wall. One is of the two of them in their dress blues. Maz is shaking Sean's hand at what appears to be his police academy graduation.

Delaney touches the wood trim. "Jason said you lost your son. Is this him?

Maz sips his whiskey. "Yes. That's Sean. His first day on the force."

"I'm sorry for your loss."

Maz frowns at me. Was I supposed to keep that a secret?

"Grandpapa!" A red-headed boy runs into the living room through the open glass doors leading to the in-ground pool. He's wearing swim trunks and holding a water gun, which he aims at Maz.

"Don't you dare, young man," Maz says and snatches it. "What did I say about water toys in the house?"

He bows his head and mumbles. "I'm sorry."

Maz ruffles Brian's matted hair. "Run upstairs and change. Then you can watch cartoons."

Irina clasps Delaney's hand. "I will get you settled in while the boys talk."

"That's kind, but I'm not sure I'm staying."

Here we go again. I motion Delaney to follow me into the foyer. "You're behind a gate with cameras everywhere. There are no better options without putting someone else in harm's way."

"But I'm putting his grandson and Irina in harm's way by staying here," she begins.

"Maz is a former police officer. He's more than capable of protecting his family—and you."

"My father is alone."

"I'll make sure Maz finds people to watch over him before I leave town."

Delaney's head tilts in a deliberate, mechanical fashion. Like a human computer analyzing new data. I have no doubt she's processing the unintended disclosure of my travel plans. My mouth was moving faster than my brain, and it slipped out. Then again, I had to tell her.

"Where are you going?"

"We'll get to that in a minute. Let's do a test run. Spend the night here. If things go sour, we'll devise a new plan."

She sighs and looks over at Maz, who's pouring himself another drink. "Maybe."

"Grandpapa, I want ice cream." Brian barrels down the stairs and plops himself next to Maz on the couch.

Maz lifts him onto his lap. "Gramps has company. Maybe later."

Brian pouts and crosses his arms.

"I'll take him," Irina says. "Go put on your shoes, and we'll get ice cream."

"Yay!" Brian screams at an eardrum-piercing decibel. He jumps off Maz and sprints up the staircase.

A great idea. With them gone, I can tell Delaney where I'm headed.

After they leave, Maz says, "Do you like my new digs?"

"Impressive. It must have set you back a pretty penny."

"Yep. A buddy on the force put me onto crypto a few years back. There were some ups and downs, but I got out with a nice nest egg."

Maz, the crypto tycoon. This guy is full of surprises.

He continues, "Dr. Martin, I am also deeply sorry for my language about the drug dealers earlier. It's the cop culture. Irina is working with me to be more of a gentleman."

In the time I've known him, Maz has never apologized to anyone in my presence. In fact, he usually digs in and doubles down when he's in the wrong.

Delaney opens her mouth, and I tense, waiting for the explosion. If there's one thing I've learned, she doesn't suffer fools or cavemen. Much to my surprise, she says, "Thank you. Apology accepted."

"Give me your dad's address, and I'll have an off-duty cop sit on his place a night or two," Maz says.

Delaney shakes her head. "I guess there's no choice unless we're going to the police and telling them we were on the bridge."

She's right. There isn't, though they will figure it out eventually. But first things first. We need to stay alive.

Maz says, "Feldman, come upstairs. I have a travel gift."

I follow him to his bedroom. He opens a dresser drawer filled with socks and underwear and takes out a revolver. "This was my backup gun on the force. Have you ever fired a six-shooter...or any weapon?"

"Hard pass," I exclaim, stepping back as if touching it will result in spontaneous combustion. I don't know how many bad guys Maz has shot, but adding to my body count is unacceptable.

Ignoring my objection, Maz says, "This is an easy-peasy Smith & Wesson .38 caliber. It's ideal for concealment, but because of the short barrel and site radius, harder to aim with precision at long distances. You want to be close and personal with this baby."

"Is it loaded?" After staring at it for a few seconds, I wrap my hand around the grip. My breathing quickens at the memory of the last weapon I touched. Two men died. But that was before, a nightmare I've had to put behind me.

"Wouldn't do you much good if it wasn't."

I aim the gun at my reflection in a mirror, then lay it on the dresser and back away as if it's a live grenade. I also contemplate the myriad ways my plan might explode, with innocent bystanders injured or killed like the good Samaritan.

Maz disappears into a walk-in closet more spacious than my kitchen and returns with a leather ankle holster. He sets it next to the .38.

No matter my misgivings, we both know what I'm going to do. There's too much at stake. I take the gun. Now, I need another car. The rental needs to stay here. I don't know how long I'll be gone, and Delaney might need emergency transportation.

"I saw a new Cadillac parked in the driveway when we pulled in." I gesture toward the bedroom balcony. "Did you buy that with your crypto bonanza?"

"Yep, fully loaded," he says.

"What about the Crown Vic you drove to work? Is it still around?"

"I can't bring myself to dump it. Had lots of good times in that baby."

Great. Old cop cars are like tanks. They can take a beating and still run.

"I'm in dire need of wheels."

"What happened to your car?"

"It's a long story."

Maz doesn't press and rummages through another drawer, coming out with a set of keys. He jingles them and says, "It's hard to believe only a couple weeks ago, I hated your guts. Now, you're in my house, and I've offered a safe haven for your friend, a gun, and my car."

"Delaney and I are grateful. We'll make it up to you."

"You bet your ass you will. I'll pull the Vic around front." He gestures toward the gun in my hand. "Firepower. Never leave home without it."

"Don't you want to know where I'm going?"

Maz raises his hand. "No. Just return it in the same condition, with a full tank. Let's go downstairs."

Back in the living room, I take Delaney's arm and motion to the front door. "I'm leaving. Let's talk outside."

On the front porch, she says, "Where are you going?"

"Philadelphia."

Her penetrating stare causes me to turn away.

"Why?" she asks.

"To reconstruct a life."

"Emmi's? I'm going with you."

No, she's not, and I'm not budging. We don't need the equivalent of another Warhol Bridge fiasco if Mary Lou and Phillip find us.

A honk and engine backfire signals Maz's Ford Crown Victoria sputtering its way over from the garage. He gets out and says, "It was my first patrol cruiser. After being decommissioned, it went to auction, and I bought it."

I whisper to Delaney, "This isn't negotiable. If we're together, it's easier for them."

She crosses her arms. "You stay here, and I'll go. I'm as capable as you."

Instead of Delaney, it's my ex-wife, Sonya. I'm not in front of Maz's house but strolling into Kennywood park, holding hands with my five-year-old son. "Daddy, am I tall enough for the roller coaster? I'm a big boy now."

I don't need a calculator for the exact math. It's been two years since Sam and I last saw each other.

"My father has a month or two left," I tell her. "He sporadically recognizes me. Your dad is waiting for you. You're not going. End of story."

What I don't tell her is that she makes a daily difference in this world, saving lives. It's been a long time since I made anything better. This is my opportunity.

Chapter 21

*A*fter a detour to spend time with my dad and ensure my no-visitors instructions are clear, I hit a convenience store for road snacks and head for the Pennsylvania Turnpike. I wouldn't classify this as a seat-of-the-pants harebrained scheme, but worry about the countless pool ball variables bouncing in unpredictable directions. In any good plan, a hundred things can go wrong. If you think of half, you're a genius.

Four diet sodas and a package of trail mix later, I pull into Breeze-wood, Pennsylvania, still three more hours to Philly. It occurs to me that this is my first drive through the "city of motels" since I was a teen with my dad on our annual summer trip to the Catskills.

To him, Breezewood was a rest stop to stretch his legs, get gas, and refill his thermos with coffee. For me, if we arrived after dark, it was a magical kingdom like Disney World, a fantastical light show of neon signs as far as my eyes could see.

At the first stoplight, I fixate on a Holiday Inn Express where a Howard Johnson's motel and restaurant once stood. If I begged my dad enough, maybe we'd stop for dinner, gorging ourselves on fried clams. It was a battle of wits, with me wailing like I'd starve to death if we didn't eat right then. My dad preferred arriving at our destination as fast as possible. My mom would take my side and say, "We'll eat a few and get on our way." She also knew Dad would stuff himself, and she'd have to drive. He'd fall asleep in the passenger seat, head hanging over the seat rest, mouth agape, and snoring.

The phantom tang of tartar sauce nips my palate as the light turns green, but like my dad, I'm focused on the destination.

Merging back into highway traffic, I see Keane's name flash on caller ID.

"Detective, I'm driving. You're on speaker."

"Did you talk to your lawyer friend? She was on the receiving end of an attempted carjacking. That woman has stones. She dropped two perps, one with a center mass shot."

Only two shooters? What about the concrete ricochet that got me in the neck?

"Scary stuff. I spoke to Andi. She's shaken, but okay. What happened?"

"Can't say beyond what I told you."

She can't, or won't say? "Did Crime Scene turn up any forensics at my place?"

The only sound is the buzzing of my tires on the pavement.

"Detective, you there?"

"Jason, we didn't find a thing. I'd hate to think you're playing me for a fool."

I knew it. Our history is clouding her judgment. "You believe I've concocted an elaborate hoax to waste your time? It's ridiculous. What's my motive?"

"It's simple. Two years ago, I arrested you, and now you want payback. You put the tracker behind the license plate and concocted the home invasion."

If I could, I'd head back to Pittsburgh and shake some common sense into her. She can't believe I'm that vengeful. Keane may also think I killed Emily. I struggle to stay focused on the road despite my skyrocketing blood pressure.

"What about Mary Lou and her brother?" I counter.

"You're the only one who's seen them."

"The zip tie I gave you?"

"Available for purchase on Amazon. Ten bucks."

Trail mix and bile work their way up to my throat. I chug what's left of my diet soda and force back a coughing fit as some goes down the wrong pipe. Keane thinks I'm full of shit. That won't change over the phone.

"I have to go."

"Where are you?"

Keane's already talking to the Philly cops. If she thinks I'm a liar, the hell if I'm giving her a roadmap to my plan. "Out for a drive," I reply and end the call before she can say anything else.

Chapter 22

*M*y turnpike exit across the Schuylkill River comes into view. I call Delaney's number. She answers on the first ring.

"Jason, are you there yet?"

"I'm just outside of Philly. How are things on your end? Is Maz driving you nuts?"

"He's been a gentleman. I'm in the kitchen with Irina. She's teaching me how to prepare banosh, a native Ukrainian dish."

"Impressive." There's a relaxed cadence in her voice that I haven't heard since we met. I'm happy one of us is able to let our guard down for a short time.

"Irina is a sweetheart," Delaney continues. "From all appearances, she loves Maz."

Google Map's AI-generated voice interrupts us. Your destination, Sunny Awakenings Treatment Center, is coming up on the right.

"Gotta go. I'm at the rehab where Patrick was a patient."

"What are you going to do?" she asks.

"For now, park out front and observe. I'll call again soon."

Sunny Awakenings resembles a Depression-era flophouse in contrast to the rendering of the Pittsburgh facility I saw in King's office. How did Emily's son end up in this sewer of graffiti-stained walls and windows so dirty they might as well be car tint? Above the door, a blue banner reads, "THE FIRST STEP TO A NEW AWAKENING IS THROUGH THESE DOORS." A small group of men mill around the entrance. They are all either vaping or smoking cigarettes. Not much different from the routine before an AA meeting. I wonder how many of them knew Patrick. This isn't the time to ask. First, I need to figure out who the players are.

A petite woman, maybe mid-twenties, exits the building and sweeps the sidewalk. Tats adorn each arm from wrist to elbow. Ink also peeks above the collar line of her T-shirt. I drive down the street, execute a U-turn, and pull up alongside her.

"Is this Sunny Awakenings?"

She responds with perky cheerfulness that's out of sync with the bleak surrounding her.

"Yes, it is. Can I help you?"

Yep, but not in the way she thinks. Maybe she knew Emily and Patrick? Someone behind those doors knows something.

"A close friend struggles with addiction, and someone recommended this facility."

"This is the perfect choice." She sweeps her hand toward the entrance. "Would you like to take a quick tour and meet one of our treatment reps?"

"As I said, it's for a buddy, but I'd like to return and look around."

"Where's your friend?"

"Nearby. He lost his job, and his wife kicked him out."

With an empathetic nod, she replies, "A sad but not uncommon scenario. Is he in active use? What are his drugs of choice?"

"Fentanyl and booze. He's a huge fan of Jack Daniels."

"Right up our alley. Most dope around here is fentanyl mixed with adulterants such as Tranq."

Her response drives home my lack of preparation, having never heard of the latter substance.

"It's fentanyl. We've tried everything, and I'm terrified he'll overdose and die."

"Your friend has an excellent chance of finding sobriety here." She hands me her business card.

Brenda Winton
Marketing Representative
Sunny Awakenings Treatment Center

"Take this and talk to your friend. Either of you can reach me day or night. Where is he living?"

"Some roach-infested dump. I forget the name." If she presses me on an actual address, I'm screwed.

"There are a few of those around," she says. "We happen to have a relationship with a sober living facility close to here, Safe Harbor. It's a converted motel, clean and drug-free."

"Who's the owner?" I ask, wondering if she's in on the treatment center scam Emily described in her letter.

"Ask for Clyde," she says.

Bingo. It has to be the same guy from Emily's notebook.

"I'll do that. How long have you worked here?"

Brenda smiles, her eyes emanating a blue-sky hopefulness. I've seen the same look in the rooms of AA. Newcomers show up defeated. Their eyes are often dull and lifeless. As the days, weeks, and months of sobriety pass, a glimmer reappears. Then, the hint of a smile. I know it well. One of those newbies was me. I rediscovered the hope of a new life. So did Emily.

"I've been here six weeks," Brenda tells me. "The people are incredible. Does your friend have health insurance?"

I hadn't thought about how I would pay for this. Using my health coverage is a nonstarter. I haven't relapsed, and I'm here under false pretenses. Going to prison for insurance fraud isn't one of the outcomes I'm shooting for.

Brenda must sense my uncertainty. "It's not fatal if he's uninsured. The vast majority of our residents use Medicaid, which we help set up." She leans through the window and whispers, "We don't reject anyone for lack of funds."

I nod and smile. "Good to know. I'll speak with him today."

"Call me if I can help. What's your name?"

On the journey here, I thought about an alias in case things go bad, but a minimum of due diligence will unmask me as a liar. "Jason Feldman."

"It's a pleasure meeting you. I look forward to hearing back."

As I start the car, she says, "Almost forgot. What's your friend's name?"

"Ahh, well, I'd rather not say until I've spoken with him."

The drive to Safe Harbor is two miles of uncertainty and anxiety. How do I reconstruct a young man's last days in what will surely be suspicious territory? Why would anyone there help me? There has to be at least one person besides Emily who cares about Patrick.

Chapter 23

Safe Harbor's lifeless exterior blends into a drizzling, overcast sky as I drive into the lot. Two levels and painted drab gray, it looks like the kind of place that rents rooms by the hour as a refuge for addicts without options. Behind the building, a white metal cross in front of a church towers at least four stories over the roof, as if it's keeping watch and waiting on prayers from the downtrodden unable to find sobriety.

Perusing the smattering of parked vehicles, I'm grateful for Maz's beater. Even my late model Honda would stand out against this assortment of junkers, some with tarped windows, tied-on bumpers, and expired tags. I've cycled through countless schemes to get the needed information about Patrick, but with each step to the office door, the flaws and danger of each one magnify. My biggest concerns are Mary Lou and Phillip. I have to assume they are educated, chapter and verse, on Emily's background. I would be. If that's the case, they may already be waiting for me. Regardless, I've come too far, and the consequences of turning around may be dire for Delaney and her father. The safest and most logical plan is to stick with what I know—my life. I'm an addict.

From the second floor, an older guy leaning on the railing gives me a pseudo-military salute. I wave back and enter the main office. It reminds me of a run-down Route 66 motel. An old-fashioned reception bell sits on the Formica-clad front counter. Against the back wall, a dorm-style mini-fridge rests on a cheap, faux-wood bedroom dresser. I tap the bell.

A bald, hulking steroid monster emerges from a doorway in the back of the room. A black T-shirt stretches over his upper torso like a second layer of skin, straining against the tattooed phrase on his right bicep: "Work it." There's a disquieting *don't fuck with me* aura about him. He clears a stack of paper off the counter and says, "What can I do for you, friend?"

"Brenda at Sunny Awakenings suggested I come here. I'm an addict looking for shelter and sobriety."

"She did, huh? I'm Clyde, owner-operator. Follow me to room 101 for intake." Outside, he waves his arm across the sky. "This is a converted motel, which allows us to offer amenities other sober houses don't."

"Such as?"

"Private bathroom and air-conditioning for starters. Have you been to any of the other shitholes on Kensington Ave? Community showers are the norm. If you're lucky, the heat is occasionally working in the winter, and your room isn't an oven in the summer."

We enter the intake room, and he gestures to a plastic chair at a portable conference table. In the rear, there's a mini kitchen with a stainless-steel buffet server, coffee maker, and refrigerator.

He sets a form in front of me. "Fill this out. Afterwards, you'll go to the bathroom in the back and piss in a specimen cup. By signing, you agree you're not a tenant, and we can evict you for nonpayment of the monthly fee or breaching any of the rules outlined on page two. Are you employed?"

"Not at the moment."

"How are you paying for your stay? Do you have Medicare? If not, we'll assist with the state assistance application, and if you manage employment, we'll take your paycheck and kick back the balance after rent and food. Sign at the bottom."

Take my paycheck? I've never heard of such a thing. There's some kind of grift going on here.

"Is that standard procedure?" I ask. "What if I need the money?"

He flexes his right bicep into a small mountain as if to make a point. "It's how we guarantee rent payment. We get our money first. Do you want the room or not?"

I flip to the page of rules, but don't bother reading any of the fifty reasons they can boot me. What's the difference? I'm not staying one moment longer than needed to learn what happened to Patrick.

"I'll pay by credit card, and I'm not signing without reading it first."

He frowns and checks his watch. "Most don't bother. They're happy to have a roof and grub in their bellies. Who did you say referred you?"

"Brenda Winton at Sunny Awakenings."

He gets on his phone. "Brenda, I got a guy here who says you referred him. His name is Jason Feldman."

Every few seconds, he nods and utters, "Uh huh," then disconnects. "She said it was for a friend. We hear that one a lot."

I sign the completed form and slide it to him.

He reviews it and says, "A lawyer, huh? No wonder you read the whole thing. You're the first one of those we've had here. How much clean time do you have?"

I process how much is appropriate and easy to remember. "Two days."

"Congratulations," he says, attaching a point-of-sale device to his phone. "We take cash, Visa, or Mastercard. Come to the office the first of every month to pay the rent. If you no show or it's declined, you're out."

"Works for me," I say and slap the plastic on the table.

He slides it through the handheld terminal and, after getting approval, tells me, "After your piss, I'll give you the nickel tour."

I follow Clyde back to the office. It's weird he hasn't asked how I ended up here from Pittsburgh or anything about my past. Maybe he doesn't care as long as my credit card clears. Like Delaney told me, it's about more bodies and filling beds.

He points to the bathroom. "Piss in the cup and leave it on the shelf above the toilet. If it comes back dirty, you'll have to leave."

The looseness of the process shocks me. When I entered rehab, an employee stood at the door and made sure I didn't use someone else's clean urine.

When finished, I follow his instructions and return to the front desk.

He picks up a clipboard from the counter and says, "Let's get you settled in."

As we pass under the second-floor walkway, he points up. "We're pretty full but have an empty self-pay room up top."

"What's the difference?" I ask.

"All welfare residents have roommates. Cash buys you a single."

"How many self-pays are there?"

"At the moment, you and Doc are the only ones shelling out green-backs. He's your next-door neighbor."

I flash back to the "DOC" next to the disconnected number I called at Delaney's. It can't be a coincidence.

I follow Clyde up the metal staircase and down the concrete walkway, stopping at room 202.

"This is yours."

The guy who saluted me is lounging on a lawn chair next door, smoking and reading *The Open Society and Its Enemies*, the light from his room illuminating the settling dusk.

"Welcome to Mister Rogers' Neighborhood." He takes a drag and puffs a smoke ring over the railing.

"This is Doc," Clyde says. "He's been here the longest and doubles as community manager. He then nods in my direction. "This is Jason. He's a shyster."

I grimace at the slur. At least I know right off the bat that Clyde is an asshole.

Doc sets the paperback on his lap and snuffs the butt on the pavement. His sunbaked face, trimmed graying goatee, and almost shoulder-length, dirty-blond hair exude more a professorish, 1970s hippie throwback than a down-and-out addict.

"When you're settled, bring a chair out, and we'll shoot the breeze."

Clyde unlocks my door and leans against the wall as I inspect the rusted-metal-frame bed, a veneer faux-wood chest of drawers, and a desk.

"Were you expecting a chalk body outline?" he asks.

It wouldn't have shocked me. This place had to be the last or only option for anyone living here. Clyde is no better than a slumlord.

I pull back the blanket and sit. *At least the sheets look clean*, I think and wonder if I should have purchased a bedbug cover.

"I noticed you referred to my neighbor as Doc. Is he a doctor?"

"He was at one time." He hands me a sheet with "Outpatient Therapy Pickup Schedule" printed across the top.

"What's this?"

"As it says in the rules, daily outpatient counseling at our sister facility, Sunny Awakenings, is mandatory. Sessions are at nine, noon, and three. You can choose, and they take attendance."

"Are you business partners with them?" I ask, digging for information nuggets.

"We have a relationship." He checks his watch. "I'm late for a meet. Doc can answer any questions."

The moment Clyde is back in the office, I go downstairs, open the car trunk, and extract Maz's backup weapon from the wheel well, shoving it in my waistband. The chill of steel against my belly button reminds me of what's at stake.

Chapter 24

*A*m I prepared to kill again? If not, why did I bring that weapon along? I know how to pull the trigger and have been up close and personal with the inevitable result. Two people died. Bad people, but I still see them in my sleep. In the months after, I learned they had families and children, mothers and fathers.

A knock at the door hastens my search for suitable weapon concealment. I lift the mattress and slide it underneath. After ensuring there's no abnormal bulge, I check the peephole and open the door to Doc's outstretched hand.

"What do you think of our little community?" he asks.

I toss a package of new underwear and T-shirts in a drawer. "It's not my first sober home."

He taps a cigarette package against his palm. "Where do you hail from?"

"Pittsburgh. And you?"

"Lived in Philly all my life."

"So, you're a physician?"

"Was." Doc blows a smoke ring toward the open door. "My Christian name is Edgar, but everyone around here calls me Doc. Are you counting days?"

"Forty-eight hours, one at a time," I say, trying not to inhale the secondhand cancer cloud.

"A great start. After you get settled, join me on the balcony."

I finish situating myself and inspect the bathroom. Dark mold and mildew splotches decorate the once-white shower curtain. Water drips from the rusted washbasin spigot.

The toilet bowl boasts a nauseating collage of off-yellow stains and darkish remnants of past usage. I limit myself to half-breaths so as not to breathe in the stale urine fumes. Cleaning products are number one on my shopping list before I set foot back in this disease incubator.

Outside, Doc sits in a plastic chair, his feet outstretched onto the railing. His eyes are closed. If it was a sunny day, he could be anybody catching rays, along with a restful nap anywhere in the world. Instead, he's on the balcony of a decrepit building that might be two steps from condemnation. What path brought him here? Did it intersect with Patrick?

"How much sobriety for you?" I ask.

He pulls at his goatee and then says, "Roundabout twenty years. Most of these characters don't last more than a month or two before relapsing—or Clyde kicks them out for rules violations."

"What's his story?"

"About five years back, the feds busted him for conspiracy to distribute anabolic steroids. He served eighteen months at Allenwood."

"How did he end up here?"

"The scuttlebutt is he's pals with the owner of Sunny Awakenings, King Fox."

That's a connection I didn't anticipate and centers Clyde on my radar for not only information about Patrick but King as well.

"What type of physician were you?" I ask.

"Anesthesiologist." He clicks his butane lighter. "Damn, out of juice. Do you have matches? Never mind. There's a spare on my desk."

I follow Doc into his room, which, to my surprise, is tidy, but reeks of citrus disinfectant spray layered over rancid cigarette fumes. It reminds me of a summer temperature inversion trapping lung-hacking pollutants close to the ground. A worn IKEA wood dresser is flush against one wall, supporting a mini-fridge, a hot plate, a stack of copy paper, and piles of books. I peruse literature ranging from *The Big Book* and biography of Bill Wilson, the founder of Alcoholics Anonymous, to medical treatises, Socrates, and Plato.

"You're well-read." I pick up the top page of what resembles a manuscript titled *Pain Kills*. "Are you writing a book?"

"A memoir of sorts."

"Do you mind?" I ask.

"Help yourself."

I slide the first page out. *When she flatlined, I knew my career and my life were over.*

"Quite the opening hook," I stick the page back in the stack, ensuring each corner aligns with the other pages below.

"With any luck, I'll finish before I'm six feet under."

He double-taps a pack of Marlboros on his palm and holds it out to me. "You want a cig?"

"I never got into the habit."

"Smart man." He slips two cigarettes out and sticks one behind his ear. "You're a unicorn around here in that regard. Everyone smokes or vapes. Did Clyde say you're a lawyer?"

"It's a long story." I cycle through potential responses, wanting to reveal enough so that if he googles me, it checks out. "I struggled with cocaine and alcohol for much of my adult life. There were some legal troubles as well."

He lights up and takes a draw. "No matter. You're here, and if you want to get clean, I can help. If you don't, this is Kensington, and dope is everywhere. Though these days, it's Russian roulette."

"What do you mean?"

He drags again and hacks a wheezing smoker's cough like my grandfather used to after ten cigars a day.

"The supply around here is almost entirely fentanyl. The good old heroin-high days are over. We're also seeing xylazine and other adulterants."

Doc's abundant knowledge drives home how unprepared I am. I feel intellectually naked.

"What's xylazine?" A warm breeze blows in over the balcony, forcing Doc's smoke into my face. I fan it away with my hand and wonder if I'll leave here with information or lung cancer.

"The street name is Tranq. It's an animal tranquilizer infiltrating the drug supply. Causes skin lesions and rotting flesh. Andy, on the first floor, lost three fingers and two toes. Hold on. I'll show you."

Doc snuffs out the butt on the sole of his shoe.

Before I can decline, he disappears into his room and returns with a printed article titled "Treating Xylazine Wounds." He turns the page to a gaping hole in someone's forearm, leaking pus. "You can see the necrosis and beginnings of gangrene."

I tighten my lips and nod without allowing my eyes to focus, desperate to change the topic. "The rules sheet says something about daily IOP and twelve-step meetings?"

"Correct. A white van comes every morning and at set times throughout the day. You can also attend either Alcoholics or Narcotics Anonymous meetings at the church behind us with the giant cross."

When was my last AA meeting? They blend together, but despite the foggy timeframe, I can still see Emily, the way she looked when we met in group. She was in an oversized, grey sweatshirt that read, One Day At A Time, on the front. I asked her if that was her recovery motto. She said, "No, it's my life plan for survival."

I refocus on Doc. "What happens if I miss a therapy session or two?"

"You'll get a visit from Clyde. He gets paid by Sunny Awakenings for every session you attend. Three strikes, and you're booted out on the street. They stuff your clothes and anything else you own in a garbage bag. Then they hang it by the dumpster behind the building. We call it skid row. The bums pick them clean within an hour unless you stand twenty-four-hour guard or steal a shopping cart and take your stuff with you when you go."

I think about how precarious the line is between belongings in shopping carts and a warm roof over the heads of addicts. How many of these people were once successful, with families who loved them?

"Do you have a *Big Book*?" Doc says.

"Nah, I left it in Pittsburgh."

Doc hands me his copy. "This is a loaner, and one more thing: If you're going to use, do it with me present. I have naloxone on hand, as well as xylazine and fentanyl test strips."

Is he encouraging me to use? How does that fit with being a doctor?

"You won't try to talk me out of it?" I ask. "What about 'do no harm'?"

"As to the Hippocratic Oath, what I'm doing is the antithesis of harm. I'm keeping people alive in a city where it's difficult for an addict to stay above ground."

My phone vibrates to Delaney's name on caller ID. Damn, I should have called an hour ago.

I stretch and say, "Thanks for the conversation. I'd better get some sleep."

Doc nods. "I'm a night owl. Going to read for a while. If you need anything, bang on my door."

Getting ready to sleep, it's déjà vu back to my first night in jail two years ago. There was no one I could trust, and I worried about a fellow inmate entering my cell and assaulting me...or worse. I move Maz's .38 from under the mattress to under my pillow. Amidst the angst of the unfamiliar surroundings, there is a speck of comfort. I'm sure the "DOC" in Emily's notebook is the same person. He's the wormhole from Emily's past to my future.

Chapter 25

The plastic-wrapped mattress sinks at least two inches when I lie down, reminding me of the giant piece of foam rubber used as a bed my first year in law school. With the fading prospect of even a few hours of sleep, it's a good time to call Delaney.

"Jason, thank god you're okay. I was worried."

"I'm at the sober house where Patrick died. How are Maz and Irina treating you?"

"They've been wonderful."

"Have you spoken to Andi or Keane?"

"No. My phone shows two missed calls from the detective."

If Keane hasn't figured out by now that Delaney and I were on the bridge, it won't be long. There were security cameras everywhere. "Wait, a sec. I'll call you right back."

When I was in trouble, internet detectives and true-crime bloggers were relentless in hounding me with their phone videos. Every minute aspect of my life made its way to YouTube or Instagram, racking up views in the hundreds of thousands. Why wouldn't this be the same?

I open my Instagram account and navigate to Pittsburgh Gone Crazy, a site where users post eyewitness videos of car chases, arrests, airplane Karens, and customers going berserk over not getting enough ketchup for their fries.

As suspected, there are multiple recordings of the incident. Three are from the perspective of the pedestrian walkway parallel to Andi's car at a distance of about fifteen yards. The Impala disappears from view as it pulls alongside her Bentley, followed by hysterical shrieks mixed with car horns, forming a grotesque, slasher-flick symphony.

I breathe easier with each preview as there are no recordings that catch me on camera. Delaney is another story. There are multiple vantage points of her struggling with the would-be kidnappers. Andi is also prominently featured. I watch in disbelief as she fires her gun with pinpoint accuracy like a Navy Seal taking out Bin Laden. The entire incident covers less than sixty seconds. On the bridge, it seemed like hours.

I text each upload to Delaney and then call her back.

"Where did you get these?" she asks.

"Social media. There are probably others floating around. Law enforcement will also have access to city CCTV cameras."

"I'll search for more tonight," she says. "It's not like there's anything else to do here. It's killing me leaving the ER staff even more shorthanded."

"I understand, but if something happens to you, it's not going to make that situation better."

"When you put it that way, I guess it's for the best."

I lie back and close my eyes, relieved that Delaney is under Maz's protection. She also seems content to stay with him for the moment. The sirens in the distance lurch me back to reality. I'm anything but secure.

Chapter 26

Someone banging on my door jolts me out of the worst night's sleep I've known since my fugitive days. Fear of Phillip busting into the room, the low-quality wool blanket acting as an itching machine, and the paper-thin curtains limited me to about thirty minutes of uninterrupted slumber.

"It's Doc. Come on out for chow."

When I exit the room, he says, "We need to build a nest for the crow's feet under your eyes. It's like the first night in the joint. No one sleeps, and if you have spare change, invest in blackout curtains and a security bar for your room."

He's right. I spent my first night in the Allegheny County Jail crying in fear of gang rape.

"Where's the nearest Walmart or Target? I need to pick up a few things."

He closes the book. "About a mile from here, and as you have one of the few running automobiles, I'd be grateful for a ride to the public library."

"Sure. Do you want to eat first? What are they serving this morning?"

Doc stands. "Slop, as usual. If you have the financial means, my advice is to eat out. "Let me get my flash drive so I can work on my manuscript."

With only one hard copy, he'd be safer backing it up to the cloud.

"Don't you have a laptop or cell phone?"

"I got rid of them a while back. Around these parts, laptops are stolen faster than addicts overdose. How about that ride?"

"Not a problem. Let's go."

Doc gets in the car and says, "I usually walk, but it's supposed to hit ninety-five today."

We're a mile into our drive, with me continually eyeing him. The appropriate moment to ask will never present itself. I need to learn these streets to understand how Emily's son ended up on them, then at Safe Harbor. Privilege was woven into my drug addiction. My dealer made home deliveries. I knew the product he supplied was relatively pure. How can I possibly come to understand this level of suffering?

"Here's the Kensington Library." He points, and I pull up to a building with a mural depicting strawberry and dandelion vines. As a child, I picked the yellow, starburst-looking flowers out of our backyard and gave them to my mother for her birthday. Maybe that's the point of the artwork. A reminder that beauty and innocence exist within the despair.

"Call me when you're done, and I'll come get you."

As Doc pushes on the library door, I sink low in my seat, removing Patrick's obituary from the glove compartment, dissecting what appears to be his high school graduation photo. I examine every detail: the over-touched red hair, smooth photoshopped skin, and brown baby eyes with a hint of hope. Had he already tasted the devil, or did it come later? His hologram materializes on the sidewalk. Matted locks, a faded and torn Sixers T-shirt hanging over his saggy jeans. Emaciated, hollow-faced, and scratching at forearm track marks.

Pawn shops, liquor stores, and boarded-up buildings dominate the landscape in front of me. I get out of the car and walk to the next block. Discarded syringes litter the sidewalk. A woman crouches against a wood panel substituting for a door. Next to her is a shopping cart stuffed with clothes, a sleeping bag, water bottles, and assorted necessities for life on the street. Despite the already sticky morning, she's clad in a winter overcoat. As I approach, she reaches into the basket and takes out a slice of aluminum foil, stretching it out and folding it in half. She then holds a lighter under the crease, allowing the flame to run along the bottom, using a straw to inhale the vapors. Within seconds, she falls back against the building and slides to the pavement.

In my peripheral vision, Doc exits the library with a bulging cloth tote in his right hand. That's weird. He wasn't inside long. He approaches the woman, kneels, and removes a bottled water and snack pack from his bag. After placing them at her feet, he leans in and says something to her I can't make out. He then continues down the sidewalk. I return to my car and follow him from a safe distance, watching.

Three blocks farther, it's a replay. This time, Doc comes up to an emaciated woman walking in circles around a light pole while picking at her arm. She stops and screams at him, but he latches onto her wrist and inspects it. She wrenches away and continues her circular orbit. Doc again kneels and places items near the pole. He continues down the road, passing a hodgepodge of sidewalk tents and blue tarps draped over boxes surrounded by trash. Doc stops at the first make-shift shelter. A hand appears through the flap opening, taking a bottled water from him.

Doc cares about this community, I think, making a U-Turn.

Upon my return, I head to my room, and Clyde intercepts me in the stairwell. "You should be at outpatient therapy. The rules I laid out are nonnegotiable."

"I'm doing fine on my own." This jerk is going to be the problem, not Doc.

He shoves his clipboard in my face and taps on a list of names with checkmarks. "All two days of sobriety. You're a modicum of sustained recovery. There are multiple daily opportunities to get the check mark next to your name. Otherwise, it's a strike. Three, and your ass is on the street." He glances toward the Sunny Awakenings van pulling up to the office. "I gotta feed these guys. Get your butt to IOP."

I remember what Doc said about the food and regret not making a breakfast run before returning. The line to enter the makeshift cafeteria is already at least fifteen deep. I fall in and shuffle past a sign taped to the wall. "ONLY TEN INSIDE AT A TIME. WAIT YOUR TURN. NO CUTTING THE LINE." The guy in front of me, wearing a Grateful Dead T-shirt, points at my phone and says, "Hey, Bro. Mind if I borrow that?"

"You don't have one?"

"It's a prepaid on empty."

With a potential information carrot dangling, I respond, "See me outside after lunch."

He sticks out his hand. "Much obliged. I'm Lance, but everyone here calls me Beach Boy."

With dirty-blond hair, a thin but muscular build, and ocean-blue shorts, he would definitely blend in with the California surfer dudes. There are plenty of rehabs and sober homes on the West Coast. How did he end up across the country in this place?

"Jason. A pleasure to meet you. How long have you lived here?"

"Six months, and I don't plan on being around much longer. I'm headed back west."

He hasn't been here long enough to have known Patrick, but he might have something to say about Clyde. Representing plaintiffs in wrongful termination cases taught me that the best witnesses against a company are employees who are leaving or already left. They aren't afraid of retaliation.

"Are you adjusting to our slice of paradise?" Beach Boy asks.

"Settling in and learning the rules. The owner is an interesting character."

He leans in and says, "Clyde don't own this place."

If Beach Boy is right, Clyde's already lied to me. It might be ego and trying to sound important, or something more devious.

"Who does?" I ask him.

"Above my pay grade," Beach Boy says. "I'll meet you out front after we eat. I appreciate you letting me use your phone."

Assisting Clyde at the serving buffet is Brenda from Sunny Awakenings. She flashes a bleached, toothy smile. "Jason, glad you made it here. Are they taking good care of you?"

In stark contrast, Clyde's suspicious eyes drill a hole through me.

"I'm getting settled in. So far, it's okay."

"Wonderful news. I hope to see you at our intensive outpatient therapy sessions."

The thought of going into a group therapy session under false pretenses doesn't sit well with me, but what choice do I have? I need to walk Patrick's path to understand Emily's footsteps and motivations.

Chapter 27

*I*t turns out Beach Boy wanted to call his mom. I'm happy he's leaving here. This place gives off all the wrong vibes. There's more going on than addicts getting sober.

In my room, I extend the security bar I bought from Target under the doorknob. Within seconds, a metallic hum vibrates through the steel tube. My first thought is an electric short, which is problematic, given the entire building is a fire trap. The only outlet is behind the dresser, so I slide it out to a rhythmic chant emanating through a basketball-size hole in the drywall.

"Om...om...om."

I drop to all fours and blink to ensure I'm not hallucinating. Doc is on the floor naked, in a lotus position, chanting.

Without thinking, I blurt an embarrassed, "Sorry!" as if I walked in on him in the middle of a sex act. He turns his head and winks without missing a chant. I jump to my feet and push the dresser back into place. Within minutes, there's a rap on my door.

I inch it open and peek outside.

"Everything okay, Doc?"

He must sense my trepidation because he says, "Relax, I do daily yoga and meditation. You have an open invite to join me."

Emily was a huge fan of yoga and hounded me to go with her. My excuse for declining was that I couldn't even touch my toes and didn't want to embarrass myself.

"Yoga has done wonders for my mental health and outlook, and it's a vital part of my sobriety routine," Doc says. "It was also helpful in the can."

Another penny drops. Doc's done time. I join him on the balcony.

"You were in prison?"

"Five years for involuntary manslaughter."

I project out every possible crime that he might have committed. Maybe he drove drunk or high and killed someone. There were plenty of those types in AA. He doesn't look the bar-fight type, so I rule out death by personal combat.

"Can I ask what happened?"

"I killed a patient." His voice is monotone and clinical, like he's reading off of a medical chart.

Doc continues, "I was high while knocking her out. She had a deviated septum. It should have been a simple outpatient procedure."

No response is necessary. He knows his conduct was reprehensible, but I won't judge him and be the hypocrite in the room. Like Doc swore to uphold the Hippocratic Oath, I was bound by the Pennsylvania Rules of Professional Conduct. On more than one occasion, I flaunted those rules under the influence and failed to provide competent representation to clients. Like Doc, people trusted me, and I let them down. If given another chance at redemption, I swore it would never happen again.

"I didn't bother fighting it," Doc says. "Plead guilty. Did my time."

There's no need to press further. "What's up with the hole in the wall?"

"Oh, that," he says, and chuckles. "I'm not spying. The last occupant of your room came up short on funds with a sex worker. An argument ensued, and things got feisty. She chased him and kicked through the drywall."

"Did he pay?"

"Don't know, but if not, she'll never collect. About a week later, they found him dead of an overdose, floating in the Delaware River."

This may be an entrée into Patrick's life. "Wasn't there an online story about a kid dying here?"

"Pittsburgh media covered it?" Doc lets loose a vicious hacking fit. With his chain-smoking, I hope that he doesn't have lung cancer.

"It was in the *Philly Enquirer*."

"I don't remember that story," Doc says. "Fatal ODs around here are common. The media doesn't care unless it's a human interest series for Pulitzer consideration. Only then is it a crisis."

I resist the urge to kick myself. This guy is no idiot. I follow him back outside, where he lounges in his chair.

"You're not the usual addict living in this dump," he says. "Most of these mopes are destitute with no place else to go. I also did some research at the library. You have quite the backstory."

I should have known he'd go online and look. I had planned on doing the same for him.

"Yep. My life has been a dysfunctional circus of epic proportions, but of my own making."

He probes me with his eyes, offering no clues into what he's thinking. "Addiction is a disease, not a choice. You're above ground, with a lot of years ahead if you stay sober—unless you get hit by a truck or struck by lightning."

"I made a choice, and it resulted in death," I say, craving one of his cigs, though I've never smoked a day in my life.

"You were eighteen years old and it wasn't your fault." He says "Yea, you shouldn't have covered it up for thirty years, but it's behind you."

Is it? I think. The same detective. Another dead girl.

"Jason, you seem like a nice guy with the resources to get sober anywhere you want. It's not like there's a waiting list for these luxury accommodations." His voice drips with sarcasm. "Why here?"

I wondered how long it would take for someone to ask that.

"Are you going to tell Clyde?"

"I promise he's already wondering, but your cash shut him up. As long as you pay and follow the rules, he won't bother you."

I remove the obit from my pocket and hand it to him. He studies it and nods a few times, his lips curling inward. "Emily's son. You're here about Patrick."

"Yes, but also Emily. She's dead."

Doc slumps into his chair and almost inaudibly asks, "OD?"

"Yes, but I believe there's more to it."

I'm not sure Doc heard. He stares past the balcony toward the horizon, tapping the bottom of his cigarette package on his thigh in a rhythmic beat.

"Emily was a nice lady. She went through hell with that kid."

"She was my girlfriend. I don't believe her death was an accidental overdose."

The revelation doesn't seem to faze him. He huffs out smoke wisps as if nothing in the outside world matters. "It doesn't surprise me."

"Which part?" *Please elaborate*, I think.

"Go home. You can't do anything here but get yourself hurt."

If Doc knew the whole story he might feel differently. What awaits me in Pittsburgh is at least as dangerous as any situation I will face here. Dead is dead.

"I can't walk away, Doc. Not again."

"This may be hard to hear, but you won't find expiation, absolution, or divine forgiveness on these streets," he says. "What happened to you decades ago is in the books as unchangeable historical fact, as is Emily's fate, and Patrick's."

That's true, but ensuring it doesn't happen to anyone else here is a fluent work in progress, like his memoir.

"I'm aware, but I'm pushing forward, regardless, and need your help. "You know the streets."

A shout from the parking lot directs my focus to Clyde, hands on his hips. "Today was strike one, Feldman. Two more and you're out. I suggest you be at Sunny Awakenings tomorrow for IOP."

Doc jumps to his feet, leans over the railing, and says, "He'll be there. Now leave us to our conversation."

Clyde jabs his finger upward. "I'm tired of your lip. Don't forget who you work for."

Doc flicks his hand outward in a get-out-of-my-face gesture and says under his breath, "If only *he'd* OD."

Redirecting him back to our conversation, I dangle the obituary at eye level. "I'm reconstructing Patrick's last days."

"It's a waste of time," he says. "No one will help, and there's a strong chance you'll end up with a severe beating, or worse."

A week ago that scenario would terrify me into inaction. Phillip's Taser and gun changed everything. "Then come with me. You're trusted on the street."

He rests his feet on the railing, but the tension between us intensifies. "What makes you think so?"

"You helped those people on Kensington Ave."

"You followed me?"

"No, I was driving around, and there you were."

"Uh-huh." The skepticism in his tone is noticeable.

"I need your help, Doc."

He stares at the obituary again, hands it back, and says, "Believe it or not, this is the first time I've read this. A touching tribute. Classic Emily. Do you have hers?"

I didn't anticipate needing Emily's obituary, but should have brought it with me. It's proof that I'm not lying about her death.

"I'm sorry, Doc. There is one, but I don't have it."

"No matter. I'll look it up at the library. Hang on." He disappears into his room. A few seconds later, he returns with a pen and legal pad.

"You can't roam the streets haphazardly and accomplish anything. I'll give you the lay of the land."

He draws a large square with an "X" in the right upper corner. "We're here, in Harrowgate." With the tip of the pen, he then traces a straight line to the lower left corner. "This is Kensington Avenue. Without getting technical, the area immediately east and west of the street is the barrio, where the vast majority of slinging takes place."

I trace my finger along the line. "So Kensington Avenue is where I want to be?"

"Correct. Your best bet is to get there early morning and hit one of the drug corners, or after dark, which, as you might expect, carries more risk." He then draws a miniature square. "This is the metro station at the intersection of Kensington and Allegheny Avenues. Start there, walk east, and you'll figure out who is dealing. They're not shy about it, and the cops don't care."

I fold the page and stuff it in my pocket. "Thanks for your help."

He shrugs. "It won't matter. They don't take kindly to anyone not buying and wasting their time."

Chapter 28

*D*oc's yoga chants serve as my morning alarm clock. I drag my butt into the shower, which I've used as little as possible. Even after a thorough scrubbing with every type of disinfectant, it smells like there's a sewage leak under the drain. A trickle of hot water finds its way to my chest and cuts off. I want to unleash a primal scream, but someone might call the cops. I drench myself with a deodorant body spray and head outside to Doc in his customary chair.

"My fucking shower doesn't work."

Doc stands and says, "Most of them don't, despite Clyde's puffery about this place."

"He said I get a private shower."

Doc flashes a PT Barnum "There's a sucker born every minute" smirk. "I thought lawyers had fine-tuned bullshit detectors."

Mine used to be, but two years of nonuse has degraded its sensitivity. "So I'm supposed to stink for the duration of my stay?"

"Don't sweat it," he says. "You can use mine. It works fine."

Of course it does, I think. He has the equivalent of the penthouse suite.

A white van pulls into the parking lot and stops in front of the office. "Time for group therapy so our hosts can pay the rent," Doc says. "Are you coming?"

It's the last place I want to be, but I need to buy time and don't want a confrontation with Clyde, at least not yet. "Let the healing begin."

Even with air-conditioning, the stench of unwashed clothes, urine, and body odor in the van is overpowering. My seatmate picks at a wound on his forearm, jogging my memory of what Doc said about xylazine.

"My name's Jason," I say, extending my hand.

The man keeps digging at the scab. "They call me Jazzman. You got a smoke?"

I point at Doc. "Ask him."

Doc raises his head from a book. "You're into me for a pack already. I'm not a commissary."

Jazzman skulks away, and Doc whispers, "Tranq caused those wounds. Unless he drags himself to the county hospital, infection will set in."

"Why does he call himself that?"

"His real name is Alonzo. Before the beast slew him, he was an accomplished saxophonist with a hell of a voice. Back in the day, I saw him perform at Zanzibar Blue. He's accompanied the likes of George Benson and Chick Corea."

"Benson's a Pittsburgh guy. Saw him at the Syria Mosque," I say, as the vehicle stops and the back door swings open to a guy with a clipboard.

"Newbies who haven't drug tested proceed to the bathroom for a urine sample."

I fall in behind Doc, who says, "Enjoy your piss! They sure will."

"I hope they don't guzzle it," I joke.

"They'd be drinking the profits. Your urine is gold to them. Why do you think they test so often?"

"To make sure I haven't relapsed?"

Doc laughs. "They *want* you to use. Sunny Awakenings has its own testing lab and a doctor on staff authorizing the tests."

He must sense my confusion and says, "These people are not in business for charity's sake. They overbill Medicare and private insurance for group therapy and urine tests. It's only the tip of the cash iceberg."

Doc points to the bathroom. "They're waiting on your sample."

Sitting in group therapy, I realize with stark clarity how good I had it when I went to treatment after my relapse. A clean bathroom, working shower, and full-service cafeteria were some of the niceties.

A woman in her mid-to-late-thirties, wearing a Sunny Awakenings T-shirt, enters and sits in the center of our group as if she's the sun and we are planets in rotation. "My name is Angie, and I'm the therapist. Welcome, familiar faces and new attendees. I'm glad you've chosen the path of sobriety and a sunny awakening."

She studies her clipboard, looking up and around the room every few seconds and nodding as if she's matching names to faces.

"Let's start with a show of hands from our new attendees so we can congratulate them on taking this gigantic step toward a life of sobriety and positive change."

No arms raise until Doc reaches over and jerks my hand toward the ceiling.

Angie points at me and says, "Why don't you start us off with your name and a little about yourself?"

I shoot Doc my meanest "fuck you" glare and decide to go with a basic AA-type share. "My name is Jason, and I'm an addict and alcoholic."

The group responds in unison, "Hi, Jason."

After a group clap, my posture relaxes, having cleared a hurdle. I spot Beach Boy across the circle. He gives me a sheepish wave and raises his hand.

Angie acknowledges him. "I know you have exciting news for us."

"I have one year sober, and I'm going home." He jumps up and down like a giddy teenager.

A crisscross of congratulations echoes through the room. He continues, "My mom is flying here to get me, then I'm going back to school in LA."

I think about the pain and anguish Sonya and Sam went through watching me slowly kill myself. The multiple times she picked me up from rehab, glowing with the hope of a fresh and sober start to our marriage. Beach Boy's mother will experience the same emotions. I hope his sobriety sticks.

As others share, I study faces for hints of usefulness.

As if Doc is clairvoyant, he elbows me and whispers, "You're wasting your time. None of these people can help you."

I respond in a low, hoarse rasp. "Who can, then? You?"

He touches his finger to his lips. "Shhh...."

Jed's up next. Doc elbows me and whispers, "He was a decorated sniper in Afghanistan. An IED explosion took his legs. Now he earns at the subway, directing customers to drug corners."

All of these people willing to share their pain, yet I bury mine. Even in therapy, there was always a brick wall around me. As if it has a life of its own, my hand shoots skyward. "A couple years ago, I killed two people."

The room goes quiet. Goosebumps raise like micro-mountains down my back and arms as the room converts to a sauna on maximum setting.

Doc whispers, "A ballsy share. Good for you."

A straggly haired guy wearing a military field jacket and a faded Flyers cap says, "Son, you a rookie. Some of these bangers have a higher body count than Scarface."

The room erupts in laughter.

"Everyone settle down." Angie wags a finger. "What have I said about this being a no-judgment zone?"

Jed says, "Relax, sis. No one here's judging. I got ten certified kills in combat. Fuck anyone who has a problem with that."

Angie returns her focus to me. "Jason, do you have anything more you want to share with the group?"

Still mortified and perplexed at my admission, I say, "It was self-defense. The cops cleared me of wrongdoing."

"This is a safe space," she tells me. "You're welcome to see me during office hours if it's something you want to discuss in private."

After a few more shares, Angie says, "We'll close with our group affirmation. Take the hand of the person next to you. Jason, would you like to lead the Serenity Prayer?"

"Ahh, I'd prefer not."

"What about you, Jed? Maybe today's the day you close us out?"

He maneuvers his wheelchair facing the exit and rolls himself to the door. "Unless the man upstairs can give me my legs back, I got no use for it."

We'll be here forever if someone doesn't volunteer. I reach back into my AA memories for the correct words and recite the prayer. The moment I finish, the chairs empty, and everyone stampedes to the exit. I loiter until Angie and I are alone. As she adjusts each seat into a double-row formation, I unfold Patrick's obit and help her adjust the last few.

"Thanks for helping," she says. "Did you enjoy your first meeting? That was a provocative first share, but in a good way."

"I'm not sure why I did. It popped out."

"Remember, Jason, no one is in here because everything is blue skies and angels in their lives," she tells me. "I know the van is waiting, but remember my offer if you ever want to talk in private."

This is my only chance to find out what she knows about Patrick. I'm not coming back.

"I'll keep it in mind. How long have you been a therapist here?"

She picks up an empty Styrofoam cup by a chair leg. "I wish they'd clean up after themselves. This isn't kindergarten. As it happens, tomorrow is my five-year anniversary."

Perfect. There's no doubt their paths crossed.

"Congratulations. Can I ask a question?"

"As long as it's about recovery. You wouldn't believe how many of these guys hit on me."

It kind of is, I think. Just not mine. "Nothing like that." I hand her the obit. "Was this person part of the therapy group?"

She reads it and nods. "Patrick. So sad. He was a sweet boy. Did you know him?"

"I was close to his mother."

"Emily attended several sessions with him," she says, and hands it back to me. "I last saw her at Patrick's funeral. Is she doing well?"

Should I tell her Emily is dead? It may open up a new can of worms that I don't have time for. It's best to learn what I can while divulging as little as possible.

"Not really. Did Patrick ever discuss how he ended up at Safe Harbor Recovery Home?"

She glances at the clock on the wall. "I referred him. Patrick showed up in the winter when it was zero outside. He had been living in an abandoned row house. After detox, we sent him there. What happened was such a tragedy."

"I heard he was also working drug corners. Do you know anything about that?"

Her body stiffens, and she steps around me, fast-walking to the door. "My discussions with Patrick are private. You'd better hurry, or you'll miss your ride back."

Is she worried about confidentiality or something else? Either way, I'm not going to get anything more from her. I bolt for the exit and into the back of the waiting van, resolved to not return to the group and be on my way back to Pittsburgh before the third strike.

Chapter 29

*D*oc's advice on eating out was sound. After tasting Clyde's pizza, I decided that eating in the makeshift cafeteria is another activity I wouldn't participate in again. After the van drops us off, I get in my car and drive to a fast-food joint. Then I stop at the Kensington Public Library and print out a copy of Emily's obituary. I also scan the internet for news of the bridge shootout. The front page headline reads:

Cop Dies From Wounds in Attempted Carjacking

Did I get him killed? I can still hear the splash when he hit the water. It's not like I didn't try to convince Keane that the danger was real. I print the article and head back to Safe Harbor. As I pull into a parking space, Delaney messages me.

In Philly, at a Holiday Inn, Center City.

I'm stunned. Her being here adds an unstable variable to the situation.

I text back: *It's not safe. GO HOME!*

Are you picking me up, or am I on my own?

Goddammit. She marches to her own drummer, and I need to accept it.

Give me the address.

I'm about to pull back out of the space when Doc yells down, "Where ya going? I need a ride."

I'm not driving him around with a pissed-off Delaney waiting on me.

"Can't. I'm running late for an important meeting."

"I'm only going a few blocks. Don't you want to get in the game? This is your chance."

I text Delaney: *Making a quick stop first.*

Doc tosses his tote bag into the back seat.

"Handing out water again?" I ask.

"No."

I reach back into his sack and open it. Inside are USEsafe fentanyl test strips, as well as packages labeled "Naloxone Hydrochloride INJ."

"I've never seen one of these before." I turn the container front to back. It's similar in shape to a toothpaste carton.

"They're prefilled syringes to reverse overdoses."

Thinking about the paramedic trying to save Emily, I say, "Jabbing this into someone? I'd rather have the nasal spray."

"If you need it, you're in no position to object. These are also much cheaper. They don't play as well in the suburbs. But here, people understand their value and know how to use them."

"How do you come by these supplies?" I ask.

He places the bag on his lap. "I have contacts in the medical and recovery community who donate them. Let's go."

"Where to?"

"The El. I mean, SEPTA station."

The tires spit gravel as I gun the gas and wonder whether to canonize Doc or resent him for holding back on Emily and Patrick. I'm positive he knows more.

We pass the light pole where the woman was smoking, prompting me to say, "The woman you helped the other day. She used a straw to inhale something off tinfoil while holding a lighter under it."

"Fentanyl. You've never seen anyone smoke dope before?"

"Only on television—crack with pipes and such. I thought people only injected fentanyl."

Doc snickers. "You privileged suburbanites don't know much. Illicit fenty can be smoked, snorted, or injected. There he is. Pull to the curb and wait."

As Doc ambles across the street, I roll down the window. Even with dusk taking hold, a potpourri of noxious grease and trash odors find their way inside, along with the click of wheels along elevated tracks. Rolling his wheelchair around the stairs to the platform is Jed from group therapy. Doc reaches into his bag and hands him a bunch of injectors. While they're talking, the train above screeches to a stop. The doors open and passengers rumble down the stairs. Jed holds up an injector.

A twenty-something male plucks it from his hand without making eye contact or breaking stride. Doc shakes Jed's hand and returns to the car.

"What was that about?"

"Jed is a corner guide. Addicts come in on this line to score. He directs them to the appropriate corner and if they want one, gives them an injector. Like me, he wants addicts to stay alive."

After two stoplights, Doc says, "See those two characters in front of the bodega? They're trappers. Street-level dealers. It's one of four drug corners, called a block."

A white Tesla pulls up to the curb. A dark-haired male in his twenties exits the passenger side. His cufflinked shirt and shined dress shoes are decidedly out of place among hoodies, ball caps, and low-hanging jeans. I can't help but wonder if he's a lawyer. As he approaches one of the trappers, I can make out the cash he's holding. A lighting hand-to-hand exchange ensues. Seconds later, he's back in the car and down the street. The trapper turns and hands the money over to a third guy with dreadlocks hanging below his shoulders.

"That's how it happens," Doc says. "All day, every day."

"Who's the dreadlocked guy wearing the Sixers jersey?"

"Billy B. He's the caseworker, like a supervisor for his territory. The two trappers report to him." Doc gets out of the car. "Let's go."

My heart rate skyrockets as we approach the corner. "This might be a mistake."

"We're here," Doc says. "Keep your mouth shut and your phone pocketed."

The moment Doc steps onto the sidewalk, Dreadlocks blocks his path. "What you doing on the corner, Doc? This ain't your game no more, and we don't need a street preacher scaring away the dope fiends." He then points at me and says, "Who's that?"

Every eye is on me, and my hand trembles as I unfold the obit. "This kid overdosed and died at Safe Harbor. Is there anything you can tell me about him?"

Doc glares at me and says, "This is Jason. He's a friend. Any information you can give him puts a favor in my bank."

The trapper leaning against the building mumbles, "That wasn't no accident."

Billy B. frowns at him. "Shut up, Jolly." Then he turns to Doc. "Is this lily boy for real? He ain't no dope fiend. Why are you asking about Sad Boy? He dead and ain't comin' back."

Doc raises his hand. "Relax. We're trying to get the mother some closure. Wouldn't you want us to do the same for yours?"

"Shit, I ain't see my moms in years," Billy B. says. "Why you bringing her into this?" He raises the hem of his shirt, exposing a Sig Sauer. "You over-steppin', Doc. Take this narrow-ass pasty back where you found him before he learns what permanent closure is. Don't do this no more."

"Let's go." Doc pushes me towards the street.

Back in the car, I say, "Who's the kid Billy told to shut up?"

"His street name is Jolly. He and Billy B. live in one of Clyde's other facilities."

"So, Clyde has residents working the corners for him. These aren't legitimate recovery houses. They're drug operations."

"You're catching on."

Did Emily catch on as well? If so, no wonder Mary Lou and Phillip will do anything to get the video back for King.

Chapter 30

I drop Doc back at Safe Harbor and text Delaney: *On my way.*

I walk into the lobby and eyeball as many people as possible. The masked shooters didn't materialize out of thin air. Mary Lou has help beyond Phillip. Delaney is seated in the lobby, dipping a tea bag into a cup.

"When did you last sleep?" I ask, noting her drooping eyelids.

"Is it obvious?" She sips her tea.

"You look worn out. Why did you come? There's nothing you can do, and it complicates the situation."

"I couldn't sit around Maz and Irina's place like a slug. This is my battle as well, and frankly, I'm not happy with how you've commandeered things."

I fight back a reflexive desire to defend my actions. She's hyper-analytical and smarter than I am. Most importantly, she's here, and nothing can change that. "You're right. I'm sorry."

"Have you learned anything?" she asks.

"I connected with a guy who may know something. Believe it or not, he's a doctor."

Her eyes go wide. "Really? I want to meet him."

Who knows when Doc last talked shop with another physician? Delaney may be the perfect weapon to break down his defensiveness.

"He has quite a story."

"Give me five minutes in my room to freshen up."

The moment she's in the elevator, I text Maz: *Are you crazy, letting her come here?*

She didn't ask my permission, and it's a free country. Put on your big boy pants.

I text back: *Have you spoken to Keane?*

Yeah. The cops think you're nuts.

Did you say anything to her about us or Philly?

No.

Delaney exits the elevator. "I'm excited to meet the doctor. Let's go."

On the way to Maz's Crown Vic, we pass the car I rented. It didn't occur to me that she'd use it to follow me here. But it should have. Another misstep on my part. Now it's easier for them to take us both out at once.

As we pull into the parking lot, I say, "It's not the Garden of Eden. Prepare yourself for an abundance of suffering."

"I'm an emergency-room physician. Many of the people I treat are no different."

I wonder how condescending that must have sounded. Of course, she understands.

Three raps on the door, and I shout, "Doc, it's me. I'm with a friend."

No response. I place my ear up against the rotting wood. "Om...om..."

"Follow me." I take Delaney's arm and pull her to my door.

Inside, Delaney examines the security bar. "Is it that bad here?"

"It's not the Ritz." I slide the dresser out from the wall, exposing the porthole. Doc is once again in the buff, doing his thing.

"Put some clothes on and open your door," I tell him. "There's someone I want to introduce you to."

"Why is there a hole in your wall, and who were you speaking to?" Delaney asks as I guide her outside to the balcony.

Seconds later, Doc's door opens. He rests his hand on his chest.

"Be still my heart. Jason, you out-kicked your coverage."

Delaney offers an indulgent smile, and I correct him. "We're not a couple. She's a good friend and a doctor."

"What's your name?" Delaney asks in a gentle tone.

"My Christian name is Edgar, after Edgar Allan Poe. But here, I'm only Doc."

"How interesting. I'm Delaney, named after the first Black doctor in Pittsburgh. There's quite an eclectic selection of books on your dresser. It's nice to make the acquaintance of a fellow bibliophile."

"Now I do love you," he says, and drags a chair out of his room. He wipes the seat with a paper towel. "Please sit."

"What kind of medicine do you practice?" Delaney asks. "I'm an ER physician and teach toxicology at Pitt Medical School."

Doc takes a pack of cigarettes out of his pocket. "In another lifetime, I *was* an anesthesiologist. Do you mind?"

"I'm not a fan, but they're your lungs. Is it too personal if I ask why you no longer practice medicine?"

I wasn't expecting her to be so forward seconds after meeting him. I hope it doesn't push Doc away.

"Demerol addiction," he tells her. "I botched an operation under the influence. A young woman died. Her name was Melanie. I got sober in the can, did my time, and here I am. What brings you to my neck of the woods?"

Delaney glances at me and says, "I was Emily Williams's best friend."

I'm about to correct her on the last name when it occurs that, given the timeline, Emily wouldn't have changed it to Wilson yet.

Doc nods and takes a drag as if he already knows why we are here. "She was a wonderful lady."

The sound of footsteps redirects my attention down the hall to Jazzman from the van, shuffling in our direction, scratching his Tranq wound. "This thing is itching worse than ever. Can you take a look?"

Doc crouches on the concrete, takes hold of Jazzman's wrist, and rotates it. "It's infected and getting worse. Get your butt over to the County Hospital so they can clean this and give you antibiotics."

Jazzman shoots a suspicious glance at Delaney. "Who are you?"

Doc releases his arm. "She's a friend. Come into my room, and I'll clean it the best I can, but if you don't deal with this soon, it will go gangrene."

"I'd like to observe," Delaney says. "I'm a doctor."

Jazzman hesitates and then says, "Suit yourself."

Inside, Doc reaches under his bed and slides out a shoebox filled with gauze, nitrile gloves, plastic bottles of alcohol, and tubes of store-brand Neosporin ointment. After he wipes the desktop with an alcohol swab, he says, "Lay your arm here, wrist facing the ceiling."

As Doc cleans the wound, Jazzman closes his eyes and growls through gritted teeth, "This shit burns."

Doc then unscrews the cap off a generic Neosporin tube. "Do you wish to examine this, Dr. Martin?"

She tears an alcohol swab open and disinfects her hands. Then she removes a Q-tip from the box and traces it along the outer rim of the infected flesh. "We're seeing more of this in the ER."

While Doc cleans and bandages the wound, Delaney lays her hand on his shoulder, squeezes, and says, "You're a kind soul, Edgar."

As Jazzman leaves the room, Doc says, "Remember what I told you about getting back here to have the dressing changed and not injecting near the infected site."

Jazzman grunts and says, "Yeah. Yeah," then pulls the door shut behind him.

Doc removes his gloves and drops them with the used swabs into a plastic trash bag. "I do the best I can with limited resources. Jazzman is a microcosm of what's going on in this town."

Delaney picks through the box. "Where do you get these supplies?"

A great question, I think. The Narcan, fentanyl strips, assorted ointments, and antiseptics in that box all have a cost attached.

"Kind people in the community who know what we're facing. Every week, I make the rounds, and they donate. Let's go back outside. It's suffocating in here."

He points toward the office. "Look down there. Clyde's watching us from the window."

"What's his problem?" I say, returning the stare.

"An attractive woman is here. He's wondering why. Make no mistake, he'll confront one or both of us about it. Other than immediate family, there's a rule against females in the rooms."

Clyde exits the office and heads toward the stairs.

"Here he comes," Doc says. "It's been a pleasure, Dr. Martin, but you should return to your hotel. Come back tomorrow, and we'll chew more fat."

Delaney and I hustle down the steps, but Clyde is standing next to my car, blocking the driver's side door. He juts his head at her. "Who is this?"

Before I open my mouth, Delaney adopts a baritone, authoritative voice and says, "I'm Miss Martin from welfare, checking some addresses in this building."

"It's kind of late in the night for that, and why are you with this guy?"

"What are you, a cop?" I say. "Move away from the door so I can get in."

Delaney circles to my side of the car and gets right in Clyde's face. "Mr. Feldman was at the office earlier today, inquiring about benefits. I saw him on the balcony and went up to confirm his address."

Clyde backs away from her. "You're not the usual person who comes here, and it's late. Show me your badge," he demands, hands on hips.

"Listen, mister. My car won't start, and Mr. Feldman was kind enough to offer a ride back to my office. If you don't want me coming back with city code inspectors climbing up your ass, you'd better step off."

The threat has the intended impact, and he backs away from the car. As I start it up, he says, "I don't know what your deal is, but if you weren't self-pay, I'd toss you out on your ass."

"You're the one creating drama," I retort, slamming the door. "I'm paid up and going to group. The rest of my life is none of your damn business."

As we pull away, I tell Delaney, "Your impersonation was impressive. How'd you know how welfare works?"

"I've helped many with the process so they can get basic medical care and feed their families."

As we pull out of the parking lot, I decide that a detour is in order and head for Kensington Avenue. After a few blocks, Delaney says, "This isn't the way to the hotel."

"I know. There's something I want to show you."

Delaney stares out the passenger window as I drive toward Billy B.'s corner. She says, "I've read stories about how bad it is here, but seeing it for myself is heartbreaking."

"Yes, it is." I pull to the curb across from the corner. Billy B. and Jolly are still there. I slide down in my seat so they don't see me.

"See those kids in front of the bodega? It's a drug corner. They're dealing fentanyl and other illicit substances."

"How do you know that?"

"Doc brought me here. I'm sure he wanted me to meet these specific people."

I proceed to recount everything that happened on the corner.

"I'm paraphrasing, but when Patrick's name came up, this one kid claimed it wasn't an accident. His boss shut him down with a dead-eyed glare that would terrorize Freddy Krueger."

"Are we going back over there?"

"No way. They all had guns and made it clear I was an intruder on hallowed ground. I just wanted you to understand the obstacles in front of us."

"One of them is crossing the street in our direction," Delaney says.

I didn't see Billy B. step off the curb. He's craning his neck forward as if to get a better view of us. I cut the car into traffic and gun the gas.

In the hotel lobby, Delaney says, "If one of those kids knows something about Patrick or Emily, we need to go back."

Didn't she hear what I said about guns? I'm not stepping back on that corner without an armed escort.

"Won't work," I tell her. "They made it clear that neither of us was to show our face there again. Get some sleep. Tomorrow, we'll figure out an alternate plan."

What I leave unsaid is that the road to justice for Emily runs through that corner. I'm certain one or more of those corner kids knows what happened to Patrick. The obstacle is that this isn't a game. It's their livelihood. I'm going to have to get them to come to me.

Chapter 31

The pounding on the door wakes me out of a nightmare. Cat-sized rats were nibbling at my toes while cockroaches covered the floor like a grotesque, living carpet.

"It's Doc. Call 911!" I kick the security rod loose and yank the door open. Doc's eyes are wild. His breathing quick and shallow. "Follow me." He sprints down the balcony. I try to keep up as I dial.

We reach the open door of Jazzman's room. He's prostrate on the floor. Open tuna cans, shards of pizza crust, empty water bottles, and cola cans are strewn about. Next to his right hand is a syringe with the plunger pushed all the way to the barrel.

Doc's previously frantic tone is now clinical, as if he's still a practicing physician. "Give them this address for an unconscious sixty-five-year-old male in respiratory distress. Probable OD."

Like a child reciting the ABCs, I repeat the information to the emergency operator.

"They want to know—"

"Shut up," he says, opening one of the Naloxone cartons and removing a prefilled syringe, which he jabs into Jazzman's thigh. After checking his vitals, he repeats the procedure with a new needle. His shoulders slump.

"Forget it. Tell them there's a dead body at Safe Harbor." Doc runs his hands through Jazzman's hair, leans over, and says, "You're free, my friend. Jam that sax with the greats."

I disconnect and rest my hand on Doc's back. "I'm sorry."

From the doorway, Clyde says, "Best thing for him."

Doc turns, and with the dexterity and speed of an NBA point guard, lunges at Clyde, clawing his throat. His legs piston forward, slamming the much bigger man against the balcony railing.

"Are you out of your mind?" Clyde rasps. His hands have a death grip on Doc's wrists, but they're unable to pry him off.

Doc thrusts forward, bending Clyde backward, halfway to falling onto the pavement below. "The corpse mover is on the way again, you drug-dealing piece of shit. A second body won't matter."

Clyde struggles to breathe, squeaking, "Feldman, get this lunatic off me."

I tap Doc's back. "Ease off. This won't help."

"Like we say in AA, 'It's a good start,'" he says, eyes locked on Clyde, who is limp and moaning.

"Take a deep breath, step back, and release. You can do it."

Doc closes his eyes as his chest expands and contracts. His breathing becomes more rhythmic.

"Good. Now let him go, and walk away."

He complies, and Clyde drops to his knees, gasping for air. "You're finished. I want you out of here tonight. Feldman's my witness."

"Fuck you." Doc turns to his door. "Call the cops, and we'll all have a chat about what goes on here." Then he mutters, "This is the last time."

The paramedic's gurney clatters down the concrete, stirring memories of Emily being wheeled out. As they pass, one says, "Why hasn't the city shuttered this shithole?"

Doc accompanies them to the stairwell in silence. As he passes, I say, "Are you going to be okay?"

He locks eyes. "What do you think?"

After a sleepless hour waiting for the adrenaline surge to subside and worrying about Doc, I decide to ride out the night in my balcony chair in case he does the same. Fireflies flick against the streetlight haze. An internet search confirms that Andi's carjacking story is holding, though it's a short matter of time until video of the incident tells the real story, if it hasn't already.

I scroll to a thumbnail of my son in phone favorites. After two years, maybe now's the time. Isn't that what the father is supposed to do? Be the peacemaker? Tell him I'm done with drinking and blow. Ask how I can make things right. My finger then hovers over Sonya's number. It's been at least six months since we last spoke. Some of her remaining possessions were still in my attic. She asked me to ship them to her place in DC. Much like my hand shot up in group therapy, without thinking, I press. After four rings, I'm about to disconnect when she answers, soft and scratchy, with a touch of sleep disorientation.

"Jason? It's two in the morning."

A hollow, irritated voice chimes in. "Who is it?"

"My ex-husband."

"Does he know what time it is?"

"Jason, what's wrong? Is Sam okay?"

That's what I want to know, I think, regretting my impulsive act.

"Mister."

My heart leaps into my throat. It Jolly from the corner. I end the call and pocket my phone. Even in the low light, there's no mistaking the gun butt's outline under his T-shirt.

"You frightened the hell out of me."

"Which one's yours?" he asks, nodding toward Doc's door.

"This one."

"Inside."

My eyes dart to the stairwell, searching for stall tactics. If I yell for help he'll shoot me and slip out the same way he crept in. It's not like screams and gunshots are out of the ordinary in this part of town.

"Get inside."

He follows me in and says, "Sit your narrow ass down." The odds of me getting to the .38 under my pillow before Jolly fires are close to zero. He slides a 9mm from his waistband, pulls the chair from my desk, and sits facing me.

Sweat pours down my face and back as I close my eyes to a lifetime of home movie vignettes. Sonya holding Sam for the first time. Our first kiss. Sam's first trip to Kennywood, bawling because he was too small to ride the Jack Rabbit. His bar mitzvah. Emily's lifeless eye. Blue foam puddling on the carpet.

"Open your damn eyes. If I was here to kill you, you'd be dead, and I'd already be gone. I'm here about Patrick. You got ten minutes to ask."

"Why are you doing this?"

"I was his roomie here. Miss E and Doc were good to me. Patrick wasn't cut out for the game. They did him dirty when he wanted out."

"Who?" I say.

He nods toward the office. "Clyde gave the order."

"For what?"

His shoulders rise and fall. "It's how they do you when it's your time. No one pays attention to fenty bodies in these parts. Eight minutes."

Big-boned and at least six feet, Jolly seemed older on the corner. Up close, I question whether he's more than sixteen. Soulful doe eyes belie the bravado. A child in a man's body.

"What did Emily do for you?" I ask.

"She brought food every week and made sure Patrick had clean clothes. Me too."

"Why didn't she take him out of here?"

"Man, when you in, you in. We keep a piece of the dollars, and the rest kicks back to Clyde. They also turn you into a dope fiend for good measure."

"You too?"

Jolly checks his watch. "We ain't here to talk about me. I take care of myself. Time's up." He stands but doesn't conceal the gun. With it at his side, finger on the trigger, he cracks the door open and peeks out. After looking right and left, he's gone.

Chapter 32

The adrenaline surge doesn't subside until the morning sun peeks through the slit in my blackout curtains. In the old days, last night would have been an excuse to drink until I passed out. Instead, I'm forced to deal with the vivid snapshot of Jolly's childlike eyes and the stark contradiction of the gun in his hand. What could a different timeline have meant for his life? For Patrick's? College? Law or medical school? Maybe a startup? I read an article about how fatal overdoses have wiped out the promise of an entire generation. After witnessing the suffering along Kensington Avenue, I now understand.

Delaney arrives as residents file into the van for their group therapy session at Sunny Awakenings. I have no intention of attending another one and rush down the staircase to greet her. Clyde, who is holding court with a group of residents in front of the intake room, says, "Hold up, Feldman."

Pretending not to hear him, I open her car door and say, "Get up to my room." Delaney grabs her laptop and a file folder off the passenger seat and hurries upstairs.

"Who is she?" Clyde asks. "And don't hand me that line about the welfare office. I checked. They didn't have anyone here yesterday."

"A friend. The rest isn't your concern."

He positions himself at the base of the stairwell, blocking my ascent. "I don't think you're even an addict. Either I get answers, or you're gone."

It's obvious Clyde hasn't bothered to do his homework, which tees up my response like swinging at a grapefruit-sized baseball. I surf to an article mentioning my addiction struggles and license suspension.

Clyde scours the story and says, "I guess you're not lying, but your belongings can end up in the dumpster any time I please. Doc's too. Just remember that." He then steps away from the stairs and gestures toward my room. "I can't put my finger on it, but something else is going on with you two."

He can't throw Doc out now. Not with the threat Doc made about outing his whole operation. All I need is another two days.

"You're getting paid. I'm attending therapy and building clean time like any other resident."

Clyde starts back to the office and then pauses and looks back at me. "We'll see."

In my room, Delaney is seated at the desk, laptop open. "I've been going through the documents in Emmi's cloud account."

I collapse onto my bed. "I had a visitor last night. How are you online? There's no Wi-Fi here."

"I'm using my cell phone as a hotspot. Who?"

"A kid from Kensington Ave. Doc introduced me. He lived here with Patrick and filled in some gaps. What did you find out?"

She took out documents related to King's nonprofit, The Sunny Awakenings Foundation. "I have the board of directors and a spreadsheet of annual donors marked confidential."

The directors are public record. It's the donor's list they're worried about. I bolt upright, striking my head on the bed above me. "Goddamn, that hurt," I exclaim, rubbing the impact point. "Who's on the board?"

"Two of the directors are King Fox and Mary Lou Dubois."

I'm now wide awake. "Who else?"

She scrolls the page. "The only other one is Clyde Brown. The major donor list goes back two years, but there is only one."

"If Mary Lou is a director, I don't have to guess where the money comes from."

"Bayou Intelligence and Analytics."

"Correct. Last year, $5 million dollars. This year, $5 million."

They are clearly not putting that money into this facility. It's possible that it's going to the new McKees Rocks operation, but how the hell is a private investigating firm generating that kind of revenue for philanthropic endeavors? Unless it's coming from some other lucrative business. Of course. A secret they'd kill to protect.

"King's into more than opening rehab centers and recovery homes," I tell her.

"Now, you're catching on."

I wheel around to Doc standing in his doorway.

"How long have you been creeping?" I ask.

"Less than thirty seconds. You're looking refreshed and radiant, Dr. Martin. Would you care to accompany me outside?" In his chair, Doc upends his cigarette pack, but nothing drops. "Shit, I'm out," he mumbles.

That's a good thing, I think. I may get out of here without developing lung cancer.

"What about Clyde's threats?" I pull my door shut and lean against it. "Will he evict you?"

With a dismissive wave, Doc says, "I'm not going anywhere."

"Jolly, the kid who said Patrick's death wasn't an accident. He showed up here last night."

"I know. Did you forget there's a hole in the wall?"

There's no point in moving the dresser back, I think. He hears everything regardless, and it's not like I'm doing anything I don't want him to see.

Delaney pulls her chair around until she's facing Doc. "You said we're catching on.

What did you mean?"

My text message alert vibrates in my pocket. It's Maz.

You alive? When are you and the doc coming back? Wedding in two weeks!

Won't be here much longer. Heard from Keane?

Yep. Closing your girl's case as an accidental overdose.

There's an oddly calming resignation to the news. At least I know it's up to me now.

"Patrick showed up here on a bone-freezing night," Doc says. "He'd been living in a shooting gallery. Clyde bunked him with Jolly, and I walked him through the hoops."

"Jolly told me—"

"I'm aware of what he said. If you allow me to continue without interruption, you might learn something."

Delaney elbows me. "He's sorry, Edgar."

"Patrick was terrified. He only wanted a warm room and some food. These are the vulnerable marks they manipulate to do their bidding."

And then there's Beach Boy, I think. They both had caring mothers. Now he's going home, and Patrick is dead. What set them apart?

"Jolly said they worked a corner together," I say.

Doc scowls at the second interruption. "Patrick kicked most of the drug proceeds back to Clyde, who paid him mostly in product. One night, he overdosed and died. I told him not to use alone. He only had to knock on my door for supervised consumption and testing but never did. Like so many of these new kids on the street, Patrick thought he was invincible. I told him, 'Even if you're Superman, this shit is kryptonite.'"

His analogy brings the multiple lectures from my sponsor front and center. He pounded home that my addiction would only end one way, below ground. I scoffed at the notion that anyone died from cocaine or that my drinking would take me that low. What I learned is that there are many forms of loss. I was the walking dead.

Risking Doc's wrath again, I ask, "What did Jolly mean about Clyde giving the order?"

Doc shifts in his chair. "What do you mean?"

He listened to every word spoken in that room and is playing dumb? "Cut the crap. You heard me."

"They get rid of people who risk exposing the true nature of their business."

Delaney gasps. "You mean Patrick was murdered?"

Doc stands and says, "I need a smoke. There's a fresh pack in my room."

Delaney jumps up from her chair and blocks his door. "Don't you dare walk away from me. We're going to the police."

Now it's my turn to freak out. Has she lost her mind? Not only would we be outing ourselves, but what's the proof? Who's going to testify? Doc? Jolly? Not likely.

"You are free to do as you choose, but don't count on my help," Doc says.

"We're not going to the cops, at least not yet," I tell him. "We'll get justice for Patrick, but there's more work to do here."

Delaney returns to her chair and sits in silence. Maybe she's right. At this moment, I feel like we're in over our heads and drowning. It might be time to fill in Detective Keane, at least.

"You have to understand," Doc says. "When I arrived here, things were different. The owners were trying to do good but were unable to stay afloat financially. Then The Sunny Awakenings Foundation stepped in and bought this place."

He points down at Clyde, who is entering the intake room. "It wasn't long after that he showed up to run things. That's when everything changed. Within months, this place was more of a drug den than a sober living home. Anyone who pointed it out was evicted."

"Why did you stay if you knew what was going on?" Delaney asks.

Doc shrugs. "Clyde offered me the job of community supervisor, with a hefty raise and a connection to medical supplies. Before, I was begging for scraps."

Delaney pulls a document out of her computer bag. "This is The Sunny Awakenings Foundation board of directors. It owns this building. Do any of these names look familiar?"

Doc says, "Hold on," and disappears into his room. When he returns, he's wearing a pair of wire-rimmed glasses.

Delaney hands him the list. His index finger slides over Clyde, then past King. My palms seem to have doubled their sweat glands when he stops at Mary Lou Dobbs.

"This might be the pretty blond who shows up once a month," Doc continues. "She keeps a low profile. I walked by the office and overheard Clyde use the name on his cell phone. But then again, I'm speculating. Come to think of it, this is around the time frame she shows up here."

I run my hand down my pants legs to dry them. "Do you know what goes on when she's here?" There's no way this is an innocent coincidence.

Doc's veins strain outward along his neck. "Nothing you need to mess with."

I've come too far to be coddled but won't get what I need by knocking heads with Doc when he's already agitated. "We'll discuss it when you're calmer."

"Don't worry about me. My zen is strong."

"Edgar, tell me about Emily," Delaney says.

Doc closes his eyes as if he's accessing deep, repressed memories. "Emily loved Patrick more than her own life. She lost everything trying to get him sober. He overdosed multiple times and robbed her blind.

Even after he ended up here, she showed up every week with food and clean clothes for him."

Delaney's chin rests in her palm as she listens. He continues, "I promised to look out for him, and don't tell me it's not my fault. No one understands the addict life better than I."

What did Jolly say? *It's how they do you.* "If it's around the time when the blond makes an appearance, I want to get a look."

Doc jumps to his feet and kicks a pizza crust remnant off the balcony. "You now know what happened to Patrick. Go back to Pittsburgh."

"We're past that. Why did you take me to the block? You knew they wouldn't tell me anything."

"I wanted you to not only see the danger of meddling in their business but feel it."

He wanted to scare me into going home. When it didn't work, he sent Jolly.

Doc stands and takes his USB out of his pocket, rolling the plastic casing between his fingers. "You two are train passengers who got off at the wrong stop. You'll return home, but I have to live here."

Delaney touches his shoulder and says, "Come back with us."

He yanks it free. "Don't you get it? They kept Patrick broke and high. It's what they do, bringing in vulnerable addicts with no place to go and using them up. When there's nothing left to give, life becomes cheap."

"I understand," Delaney says.

Doc goes rigid and steps backward. "That's the car."

Chapter 33

A black Chevy Suburban rolls up to the office door. Hearts pounding, we backpedal into my room but with enough line of sight to view the happenings below.

Clyde exits the office with a gym bag. He tosses it in the back of the SUV and glances upward in our direction. He then gets in the car, and it pulls out of the lot.

"What's in the bag?" I ask.

"Right now, maybe nothing, but when he's finished, it will be filled with cash. He'll turn it over to the blond, who in turn sources him more pure fentanyl. Then it goes in the safe until this evening."

"What happens then?" Delaney asks.

"Clyde couriers it to a millhouse in far Northeast Philly. They'll cut it with xylazine, mannitol, and a slew of other adulterants. The end product is a street-ready, five-dollar baggie."

And where is Phillip? If he's here, we're in imminent danger. If he's back in Pittsburgh, Delaney's father is at risk.

"Have you seen her with a big guy sporting a military-style buzz?" I ask.

Doc shakes his head. "Nope, only her."

Delaney walks to Doc's desk and picks up a medical treatise, *Poisoning and Drug Overdoses.* "I have this in my office." She glides her fingers down the front cover, glances at Doc, then hurls it against the wall. The pages flutter like the wings of an injured bird. "This ends now. For Patrick, Emily, and all the others they've taken advantage of and killed."

"I appreciate your passion," Doc says. "But are you suggesting the three of us take down a Pablo Escobar type?"

"No, but we can disrupt our little corner of the world and, in the process, obtain a sliver of justice," she tells him.

"What about your dad?" I ask.

She walks to the balcony railing and leans forward, gazing in the direction of the giant cross. "There's no doubt in my mind he'd do the same."

"Have you checked on him?" I ask.

"Yes, he's fine and thinks we are still at the conference."

Doc walks away, muttering to himself. Upon reaching the stairwell, he returns and says, "The SUV will bring Clyde back in a few hours. He'll tend to business here until this evening, when he'll use his car to take the dope to the millhouse, then distribute the end product to the corners. He won't be back until after midnight. Meet me here at dusk."

I force a calm exterior, but inside I'm uneasy. Whatever Doc has in mind, I'm sure the stakes will be high.

Delaney and I sequester in my room. If Mary Lou is in town and discovers us, that would endanger not only our lives but Doc's as well. Jolly also lingers in my thoughts. He took a tremendous risk.

As the sun sets, Delaney closes the medical textbook she borrowed from Doc and says, "I still think we should let the authorities handle this."

"Here's the thing," I tell her. "There's no evidence of wrongdoing beyond the word of Doc and a corner kid."

"Om...om...om..."

Delaney points to the hole in the wall. "We should join him. Some of his zen in our lives can only help."

"Om...om..."

Fifteen minutes pass before the chanting stops. He then pounds on the plaster and yells. "Meet me outside."

I run my hand over the mattress concealing the .38. If it comes out, Delaney will object, and an argument will ensue. What was it Maz once told me? *Don't point a gun at a human being unless you're willing to take a life.* Two years ago, I pulled the trigger to save my own. The men I shot would have killed me, but the guilt's eaten away at me like cancer since then. Late night Jack Daniels and coke binges helped stave off the vivid nightmares, but eventually you have to sleep, right?

"Are you okay, Jason?" Delaney says.

"Yeah, let's go."

Chapter 34

Outside, Doc points to a red Camaro. "That's Clyde's. He'll depart for the millhouse soon."

"And then?" I ask.

"We're breaking into the back office," Doc says matter-of-factly.

I glance at Delaney, certain she's never received a traffic ticket, let alone committed a felony. To my surprise, she appears calm and focused. Maybe she's channeling Doc's zen.

"To what end?" I ask.

"You want evidence of wrongdoing? Otherwise, you should both go home."

"If we're going to take this risk, it would help to have some idea of what we'll find," I say.

"The Holy Grail," he replies with stinging sarcasm. "What do you think? These are drug dealers. Money and dope."

"You said he gave the money to Mary Lou, then distributed the fentanyl."

"It will be there. Trust me on this."

A concept that has been in short supply not only the last two days but most of my life. I have to take him at his word, or he's right. I should start up Maz's Crown Vic and get back on the Pennsylvania Turnpike to Pittsburgh.

"I'm not committing a crime," Delaney tells him, her once-calm exterior now shaking. "If we're caught, I'll be fired and lose my medical license."

Doc hacks up some smoker phlegm and says, "Which is why you're not coming with us."

He's right. Doc and I have already been through the wringer. If I can't practice law, I'll manage. Maybe Maz will take me back. For Emily and Patrick, it's worth the risk.

In as demanding a tone as I can muster with little leverage to back it up, I say, "Tell us how you know we'll strike gold, or this is over before it starts."

Part of me worries that is exactly what he wants, and I just gave him his out. I'm hoping, however, he's had enough and decided to follow this to conclusion, wherever it leads.

Doc glances at Delaney with sad eyes as if he's ashamed of what's coming next. "Clyde is skimming. He keeps it in the safe."

There's only one way he would know. "How much was your cut?"

Doc studies his feet. "Enough to buy needed medical supplies. I never kept an extra penny. In this town, dancing with the devil is a requirement to do any good. No one wants to help."

Delaney's narrow gaze broadcasts extreme disappointment. "You lied about soliciting donations."

"How do you know no one wants to help?" I ask Doc. "Did you even try the legitimate way?"

Doc's response is pure sarcasm. "What way is that in a community with no money or discretionary medical resources?"

His biting retort again reminds me that I'm not on my turf and to get off my high horse. He's keeping people alive.

"There's Clyde," Doc says. "I don't want him spotting either of you. Get in your room until I signal all clear."

Delaney and I back up into my room and hide behind the half-open door. Clyde gets in his Camaro and revs the engine multiple times like he's about to drag race.

"A substitute for his tiny penis," Delaney cracks under her breath.

"He's gone," Doc says, and motions us to join him.

"It's game time." I turn to Delaney. "Wait for us here. If Doc's right about the contents of the safe, we'll make an anonymous call to the Philly PD. It should be enough to close this place down and get them probing further."

"I'm supposed to sit in your room, hoping you return?" The familiar defiant tone signals an argument we don't have time for.

"Follow us downstairs, get in your car, and drive straight back to Pittsburgh," I tell her. "There's nothing more you can do here."

Delaney shakes her head. "What is it with you men who think you're our caretakers." She points to the parking lot. "*You* go back."

"What are you two jabbering about?" Doc asks. "We don't have all night to pull this off."

He's right. Every second we stand here is one less before Clyde returns. I sigh. "Have it your way."

As we creep down the balcony toward the stairwell, Delaney whispers, "What if we're stopped?"

Doc replies, "Most of the jokers here mind their own business. If a nosey nelly bothers us, you're a mom checking the place out for your kid."

We step softly through the dark, doing our best to stay out of ambient light. At the bottom stair, a gravelly smoker's voice from the balcony yells down, "Who's the lady?"

Delaney and I freeze like deer caught in headlights while Doc, nonplussed, glances upward and says, "Yo, Sal. I'm giving a tour. She's the mother of a kid who may be living here."

"Kind of late for a walk-through, isn't it? Where's Clyde?"

"She drove in from Allentown after work. I'll get with Clyde in the morning."

"Another soul needing saving. You are doing god's work," Sal says, disappearing from view.

Doc waves. "Amen." He then turns to Delaney and says, "It's been the pleasure of a lifetime, Dr. Martin. May your days be filled with joy and purpose."

"I'm not going anywhere," Delaney says. "Let's do this."

I know she's not going to budge but make one last plea.

"Not a chance," I say. "We're exposed and on the clock. Go home."

"Neither of you are my father or boss," Delaney shoots back. "Which way?"

The few seconds Doc stares at her pass as slowly as a baseball game rain delay. He then says, "Suit yourself. We're headed to room 101, where they serve meals and do intake. The back office access door is located there."

"Is it locked?" Delaney asks.

"A credit card will do the trick," Doc says. "I've done it before, but Sal for sure is gonna blab to Clyde. He's the community snitch."

"Let's pay him off," I say. "We only need a day or two of silence."

Doc takes a twenty from me. "It might work, but there's no guarantee he won't take your money and still rat us out."

He's right, but we're committed whether Clyde blabs or not. The bribe is a bit of insurance, nothing more.

I hand him another Hamilton. "After we're done, give him the bills."

Doc inserts the key into the lock and twists the knob, using his fingertips to push the door open. We slide into the room behind him.

He turns to me and says, "Be sure to secure it behind you." Doc then points to the back office door. "Delaney, you're the lookout. If the Camaro or SUV show up, come get us."

She nods and pulls a chair to the window facing the lot, edging the curtain aside.

Doc and I snake around the serving tables. At the door to the back office, he turns the doorknob, but it doesn't budge. "Nothing lost by trying. Hand me a credit card."

"You're going to open the door with it? I thought you were kidding."

"I've done it before. You've never locked yourself out of your mansion?"

"I live in a two-bedroom house."

Doc leans in with his shoulder, causing a slight separation between the door and the jamb. He then wedges the card into the opening, parallel with the doorknob. The door pops open.

"Turn on your phone's flashlight and hand it to me," he says.

He rotates in place, illuminating pallets with boxed dry goods stacked to the ceiling. At the front of the room is a metal desk stacked with papers. Next to it, a locking metal file cabinet with three slide-out drawers.

"Help me move these boxes from the back wall," he says, and pushes aside a bulk container of one-ply Walmart-brand toilet paper.

"What are we looking for?"

Ignoring me, Doc continues pushing crates aside, creating an opening spacious enough for one person to wedge between the drywall and the pallets. Then he shines the light on a square metallic faceplate with a numeric keypad and lever handle.

My heart pounds as if a baseball bat's slugging my inner chest wall as he motions for me to inspect the tight space.

"Do you know the combination?" I ask, running my fingertips across the keypad. Then, I push myself backward and out of the squeeze.

"Nope," Doc says.

The dread of Clyde coming back early creeps from my toes to my gut. "Then what's the point of this?"

"I can make an educated guess."

"Out of billions of possibilities?" I ask, exasperated. "We might as well play the lotto."

Doc squeezes himself back in, punches the keypad, and says, "Don't they teach you deductive reasoning in law school? The lottery is random. We only have to deal with the possibilities of Clyde's limited intellect. The key is thinking like he does. He uses variations of the office computer password for his other stuff."

"How do you know?"

"The moron told me when he locked himself out of his personal computer with too many failed password attempts."

The glare of headlights sweeps across the window of the main office. I glance back toward the door and say, "Let's get the hell out of here."

He mutters, "I know this guy. It has to be one of these variations."

On the fourth attempt, I'm stunned by a metallic click.

"I knew it," he says, opening the door. He shimmies out and hands me the flashlight, "Take a look."

I work my way to the safe and shine the light inside, illuminating multiple quart-size Ziplocs, each filled with smaller baggies of minute portions of white powder, too many to count. Further to the rear are stacks of cash bundled by rubber bands. Not clean bank notes, but bent, stained, and misshapen. I extract a wad and flip through ones, fives, tens, and twenties, but nothing bigger.

"He's back!" Delaney shrieks from the front room.

I put the money back inside and slam the safe shut. "You said he wouldn't return until midnight."

"I was wrong. Get your ass out of there."

We frantically shove boxes back in place until Doc, heaving for breath, says, "Only enough to conceal the safe. He won't know the difference."

Delaney rushes into the room. "He's parked and walking to the office with a blond woman. I think it's Mary Lou."

We sprint out into the meal-serving area. Doc presses the locking button on the doorknob and pulls it shut. We're less than ten feet from the exit when three knocks send us scurrying for cover.

"It's Sal. You in there, Doc?"

Doc turns and points to the stainless-steel serving table. Delaney and I duck walk behind it for cover. Sal enters the room and flicks the light on. Fuck, I didn't lock the door like Doc told me to. He's three steps inside when Clyde enters from the main office. "What are you doing in here, Sal?"

My teeth grind so hard I'm certain the grating is audible.

Clyde saunters toward us. Delaney covers her mouth, and I regret not bringing the gun. Doc reaches into his sock and out comes a scalpel, the sharp end covered in a plastic sheath. He removes the protection and raises it to chest level, hand trembling.

I can't take my eyes off the stainless steel blade attached to a green plastic handle. Doc crouches like a lion, ready to ambush his prey.

"Did they come in here?" Clyde asks.

Sal shrugs. "I don't think so."

Clyde cranes his neck around to the office door. "Quit wasting my time and get back to your room. You're breaking curfew." He pushes Sal outside, locks the door, and continues toward our position.

Doc raises his free hand as if he's worried either Delaney or I will give our position away before he can attack. Ambient light from the open office door glints off the blade.

Clyde is arm's length from the stack of buffet steam pans obscuring my forehead when a familiar female voice emanates from the storeroom.

"Can we finish, please? I'm on the red eye back to New Orleans."

It's Mary Lou.

Clyde leans forward and cocks his head as if he hears my labored breathing.

From the backroom, Mary Lou says, "If I miss my flight, I'll be unhappy."

Clyde turns and says, "I thought I heard something." He returns to the back office, slamming the door shut behind him.

"Let's go," Doc says under his breath. He opens the front door a few inches and peeks outside. Unnerving seconds creep by. If Phillip is here, he won't hesitate to kill us all. "Get your butts upstairs," he says. "I'll be right behind you."

"What if they see us?" Delaney says.

"I'll take care of it," he whispers. "And don't run."

My room might as well be in Pittsburgh as we tiptoe upstairs. I insert the room key and press. The door glides open as if guided by a ghost.

"I said I'd see you again, asshole." Phillip is sitting in my desk chair, his Sig Sauer zeroed on my chest. Heels click down the balcony. I twist my head around to Mary Lou approaching from the stairwell.

Phillip flicks the barrel toward the bed. "Sit down and don't say a fucking word."

Mary Lou slides by us, Sig in hand, and walks to the other end of the room. "You should have let sleeping dogs lie. Now we've come to this."

"Is Doc alive?" I grasp Delaney's hand as she trembles, never taking her eyes off of Phillip.

"As my brother said, please seat yourselves, hands on your laps."

"We don't have the video," I say, tightening my grip on Delaney, who reciprocates. "I've never even seen it, only the transcript."

"We're past that," Mary Lou says and taps her phone screen. "Clyde, please escort the doctor to Mr. Feldman's room."

They have Doc. At least he's alive.

Phillip unzips his satchel, and out comes the Taser. "Both of you, put your hands behind your back," he says, and takes a roll of black electrical tape out of his bag. After wrapping both of our wrists together, he thrusts the Taser into my neck and says, "Unlike my sis, I'm going to enjoy this."

I'm vaguely aware of Delaney's screams as searing heat jets into my heart and then fans out like serrated knives ripping through veins, arteries, and muscles. I topple forward onto the carpet, writhing on the floor like a wounded animal. As the convulsions subside I heave half breaths, unable to expand my lungs.

"Not a pleasant experience, is it?" Mary Lou says. "Phillip, please help Jason back to the bed."

I slap his hand away. "Go fuck yourself."

Phillip hoists me up by my armpits. "I've waited for this moment since Pittsburgh. It's payback time."

"What will I do with you two?" Mary Lou says, pacing the claustrophobic length of the room while tapping the muzzle against her leg. She squats, facing me. "You must have loved Emily to have gone to such lengths. Why are you here?"

Still cloudy and doubled over, my chest on fire, I spit back, "To get a cheesesteak and catch a Phillies game." I gasp for breath, unable to feel my fingers.

"Wrong answer," Phillip says, leaping at Delaney and ramming the Taser into the side of her neck. Tears stream down her face.

"Jason."

"You're the simple part," Mary Lou says to me. "After a tragic relapse and fentanyl overdose, you'll be found in the basement of a vacant row house or floating in the river. But what to do with the pretty doctor?"

"Let her go back to Pittsburgh," I say. "She's not an addict, and she's known in the community. You'll never get away with staging an overdose like you did with Emily."

Mary Lou sits back in the desk chair, facing Delaney and me. "You're probably right about that, but we'll figure something out. First, I have to know what you learned about our small but profitable operation."

Delaney squeezes my hand. "Don't let them electrocute me."

Phillip takes a washrag out of his satchel, circles behind Delaney. "Open your mouth."

Her lips clamp together, blocking the cloth's forward progress. Out comes the serrated knife. He inserts the tip between her lips. "Open it." Delaney's eyes meet mine. They are wide and unblinking. Her jaw then lowers, and he stuffs the rag in. Tears pour down her cheeks.

"We're here to learn what happened to Emily's son," I tell Mary Lou. "We don't know anything about whatever else you're up to."

"Patrick was a nice young man who got in with the wrong crowd," Mary Lou says. "Unfortunately, he became a complication. It's not something I relished."

The timeline is becoming clear. Patrick told Emily what was going on here. They killed him for it, then her. My mind probes for any words, sentences, or threats to pause this nightmare.

Mary Lou says, "I loathe violence and take no pleasure in this, but I need answers." She nods at Phillip as Delaney's gurgles and moans through the gag wrench my gut.

A bang like a car backfiring vibrates the wall, followed by a dull thud. Phillip drops the Taser and collapses. "My leg!"

Mary Lou whirls to the origin of the blast, Sig raised. Another pop, and she cries out, crumpling to the rug. She rolls onto her back, aiming her gun at my upper torso. Restrained, all I can do is force myself to my feet and fall forward on top of her as she fires and hits the ceiling. Specks of white plaster settle on her face.

Doc rushes in, Maz's .38 revolver in hand. He steps on Mary Lou's gun hand and wrestles her weapon away. I roll off her and onto the rug, ears ringing and grateful Clyde never fixed the hole in the wall and I didn't move the dresser back.

Doc removes the gag from Delaney's mouth. "Are you all right, Doctor?"

Her answer is multiple heaving gulps for air. He cuts through the tape binding her wrists, then does the same for me.

"He has a gun." Delaney shouts.

Phillip aims his 9mm at Doc, who, as if on autopilot, drops the scalpel and fires. A quarter-size red blotch materializes on Phillip's forehead. He falls backward, eyes closed. In all the excitement, I assumed he only had the Taser.

"You killed my brother," Mary Lou cries out, clutching her ankle.

Doc trains his weapon on her. I wrap my hand around the barrel. "Give me the gun."

He resists for a moment, then releases his grip. Now, it's my turn. I aim the muzzle at Mary Lou's head. A squeeze, and it's over. Self-defense. No jury will convict me. Justice for Emily and her son.

A soft hand takes hold of my wrist. Delaney's breath against my ear is calming. "This isn't the way."

"It's justice," I say, not taking my eyes off Mary Lou, who returns the stare as if she's daring me.

"You're wrong," Delaney says. "It's murder. I want accountability as much as you do, but we need her alive."

My breathing regulates as the pressure in my head subsides. She's right. King must answer for the wreckage he's caused. His new facility can't open. My lungs expand until my chest forms a barrel shape. I exhale and drop the weapon to my side.

"Doc, give me my phone and the satchel," I say, backing away from Mary Lou.

"What happened to Clyde?" Delaney asks.

Doc picks up the surgical knife and raises it to eye level. The steel shine is obscured by dried blood. "He's alive but indisposed."

I upend the satchel. Three rubber-banded stacks of bills free-fall to the floor, along with two quart-size baggies of white powder and another stuffed to the brim with pills carrying the same marking as the ones in Emily's pocket.

"Step away from that crap so you're out of the photo frame," I announce, positioning the loot and drugs above Mary Lou's head. Then I snap photos of her and Phillip from multiple angles. She grimaces, "You might as well kill me. There's no place I won't find you."

She may be right, but at this moment, I have the gun. "You've given us an easy self-defense case if I have to shoot, so don't even think about fucking with me."

Doc kneels and pulls the hem of Mary Lou's black pants up to her calf. She clenches her teeth as he presses on the tibia. "It's shattered. She's not going anywhere."

His pronouncement doesn't comfort me, but unless we kill her, it will have to do. I toss him the electrical tape and the rag that was in Delaney's mouth. "We're leaving. Secure her hands and gag her."

Without being asked, Mary Lou thrusts her wrists toward Doc. He binds them together. Before he gags her, Mary Lou says, "I wish you hadn't killed my brother."

I drop Mary Lou's Sig and Phillip's 9mm in the satchel. "Let's go."

Doc shakes his head. "I'm not leaving. This is my home. People count on me."

"You're hanging out here with Mary Lou? What will you tell the cops? Don't be an idiot. Your life in Kensington is over."

Delaney clutches his hand. "Come back with us. You have so much to offer."

"I gave it all away in the operating room. This is my penance."

His words stab at my gut as if he'd sliced me with his knife. How long will I punish myself for my past?

"There's nothing for you here," I tell him. "The cops, feds, and who knows what other agencies will be swarming. That life is over. Time to make a better one."

"So, we're running away?" he asks.

"Yes. Let's get out of here before the cops come. We'll work it out in Pittsburgh."

I open the door and jump backward. Sal is on his knees, leaning toward me as if he had his ear to the wood. He jumps to his feet and stares at the .38 in my hand. "I heard gunshots. What's going on in there?"

Doc edges past me and hands Sal the twenties. "Go back to your room. You didn't see or hear anything." He glances at the money and, without another word, double-times into his room, slamming the door shut.

I put Maz's gun in my waistband. "The satchel goes with us. Everything else stays where it lays."

Doc says, "I have to get my flash drive."

I sling the bag over my shoulder. "Hurry up; we're out of here in five minutes."

After following Delaney outside, I take one last look at Mary Lou. I didn't want it to come to this, but unlike Emily and Patrick, at least she'll live, even if it's in a prison cell. I pull the door shut and lock it.

My first instinct is for everyone to pile into the Crowne Vic, but it occurs that an out-of-service cop car might be conspicuous. "We're taking the rental. Let's haul ass."

Delaney out-sprints me to her car and gets in the driver's seat.

"Pop the trunk," I tell her.

Doc brings up the rear and gets in the back. Maz may right-hook me when he finds out we left his car in Philly.

I stick Maz's weapon in the satchel and lay it in the spare tire well. Then, I take one last look around before getting in. Other than Sal, no one else seems to have cared about the shots fired. After living here, I understand. Why get involved? A sex worker mills around the sidewalk. There are no sirens. For the moment, the outside world is oblivious to our predicament.

The rear tires spin on the blacktop, and a minute later, we're three blocks away. We merge onto the Pennsylvania Turnpike and travel the next thirty miles in silence. I replay every second in the room. Did we do the right thing by fleeing or did we create more problems? Technically, I'm a fugitive again. I can only imagine how Keane will respond to that. As she said, we are not pals.

Doc dozed off at least ten miles ago. Moans and mumbled gibberish intersperse themselves between snores.

"What do you think happened to the video?" I ask Delaney, who is focused on the road.

She shrugs. "I don't know. Maybe Emmi destroyed it or had another cloud account."

Another ten miles later, I lean back and close my eyes. The steady buzz of the tires on the pavement act as a downward force on my eyelids.

"I'm beat," I mumble. "Wake me when we hit Breezewood."

Dream-like images of Emily pop into my subconscious. Why wouldn't she trust me with her secrets? She didn't even tell Delaney. What was it Doc said?

We chatted whenever Emily visited Patrick.

My eyes snap open. I twist around and place my hand on Doc's arm, shaking it. "Wake up."

"We're there already?"

"No. Does your USB contain anything else besides the manuscript?"

He sits upright, eyes wide. "Why do you ask? It's my personal business."

"Let's not play this game. You know why."

He slides to the driver's side of the car, behind Delaney. "I don't know what you're talking about."

"Don't hand me that line of bull. The video is on it."

Delaney adjusts the rearview mirror. "Edgar, people are dead because of what Emily saw. Please tell us if you have it."

"I know he does. Why would you conceal it from us?"

Doc's shoulders slump. "Giving it to you wasn't going to bring Emily or her son back, and it would jeopardize everything I was doing in helping people to stay alive. Where will they go now?"

"We can talk about that later. Turn it over," I demand, hand extended.

He takes the USB out of his pocket and closes his fist around it. "I never dreamed things would come to this."

That makes two of us, I think, as he drops it into my palm.

After powering up Delaney's laptop, I slide the drive into the port and locate the file. The video begins with the instantly recognizable King Fox entering an office and sitting behind a desk.

Doc leans over the seat back. "I wonder how she concealed the camera."

"People hide them in all kinds of stuff. You can buy them hidden in flowerpots, clocks, even those tiny USB power adapters."

The next two minutes consist of Fox shuffling through papers. He then makes a phone call to his construction foreman and discusses various deadlines for the new McKees Rocks rehab center.

"Turn it up," Delaney says.

"Focus on the road," I tell her, wondering if the strobes of police lights are not far behind.

Two minutes and thirty seconds into the video, King is back on his cell phone. "Yeah, I'm buzzing the gate now."

"Here we go," Doc says.

King opens a translucent baggie containing white powder. He upends it, and a mini snowstorm of white flakes floats to the polished mahogany. Then, he slides an American Express Black Card through the pile, creating two equal lines. My heart palpitates, and the bitter chemical odor reminiscent of cocaine-cutting agents fills my nostrils. The air-conditioning is on high, but the car interior might as well be the surface of Venus. Sweat beads form under my earlobes and ebb down my cheeks.

Doc hands me a handkerchief. "No shame. Decades of sobriety, and I still trigger over certain sights, smells, and even sounds. It's what happens next that matters."

I dab perspiration bubbles on my forehead. "As long as you don't line out a rail of blow, I'm fine."

He laughs. "Joking about it is a sign of recovery."

Delaney blurts an impatient, "Well, what's he doing?"

King stands, steps out of frame, and says, "When did you fly in?"

A female voice replies, "This morning, honey. I'm back to the City of Brotherly Love in three hours."

"It's her," I announce as Mary Lou steps into the frame and sits, holding what appears to be Phillip's satchel, now in our possession.

She reaches in, then drops a quart-size, white powder filled plastic Ziploc on the desk. "Get this fentanyl milled, then distribute it to our dealers as soon as possible."

King stands and pulls on a framed landscape portrait on the wall behind him. It swings open, exposing a safe. He punches the keypad and puts the baggie inside. When his hand comes out, he's holding a gym bag.

"I don't need a medical degree to know it's full of cash," Doc says.

The video confirms everything we already speculated. King's addiction treatment facilities and sober homes are fronts. Bayou Intelligence and Analytics supplies the product. From what went down on the Warhol Bridge, the next step up the ladder has to be the cartel.

Entering Breezewood, I rack my brain for my next move when we get to Pittsburgh. The Philly PD may already be looking for us.

"Pull into the first gas station," I say. "I have to go."

"Get some snacks," Doc says. "I'm hungry."

In the restroom, I google every search variation of a shootout in Kensington and then dial Maz.

"We're in Breezewood, on our way back. It was a shitshow, and we have another guest for you."

"What am I, Motel 6? Irina's parents are here from Kyiv, helping with the wedding. You still have my backup weapon, right?"

I inspect my haggard reflection in the grime-streaked bathroom mirror and consider the ramifications of the full truth. For now, I'll keep it simple. "Yes, I have it. See you soon."

Inside the convenience store, I head to the snacks section where I decide on protein bars and salted peanuts. I then get in the payment line behind several customers and also watch the parking lot. Delaney is filling up the gas tank, but I can't see Doc in the back seat. Either he's lying down, or he's in the bathroom. There's still one customer ahead of me when a Pennsylvania state trooper pulls into the lot and up to the gas pump opposite Delaney. The trooper gets out and unscrews the gas cap on her cruiser. State police are a common sight on the turnpike, but right now, I'd rather she was someplace else. If the Philly PD put out a BOLO, she'll have it and be looking for us.

"Sir, can I help you?"

I was so fixated on the trooper that I didn't notice the line move. Without a word, I push the snacks toward the cashier while never taking my eyes off the trooper, who is now having a conversation with Delaney. If only I had Superman hearing right now. Delaney is smiling and appears calm. The trooper says something, and then she laughs.

"That will be eight dollars."

I slide my credit card into the point-of-sale device while working through potential scenarios if things go south. She's not onto us yet, or Delaney would be under arrest.

"Would you like a bag, sir?"

I shake my head and take the items. Where the hell is Doc? The trooper closes the gas cap and walks this way. My heart is beating so hard, I wonder if she'll hear it or otherwise notice something off about me. It's what cops do.

I silently speak to myself. *Keep your head up, Jason. Look her in the eye and exchange a pleasantry.* My back is soaked with sweat. All I see are the three guns in my trunk.

She gets to the door and pulls it open. I take a deep breath and turn toward her. As we pass each other, I smile. "Good evening, officer."

"Same to you." She waves to the cashier and walks to the refrigerated drink section. I exit the store and force myself not to look back over my shoulder. Delaney is in the car, but still no Doc.

She doesn't wait for me to ask and says, "He's in the restroom."

Smart move on Doc's part, I think. They would be looking for three people traveling together, not two. "Pull up to it, and I'll get him."

Delaney drives around to the side of the store. I get out and bang on the door. "Doc, let's get out of here."

He comes out and gets into the back seat. "Damn, that was intense."

"Roll out slow," I tell Delaney. "We're just customers who stopped for gas and snacks. No big deal." My accelerated heart rate tells a different a different story.

She merges back onto the turnpike. I twist around to the back seat and look at Doc. "You did good, staying out of sight."

"I didn't think anything positive would come of making myself known. The safe play was staying where I was."

I turn back to Delaney. "What did you two talk about?"

She shrugs. "Believe it or not, the weather. The officer said it looked like rain. I told her that was good because my car was filthy. She laughed. That was it."

I nod and exhale a nervous breath. "Stay the speed limit all the way to Pittsburgh."

Delaney looks over at me, rolls her eyes, and says, "No kidding."

The next hour passes with only the crunching sound of Doc munching on his peanuts. Delaney made a nasty face when I offered her the protein bar, and the cop encounter took away my appetite.

We're in Monroeville, fourteen miles from Pittsburgh, when Doc volunteers, "Drop me off at a twelve-step meeting. I'll take it from there."

"That's not happening," I tell him. "You'll stay with a friend of mine. He's a retired cop."

Delaney adds, "You'll stay with me at my place until we figure something out."

I shoot her a puzzled look. She's not going back to Maz's? That's a mistake.

"I appreciate that you're both concerned, but I can take care of myself."

Delaney and I glance at each other as if we've been scolded by our first-grade teacher. She says, "You're right. Tell us what to do."

"Drop me at an AA meeting, and I'll find a place to lay my head, even if it's a shelter. I've done it before."

"First, we'll stop by my place to change," I say. "Then find a cheap hotel. You're not staying in a shelter. That's nonnegotiable."

Doc's eyes flit from Delaney to me and back. He scratches his beard and says, "Okay, but this better not be a ploy. I don't want your charity."

I extend my arm. "There's one condition. Hand it over."

"What?"

His deflection bristles my neck hairs. "Give me the USB. I saw you pocket it at the gas station."

Doc shakes his head. "The only duplicate of my manuscript is back in my room. This is safe with me."

"Give it over," I say, curling my fingers in and out as if I'm challenging him to a fight.

"Go fuck yourself."

"Settle down, guys," Delaney says. "I have a compromise. Edgar, do you have an email address?"

"Yes. I check it at the library for my medical journal subscriptions. Don't use it for much else. It's Lapsed Healer at AOL dot com."

"Jason will email you a copy of your manuscript. You'll be able to access your document any time you want and not worry about misplacing it."

Doc pinches the device above my outstretched palm, exhales, and releases like a vise springing open. I activate the Bluetooth on Delaney's phone and then tether her computer.

"Give me the email again."

He repeats the address, and ten miles pass before the file uploads to my Gmail account.

I press send and say, "It's on the way to you."

Doc takes the laptop and hunches over the keyboard. His fingers tap with intensity and intention as if he's cutting an incision on the operating table.

"Got it," he announces.

As we enter the Pittsburgh city limits, Delaney says, "Please, Edgar, stay with me. I have an extra bedroom."

"Whoa, wait a minute," I say. "You're going back to Maz and Irina's."

"You can do what you want," she says, "but I'm going home, and tomorrow, I'm calling Detective Keane and telling her everything. I've done nothing wrong, and I'm not paving over my life with lies."

I know she's right, but it's too soon. How can we be sure this is over until King is behind bars? "Can we at least discuss this with Andi before you say anything? Remember, she lied to protect you. It could impact her career."

Uncomfortable miles roll by as I wait for Delaney's reply. Doc is stretched out again, eyes closed, as if he couldn't care less what we decide.

"Okay. We'll do that," she finally says.

"Which part?" I ask.

"Discuss it with Andi first."

Chapter 35

"Wake up, Doc. We're here."

"The AA meeting?"

Delaney shuts off the engine and tells him, "This is my home."

"I thought you were taking me to Jason's."

"You'll be comfortable here. I can always drive you later if that's what you want."

After popping the trunk, I lift the spare tire and remove the satchel. "You, of all people, know there's always another meeting. We'll make coffee, and you can light up."

"No smoking in my condo," Delaney says, and hands him the pack she bought at the gas station.

Doc fires up, inhales, holds it, and then exhales a white cloud. "Oh yeah, better than sex. In Philly, some rehabs won't let you smoke. It's one of my few pleasures and, for many addicts, a big part of staying clean."

"Cigarettes kill as well. My mother died of lung cancer," Delaney tells him.

He sucks a pensive drag and says, "I'm sorry about your mom. Cigs may kill me eventually." He sucks more nicotine. "But not today."

Delaney unlocks her front door. "Smoke as many as you want. Outside."

He gazes upward at summer cumulus clouds floating toward the Monongahela River. I wonder what's going through his head and ask myself who we are to decide his future.

Delaney sets her computer bag on the breakfast bar.

"I'm calling my dad and then scrubbing myself raw in a hot shower."

I power up her laptop and collapse into the reclining chair, now hyperaware of my body odor. She's not the only one who needs disinfecting. Secondhand, stale cigarette smoke seeps from my every pore.

The *Philly Tribune* page-one headline disrupts my tenuous level of calm.

Three Dead as Recovery Home Burns to the Ground

"Firefighters responding to a three-alarm fire at the Safe Harbor Recovery Home made a grisly discovery when they came upon three charred bodies. The structure burned to the ground before the blaze was brought under control. A police spokesperson said it will take some time to identify the bodies as well as the cause of the blaze."

My mind reels. Is Mary Lou one of the bodies? We made sure she couldn't get out of that room or yell for help. What happened to Clyde? I should bring Keane up to speed.

Doc enters the house, picks up a magazine off the coffee table, and sits. I reach into my pocket for the protein bar. I lose my grip, and it drops into the crevice between the seat cushion and the chair arm.

I grunt, jamming my hand into the open space, trying to pinch the edge, which only drives it farther out of reach. Frustrated, I ram my fingers in like a jackhammer, striking a hard surface. I feel around and slide the object out, an inch at a time, until it pops free—Emily's iPhone.

"Delaney," I shout. "Get out here and bring your phone charger."

Doc's head jerks back like he's been slapped. "What's wrong?"

"Nothing. For the first time, something has gone right. This is Emily's phone."

Delaney hands me the adapter. "Where did you find it?"

I plug the phone into an outlet. "Wedged in the chair. I can't believe the cops missed it."

We gather around and stare at the charging meter as it edges to the right at an agonizing turtle pace. When it hits 5 percent, I power on. As expected, the home screen password prompt blocks access, but Delaney reads it off the list Emily left, and we're in.

Doc and Delaney huddle behind me, peering over my shoulder as I scroll through text messages, the last sent to me at noon the day she died.

Hey sweetie! Going to leave work early, then run errands. See you tonight.

Delaney must sense my quickened breathing and rubs my shoulder.

The previous text is to Delaney: *Are you off this weekend? We need a girls' night out.*

Now it's Delaney who sniffles and swallows hard, with an audible throat contraction. Doc pats her hand. "She loved you a lot."

I double-take and stop scrolling.

Delaney's eyes narrow, and she says, "How do you know?"

Doc stammers. "I, well, only meant it appears that way from how you speak about her."

It occurs to me that the two things we never nailed down were when Emily planted the camera and when she gave Doc the video. She was working for King when we met, and Patrick passed a year ago.

"When did you last see Emily?" I ask.

Silence.

"Doc?"

"Edgar, please," Delaney says.

"She visited a week before her death, wanting to give me something for safekeeping. It was the flash drive. At first, I declined. My duty watching her son was over."

Is he freaking kidding me? Patrick died on his watch.

"How the hell were you taking care of him?" I ask. "Patrick and Emily both died. Sounds to me like you didn't give a damn about these people, only looking out for yourself."

Delaney rests her hand on my arm. "Let him be."

Do no harm, my ass. He's a hypocrite, but she's right. This isn't the time.

"You had obviously viewed the video before we fled Philly. In the car, you knew the truth about King and played dumb."

"Yes, we used her laptop. I didn't want any part of what was on it and told her to give it to someone else. I suggested you or the doctor. But given the contents, I think she thought it would put you in jeopardy."

His starstruck, gee, golly, great-to-meet-you line with Delaney was an act. He knew why we were there from the start.

"You knew about me?" Delaney says.

"Of course. Even saw photos."

Doc takes out his cigarette pack, but Delaney snatches it from him and says, "I've offered you respect and compassion. This is how you respond. With lies?"

"I didn't lie. You never asked."

"Oh, please!" Delaney hurls the pack onto the kitchen floor. "Intellectual dishonesty doesn't play. You betrayed us. Me."

Doc must realize he's on the brink of alienating his strongest ally. He covers his face and sobs. I'm unsure if it's guilt over withholding an important piece of the puzzle or tension release. But it's a funeral-worthy explosion of body shakes, air gulps, and tears flowing to the table.

Delaney pats his shoulder. "I'll get some tissue. It's okay, Edgar. I'm sorry I lost my temper."

When she returns, he wipes his nose and says, "When Emily showed up, I was excited to see her and thought it was a social visit. We talked about Patrick and what she's been up to. Then she hit me with the video."

"You knew King was deep in this when we broke into the safe," I tell him. "Why didn't you say something?"

Doc turns another page of the magazine. I snatch it from him. "The answer isn't in there."

"I made a promise to Emily to keep the video secret, and things happened fast. There wasn't time for a dissertation."

"Do you know what you did?" I say. "We almost got killed. You could have given that drive to me when I first showed up. I pull up the headline again on my phone and hand it to Doc. "Safe Harbor also burned to the ground. Do you really think that was an accident?"

Delaney slaps her palm to her mouth. "Oh my god. Those poor people."

Doc's eyes flick back and forth as he digests the disaster.

"Wait," he says. "We don't know it was nefarious. That place was an electrical fire trap. I'm surprised this didn't happen a long time ago."

He hands me back the phone. "And the blond and her psycho brother are no longer after you. You also have the evidence."

"And the bodies?" I ask.

"We need to make sure the residents are safe," Delaney says.

It's a noble goal, I think. But how without exposing ourselves. The hell if we're going back to Philly.

Doc shrugs. "If it's Mary Lou and company, I won't be sending flowers."

How do we know it was? I think. Innocent people burning to death or dying of smoke inhalation wasn't part of the plan.

"It might not be them," I say.

Doc stands and retrieves the cigarette pack Delany threw. "I'm not an idiot. I'll reach out to my Kensington contacts to make sure all the residents got out. What I know at this moment is that it happened and there's nothing we can do about it."

He's right. I'll pray that it's the bad guys but we have to keep pushing forward. Continuing my cross-examination, I ask, "Did Emily say anything about King?"

"Yes. She had taken a job at Sunny Awakenings and after a stint as a marketing rep, was reporting to him as his personal assistant."

"Did she mention that she was sleeping with him?"

"She was? No, only that she had learned something disturbing about him and was doing whatever it took to dig up more information. She didn't know who she could trust."

Delaney has to be thinking the same thing I am. We weren't on the trust list. Or maybe Doc's right, and Emily was protecting us.

"Did Emily say what that was?"

"King Fox was dealing fentanyl. I long suspected Safe Harbor was a front, but beyond my little world, I had no clue what the King of Clean was up to until the video."

"What was your reaction to the video?" I ask him.

"Adding to what I already knew about the illicit drug market in Kensington, it made sense how the operation worked. For obvious reasons, I feared for Emily's safety. She asked me to hold on to the device and her laptop until her lawyers reached out. She was suing King and Sunny Awakenings for Patrick's death. Despite misgivings, I agreed. We hugged, and she left."

So Doc had the laptop all along.

"Where is it?"

"I hid it under my mattress, so still in my room, I guess."

I pull up the article on the fire and hand the computer to him. "If that's the case, it's fried. Did you ever access it?"

Doc side-eyes me as if I've asked the stupidest question ever. "It was her property and none of my business. I planned on telling you both, but things got heated. I panicked and only thought about saving my USB."

"Ah yes, your non-interference policy."

"That worked out well, didn't it? I'm going outside for some air," Doc says.

When he's gone, Delaney takes two bottles of water from her refrigerator, hands me one, and says, "Was there any harm done? I don't think so. We have the video and documents from her cloud."

Delaney is right. I won't lie to myself that I give a flying fuck about Phillip, Mary Lou, or Clyde. They can rot in hell.

Chapter 36

*M*ary Lou and Phillip's quest to retrieve Emily's phone was the epitome of anticlimactic. After all the threats and blood spilled, it was right here in her home, stuck between cushions like pennies dropping out of a pocket. Delaney and I witnessed the Crime Scene Unit tear this place apart, looking for evidence. How could they have missed this? I need to get it to Keane. After her continued barbs, doubt, and distrust, it will be difficult to avoid a bit more of *I told you so* when I hand it to her.

Delaney comes in from outside. "I had a long talk with Doc. He'll stay here tonight, after all. I think he's done fighting it, at least for now."

That's good, I think. One less piece of conflict.

"Check this out." I hand her the phone. "The video is on it. What a screwup by the cops. If Keane had seen this at the start, King might already be in jail."

She doesn't bother scrolling it, and says, "Is there anything else on here we should know about?"

"Lots of photos of you and her as well as me, but nothing that tells us where she went every day after she quit Sunny Awakenings. We may never know."

Delaney hands it back and, in a choked voice, says, "Does it matter?"

"I guess not. Tomorrow, we'll hand off everything to Keane and let her take it from there. Once she arrests King Fox, the dominos should fall."

"But what about my dad and me?" she asks. "What about you? How do we know it's over?"

I struggle for an answer I'm not sure of.

224

"We need to talk with Andi," I say.

Delaney follows me to the porch, where Doc sits on the stoop.

"I'm leaving," I tell him. "You'll be comfortable here."

He pushes himself to his feet. "Aren't you forgetting something?"

I have no clue what he's referring to. There's no doubt I forgot a lot of crap over the last few days. My body temperature skyrockets. Maz's car. It's still in the Safe Harbor parking lot.

"I shot two people," Doc says.

"I was there. It was self-defense, and why we need to get you legal counsel as soon as possible. Delaney, I need to take the rental."

She tosses me the fob. "What about Maz's car? Will the Philadelphia police trace it to you?"

Dialing Maz, I can't help but shake my head at the mess. His gun. His car. He's going to explode. "No," I tell her. "They won't."

"Where the hell are you, Feldman?" Maz asks. The familiar irritation in his voice signals that he's about to tear me a new one. "What happened in Philly? I have a missed call from a detective out there. Why the fuck is my car in the parking lot of a burned-down junkie skell motel?"

Now isn't the time to break it to him that Doc killed Phillip with his gun.

"It's a long story. I have to stop by Andi Coffey's office. Then Delaney and I will be heading your way."

Before he can object, I disconnect and dial Andi's cell.

"This is Andi Coffey."

"It's Jason. We're in a mess and need to see you as soon as possible."

"Are you both okay? I've been meaning to call. The police have CCTV footage. They know Delaney was in my car."

I wince at the revelation, but it was inevitable. Until I know who else is after us, she's not safe, nor am I.

"We're fine, but the situation is too convoluted to explain over the phone. What have you told them?"

"To pound salt. I'm protecting my client. They threatened me with obstruction, but worse have tried to strong-arm me over the years."

"We're on our way to your office."

I execute a U-turn and call Delaney. "I'm headed back. Meet me outside. We're going downtown to see Andi. The police know you were on the Andy Warhol."

"I'll be out front."

The drive to the Coffey building engenders an elusive sense of calm. Everything once foggy is as clear as the waters of Bora Bora. King is dealing fentanyl and using his nonprofit recovery housing and treatment centers as cover. Emily stumbled onto his secret. That's why she's dead. We'll lay it out to Keane and give her the phone and the USB. Then the wheels of justice will grind.

Jonathan isn't at his desk when we enter the office. He's replaced by Andi, lasered on her laptop screen, fingers banging away at the keys.

"You two are a sight for sore eyes," she says and closes the cover. "I take it your trip was eventful, and we have much to discuss."

The understatement of the year, I think, walking into her office.

Andi follows us in and closes the door. "Where have you two been for the last week?"

"In hell!" I hand her the evidence that Emily was murdered.

Her eyes narrow as she inspects the USB. "Are you going to give me a verbal preview? Not to be too cautious, but you're not handing me anything illegal, are you, like child porn?"

I roll my eyes. "Just watch."

"What about the bridge?" Delaney asks. "Am I in trouble?"

Andi inserts the drive into the USB port on her laptop. "No. You didn't do anything wrong." As the video advances, her only utterances every few seconds are, "Goddamn King."

When the video ends, she leans back in her chair and says, "Who's the blond with the overly dramatic Southern accent?"

"The woman I told you about. Her name is Mary Lou. Something also happened in Philly. People were shot."

Andi raises her hand. "Stop there. If either of you, or both of you, were the shooters, I don't want to know."

"Don't worry. Neither of us pulled the trigger, but the person who did is our friend. It was self-defense. We'd both be dead if it weren't for him."

"I see," she says. "Where is this person?"

I dig into my wallet, take out a five-dollar bill, and toss it on the desk. "I'm retaining you to represent me."

Andi picks up the money. "We both know it takes more than handing me an Abe Lincoln to create an attorney-client relationship. I will, however, take it as a down payment for the damage to my Bentley."

"This will end up a media circus, the type of case you love."

Andi opens a legal pad. "Without knowing more, I'm hesitant. While I already represent Delaney on the civil matter, you might end up as an adverse party or witness. Right now, I'm operating in the dark."

Let's bring some light to it, I think and cycle through the events of the last twenty-four hours. It's Doc who will need separate counsel, though he's a hero, not a perp. Delaney and I would be dead if not for him.

"What if we execute waivers of conflict?"

"Delaney, are you good with a waiver?" Andi asks. "It means you consent to me handling this legal matter for Jason even if something turns up that would otherwise disqualify me from representing him."

"If Jason says it's fine, and you agree, I'm on board."

I reach across the desk and shake Andi's hand. "It's settled then. Our friend's name is Doc. For the time being, he's stashed at Delaney's condo."

"His name is Edgar," Delaney corrects.

"What's his last name?" Andi asks, scribbling on her legal pad.

Delaney and I look at each other as if it never occurred to either of us that he has one.

"Ah, we don't know."

"Not fatal. When do I get to meet him?"

"We'll bring him here tomorrow," I say. "He's going to need a lawyer as well."

"His conflict is not waivable," she says. "If he's the shooter, you both might be witnesses against him."

While she's right that he needs his own lawyer, we are actually witnesses on Doc's behalf. It's a clear-cut case of self-defense.

"What is it you want me to do in regard to your current situation?" Andi asks.

I can't put it off any longer. Keane will explode, but now I have everything needed to take her step-by-step to the ultimate conclusion. Phillip murdered Emily to protect King and their fentanyl distribution operation. It had to be him. Mary Lou wouldn't dirty her hands like that.

"Arrange a sit-down with Jeanette Keane here in your office."

Andi escorts us to the waiting room and admonishes again, "Unless I'm present, under no circumstances speak to the police or any other person with a law enforcement acronym on the back of their jacket."

I want to remind her that this isn't my first rodeo, but she knows that.

As we walk to the parking garage, Delaney says, "I can't stop thinking about what happened in your room. Doc really killed a man."

Would she rather it had been us? "It was self-defense. Keane and the district attorney will agree."

Nothing appears unusual as we park in front of Delaney's condo. Cars line the street in their reserved spots, while chairs protect other open spaces. The curtains are open, and Carson Street shoppers are out in force on a crystal-clear day with temperatures in the low eighties.

"I'm going home for a shower," I tell her. "Do you want me to come in with you first?"

"No need," Delaney says, exiting the car. "I'm going to convince Edgar to take a shower. He's a walking smokestack, and his clothes reek."

"That makes two of us. I'll bring him some T-shirts and jeans. He's about my size. If not, we'll road trip to Walmart or Target."

After she enters the condo, I text Maz: *On my way home.*

Chapter 37

What will become of Doc? I could pitch him to Andi as an expert witness for medical malpractice cases, but with his manslaughter conviction, she couldn't put him on the stand. Then again, as he pointed out, I'm not his dad.

Still paranoid, as I pull up to my house, I look in all directions for any car or out-of-place pedestrians and vehicles.

Even with the calamitous circumstances, stepping across the threshold into my living room makes me want to drop to my knees and kiss the carpet.

"Welcome home, Jason."

"Fuck!" I jump, spin around, and come face-to-face with Keane standing in the door jamb.

"What the hell? I didn't see you outside."

"I'm sorry I startled you. May I come in?" Keane says.

I step aside and wave her through. "Sure. How did you know I was home?"

She smiles. "I'm a cop. It's what we do."

"I guess so." I close the door behind her. It's just as well she's here, though. We face each other as we have so many times in the past. Only this time, we're on the same side.

"I found evidence proving a wide-ranging fentanyl distribution conspiracy implicating King and others. It's what Emily stumbled onto and why they overdosed her."

"I warned you about playing sleuth," she says. "You should have listened."

I open the photo app on my camera. "How about some show-and-tell from the City of Brotherly Love?"

She scrolls through the jpegs, nodding and muttering, "Wow," every couple of seconds. Finally, she's getting it. King's arrest is on the horizon.

She looks up at me. "Have you transferred these photos to anyone, or are these the only copies?"

"Delaney and one other person have seen them, but other than that, only you. The guy with a bullet in his head is Phillip, the one who broke into my house."

She nods in acknowledgment. "Do either of them have copies?"

"These are the only ones in existence."

She scrunches her eyes as her fingers move in a blur, hitting keys.

"What are you doing?"

"Deleting the evidence."

"In God's name, why?" I lunge for the phone.

She steps backward and reaches into her jacket, freeing a .45 automatic from its holster.

"Put your hands up against the wall and spread eagle."

As she pats me down, I struggle to process the moment. "You've worked for King all along?"

She yanks Maz's .38 out of my waistband. "I wouldn't take orders from that moron, but I've been tasked with cleaning up his mess and now yours. It's nothing I wanted. Truth be told, I kind of like you."

I'm unable to take my eyes off the muzzle, and the question finding its way past my lips is a raspy, "Why?"

She checks her watch. "I wish we could engage in philosophical banter, but I'm pressed for time. Where are Dr. Martin, and the other guy, Doc?"

How does Keane know his name? "I lied about the photos. Copies were sent to Pittsburgh and national media outlets."

Keane taps the barrel on her knee the way Mary Lou did. "I don't think so. My inside media sources would alert me if the shit was going to hit the fan. Regardless, at this point, we're not trying to eradicate the video, only assess and reduce risk to my employer."

My mind reels for any way to stall. She wouldn't be telling me this if I was leaving here alive.

"What about Mary Lou? If not King, then you must work for her."

"My employer's identity is irrelevant. I wish this wasn't necessary. I'm sorry."

It hits me. Mary Lou and Phillip knew I was in Philly because Keane did. They told her about Doc. But how did Keane know I was there in the first place? Maz must have blabbed. After all, why wouldn't he trust his old partner?

"Did Maz tell you we were in Kensington?"

Keane shakes her head as she threads a silencer onto her gun. "He didn't say anything. I'll have to have words with him about holding back. If you can't trust your old partner, who can you?"

I roll my eyes to the ceiling, searching for a semblance of sanity. She's not Svengali. How?

Keane rests the gun on her lap. "You have a right to know. After you found the AirTag, I got a warrant and tracked your cell phone pings to the PA Turnpike, then into Philly."

More to myself than her, I say, "She made me a person of interest in Emily's death."

Keane stands and backs toward the front door. "That's correct. A warrant was easy, and I pressed the carrier for a fast turnaround on the tower data. Sit on the couch. This has to look like I returned fire."

My mind drifts to the nursing home. Who will tell my father that I'm dead? Will he even understand? Dementia patients depend on routine, and I won't be coming back. I can only hope that Sam fills in for me.

"You're all going down regardless of what happens here."

"Have it your way. Don't sit." Keane aims at my head. "You gave or sold Emily the powder and pills. I came to arrest you. When I walked in the door, you aimed the .38 at me. It was my life or yours."

"You'll never make that stick. My prints aren't on that baggie."

"They will be. It's not a difficult process. Who's going to challenge it?" She squints over my shoulder. "Fuck me. Don't move."

Keane walks a wide circle toward the outlet by the television. Then she kneels in front of a USB power adapter with a blue blinking light. After yanking it out of the socket, she uses a fingernail to pry the back off and pulls out an SD card. "Fuck me," she says again.

"It's motion-activated and uploads to the cloud every thirty seconds," I tell her. "Twenty bucks on Amazon. Emily's idea from the grave."

Keane wheels around, stomps toward me, and shoves the muzzle flush against my forehead. "Delete the file, or I'll splatter your brains across the room."

The front door slams backward against the wall, and Maz storms into the room, his service revolver trained on Keane. "It's over, Jeanette. Back away from him and drop the steel."

She wheels around and fires at Maz, who moans as he's slammed against the front door. He pulls the trigger in rapid succession until there are only the clicks of an empty chamber.

Keane crumples to the ground, clutching her abdomen. Maz collapses to his knees, heaving, as he fumbles at the buttons of his shirt, exposing a bulletproof vest.

"Thank Jesus, I remembered to wear my bullet condom," he says, gasping and pressing into the Kevlar indent over his heart.

Keane rolls onto her back, moaning. Blood pours through the spaces between her fingers.

"I never thought I'd shoot another cop, let alone my old partner," Maz says. "This is bad."

I look at Keane writhing in pain and then ask, "Are Delaney and Doc safe?"

Maz grimaces, pushing himself to his feet. "Our plan didn't include being three places at once. Call 911. Tell them there's been a shooting, an officer is down, and retired cop Mark Mazansky is on the scene."

While I give the emergency operator the address, Maz rubs his chest. "I don't think any ribs are broken. You should get yourself one of these. Your nanny cam scheme was damn smart. I saw her prowling the backyard on my app and hustled over."

"Let me die." We both look over Keane. "Please, let me die."

"It's not up to me." Maz leans over and pulls her hand away from the wound. I fight not to pity this person who murdered Emily and god knows who else.

"Is she going to survive?"

"Three gut wounds. If she doesn't bleed out, maybe."

Within minutes, the scream of sirens pierces the walls. Keane's weak voice gurgles out. "Jason."

I kneel next to her. "I'm here."

Unable to decipher the almost inaudible whisper, I place my ear to her mouth.

"You're too late. Your friends... They're dead."

The rest is a slurred string of gibberish as Keane nods off into uncon-sciousness. What did she mean? Doc and Delaney are safe at the condo. Mary Lou may have died in the fire. Maybe more hired shooters? I need to get to Delaney's place.

Four uniformed officers sprint up the front porch stairs, guns drawn. Maz already has his badge out, holding it above his head. "I'm a retired cop. Don't shoot us."

"We have to get to Delaney's place now," I shout to him.

"We have a dinosaur-sized pile of dung to explain right here," Maz says.

I grab the .38 off the couch. "Do the best you can here and tell them where I'm going."

"You can't leave an active crime scene, dipshit, and certainly not with my gun."

"Arrest me." I bolt past him and out the door to Delaney's car.

Get your ass back here, now, Maz texts.

After transmitting her pinned address, I text: *Send the police to Delaney's*

Despite running every red light, the drive to her condo seems like it's happening in slow motion.

I park down the street and work my way around Delaney's front porch and stoop under the peephole. Dropping onto all fours, I crawl under the bottom ledge of the living room window and peek through the quarter-inch slit separating the curtains. Delaney and Doc are on the couch, hands folded on their laps as Mary Lou limps back and forth in front of them. A fiberglass boot covers her ankle. She's gripping a gun in one hand and her phone in the other.

"Hey, what the hell are you doing?"

I jerk my head around to a guy, three feet away, backpack in hand. "Fucking pervert. I'm calling the cops."

The curtain moves. All I can make out are the flowers on Mary Lou's dress. Trembling, I yank the revolver out of my waistband, put the muzzle flush against the glass where her navel should be, and pull the trigger.

The glass crackles and spiders away from the bullet hole. The guy screams, "Holy shit," drops his backpack, and runs like hell down the street. I'm about to fire again, but the dress is gone.

"Police! Stand and touch the sky. Do it now!"

The revolver still in hand, I raise my arms straight up.

"Place the weapon at your feet and walk backward toward my voice. If you turn, I'll put one in your skull."

After I back up, he says, "Drop to your knees and lock your fingers behind your head."

Seconds later, hands jerk my arms behind me, and I'm cuffed.

Two officers are hauling me to my feet when Delaney exits the house and runs toward us. "Don't hurt him."

Doc exits behind her, turns, and points inside. "She hightailed it out the back with a bullet in her gut."

As I'm being wedged into the back of a police cruiser, Delaney continues pleading my case. "He's not a criminal. The woman you should be after is getting away."

"Ma'am, witnesses saw him discharge a firearm into this home. Until we sort it out, he stays in custody."

"This is my home, and he saved our lives."

The officer raises Maz's gun and says, "Sir, do you own this weapon?"

"No, I do." The oft-irritating voice of the grouchy asshole who spent two years hating my guts is now a honey-sweet tune of rescue. He removes a metal Pittsburgh Police badge from his wallet. "Detective Mark Mazansky, retired. This man isn't a skell. Unhook him."

The cop flashes a skeptical glare. "No can do."

A black stretch limo pulls up, and a man I instantly recognize from television and other media exits the vehicle. Pittsburgh Chief of Police Joseph Falcone.

He shakes Maz's hand and says, "You've had an eventful retirement. Tell Brian to call his other grandpapa now and then."

"The chief of police is also Brian's grandfather?" I say.

"Sean's father-in-law. Soon to be former chief. He's retiring."

Falcone laughs. "Quite the mess here. This will be a scandal for the department, but if Keane flips, it could be a quality string of busts. Anything to tell me before I make a statement to the press?"

"The perp fled, but we'll get her," Maz says. "Crime scene and some DEA suits are in the house. The hostages are shaken up but unharmed." He turns to the once-defiant officer. now contemplating his feet. "Didn't I tell you to unhook him?"

The cop fumbles with the key, dropping it on the street. Maz winks at me. "He's probably never been this close to the chief before."

After the steel is gone, I massage my wrists and ask, "Where's Keane?"

"Under arrest and guarded at the hospital," Maz says. "There's a slew of agencies waiting to question her if she survives—local, FBI, DEA, and ATF for starters."

"What about King Fox?" Delaney asks. "You're going to arrest him, right?"

"He and three expensive legal suits presented themselves downtown earlier today. He claims the video depicts his private sting operation, and he knows of at least three other recovery facilities operating as cartel fronts. In other words, he's going to flip."

"I'm surprised he didn't lam it. These people are not the forgiving types."

"Where's he gonna go?" Maz says. "The Feds are national; the cartel is worldwide. It would be a suicide run."

"What about us?" Delaney says. "I'm not going into any kind of witness protection. I have a life here."

Maz rubs his chin. "Above my pay grade, but the cartel isn't in the business of dropping low-level bodies on foreign soil with nothing to gain. This isn't even a pin prick to their finances. My guess is that things got sloppy, and they'll just want to clean up loose ends. It's Keane and the blond they'll worry about."

"I don't feel any safer," Doc says. "What about Mary Lou?"

"One mess at a time," Maz replies. "You three brought down a major fentanyl and counterfeit pill distribution ring stretching from Pittsburgh to Philly, as well as a dirty cop. You're heroes."

A helicopter buzzes overhead. Around us, yellow sawhorses now block street access. Crime scene, DEA, and the FBI will all want to interview us. How can I ever not stop, turn, and wonder who is behind me?

Chapter 38

The last time I sat on my back porch and watched the sunrise, Emily was next to me. It feels almost sacrilegious to sit out here so soon after her death, but I need the familiarity of the birds singing in the oak tree and summer morning dew casting a sheen on the grass. I'd drink my coffee, while she preferred tea. We'd open our laptops and discuss whatever was going on in the news. I power mine up to catch up on the slew of news stories mentioning me in the wake of King's arrest.

I've had time to think during the two months of traveling back and forth to Philadelphia. DEA interviews, the media hounding me, and multiple delays of the Maz-Irina nuptials have been stressful. It's clear that King's discovery of the hidden video camera sealed Emily's fate. Not even the fate of her killer makes up for the loss I feel.

I'm also sure Emily quit her job because she knew King suspected her of planting the video camera. I wish she would have confided in me and Delaney. We could have helped, and she might still be alive.

This morning, the *Pittsburgh Tribune* headline is my welcome coffee sweetener.

King Fox Charged with Fentanyl Distribution, Treatment Centers Closed

A Pittsburgh addiction treatment clinic owner has been hit with federal drug trafficking charges after a joint task force raided his Fox Chapel home and his facilities in Pittsburgh and Philadelphia. A federal grand jury indicted former Pittsburgh Pirates and Philadelphia Phillies player King Tiberius Fox, 45, for felony possession with intent to distribute methamphetamine, cocaine, heroin, and fentanyl.

Federal prosecutors allege Fox, whose social media moniker was "The King of Clean," laundered cartel drug money through the Sunny Awakenings addiction treatment clinics and multiple sober living homes. He was set to open a new multimillion-dollar opioid addiction clinic in McKees Rocks.

I then navigate to a two-month-old Erin Campanara *Tribune* story. I know it by heart, but rereading has become a morning ritual.

Disgraced Lawyer Makes Hero Turn

It recounts my past and then describes how Delaney and I brought down King Fox:

Feldman and Dr. Delaney Martin, MD, set out to prove the fentanyl overdose death of their mutual friend, Emily Wilson, wasn't accidental. They were successful, but not before being drawn into the illicit world of treatment centers used as fronts for drug trafficking.

These facts were provided by Andi Coffey, a prominent Pittsburgh litigation attorney who represents both Feldman and Martin. Both declined interviews, citing a desire for privacy.

Andi's number pops up on my caller ID.

"Jason, I hope you're excited for your first day as my new associate. Small favor. Please run by Starbucks on your way and get me a tall caramel macchiato latte."

If I need to fetch coffee or her dry cleaning, it's the price of reentering my life when no other law firm would touch my baggage. I make a mental note to suggest the superior lattes at Hemingway's Boat.

"I'm happy to. Is there anything else you need?"

"That's all. By the way, we have good news in the Estate of Emily Williams versus King Fox et al. lawsuit. It settled yesterday."

"Fantastic. How much?"

"Policy limits of $2 million. At first the adjuster claimed there was no insurance coverage because of intentional acts, but I knew they'd cave. The feds also initiated forfeiture proceedings on King's assets, so Delaney and I decided to take the money and run."

"Outstanding. See you soon," I say, wondering what Delaney, as trustee, will do with the money after Andi takes her 40 percent plus expenses.

I shower, fill my "Love Your Lawyer" coffee mug, and unwrap the plastic over my dry-cleaned, blue courtroom suit. Sliding into the pants legs, I feel like a real attorney again. As I slip into the jacket, a knock at the door causes me to stumble forward, spilling coffee on my tie. Irritated at myself, I wonder if this is how I'm going to react every time someone's at my door or a squirrel scurries through the attic. It might be time for some therapy.

I pick up my week-old .38 revolver off the bedroom nightstand. Until she is behind bars, every unannounced visitor might be Mary Lou.

My heart stops as I peer out my new, custom-enlarged panoramic peephole. On the verge of hyperventilating, I sprint to the bedroom and shove the gun under my mattress. I rush back, twist the recently installed upper and lower steel-reinforced deadbolts, and open the door.

"Hi, Dad."

Two years have passed since I last heard those words. I'm at a loss as to how to respond.

"Are you going to invite me in?"

"Of course. I'm shell-shocked. It's good to see you."

Sam steps inside, and the fights, unreturned calls, and my slurred drunken claims I was sober melt away like waking up from a bad dream.

"Have a seat," I say, and shut and lock the door.

He takes his time, running his fingers over his grandfather's furniture as if attaching a memory to each item. "Looks about the same as the last time I was here."

"Yeah, I'm not a decorator like your mom. She had all the taste in the family. I also couldn't bring myself to do anything different with your granddad's stuff. Some of this furniture belonged to his parents."

"I know, Dad. I'm your son, remember?"

"Can I get you anything to drink? Your choices are water and Coke Zero."

He sits at the kitchen table. "No thanks. Have you spoken to Mom?"

I decide it's better not to mention the brief late-night call to Sonya. It will only dredge up past drama.

"Not since everything went down. It's understandable, distancing herself from this mess."

"How's your sobriety going?"

A perfectly reasonable question, I think. I've given him no reason to believe I'd survive an ordeal like this and not relapse. "I'll hit a year next week. Didn't think I'd make it."

"Outstanding, Dad. I'm proud of you on multiple fronts. Bringing justice to that poor girl at significant risk to yourself is a mitzvah. I'm sorry I never got to meet her. Speaking of good things, I have news."

"You would have liked Emily. She had spunk and a sense of social good like your mom. Am I a grandfather or something?"

He grins and waggles his eyebrows.

"You're joshing me. You had a baby?"

"My partner had one. It's a boy. We named him Miles."

My jaw drops. "When?"

"Three days ago. Mother and child are well. The bris is in five days. We'd like you to be there." He stands and says, "I'm sorry it's been so long and for what you've been through. I have to run, but can we have dinner this week?"

"Please stay a while longer. Tell me about the mother."

"Her name is Alexis. We'll talk more later. I promised to bring a Primanti's sandwich by the hospital."

My text alert pings. It's Maz.

The names of the Philly crispy-fried bodies. Phillip Dubois and a corner kid, Reginald Scurry, street name, Jolly. There was a third, Clyde Santelli.

My heart sinks. Why Jolly? Retribution for helping me? Where is Mary Lou?

"Dad, you okay?"

I sigh and pocket the phone. "I'll walk you to the door."

As I turn the deadbolts, he says, "You've gone security conscious. Those are some serious locks."

I chuckle. "You can never be too careful."

He reaches out for a handshake. *Screw that.* I bear hug him like I'm trying to absorb his body.

"It's been hard," I whisper, "but I'm sober today, and I'm trying."

"I know you are, Dad. Love you."

I watch him walk to his car, and for the first time in my life, everything is right in the world. I put my coffee cup in the sink and head upstairs to my bedroom. My legs buckle when I see her.

"You should have killed me, Jason."

My first thought is to turn and dash downstairs, but I can't move—as if the neural link between my brain and feet has been severed.

Mary Lou limps to my desk and slowly lowers herself into the chair, wincing. Sweat breaks out on my forehead as her eyes bore into mine. My mind reels. How did she get in? Every door and window lock is new and stronger. What did I miss?

"Sit on your bed. We're going to have a brief chat."

I eye every angle of the room like a wild animal about to be devoured by a lion, searching for an escape route. She scratches above the boot. "This thing itches like my grandmother's sweater."

How did she get in? All windows and doors are secure and my security cam app didn't alert me to an intruder.

"I can tell you're wondering how I found my way inside. A more pointed inquiry would be how long I've been here. I'll be out of the country soon but couldn't leave without bringing those responsible to account for Phillip."

I visualize every entry and exit from all points in the house. Doors, windows. She didn't come down the chimney like Santa Claus. Where and how did she stay hidden? I haven't left the house in twenty-four hours.

Mary Lou checks her phone and says, "I can't visit long. A private jet to New Orleans awaits, then on to a secluded beach in Mexico to heal up."

How could I be so stupid? I've never used or bothered to reinforce the flimsy padlock securing the roof access panel.

"You've been hiding in the attic."

"I cut the lock last night and waited for the right moment to climb down through the attic entrance into the bathroom. It wasn't easy with a cast and stomach wound. I have a security suggestion, not that it will do you any good. New video cam passwords are set to the word 'admin' by default. If you don't change it, bad people can hack in and shut them off."

Mary Lou removes a silencer from her purse and screws it onto the muzzle. "Losing a sibling is akin to having a part of your body amputated and your heart torn in half. Similar to how you would feel if Sam died."

Is she threatening my son? If so, why let him leave?

"Congratulations on your new grandson, by the way. Phillip, on the other hand, has a daughter. She's in a private school in New Orleans and doesn't know he's dead. I thought about dealing with Sam as well, but it would only complicate things. Once I'm healthy, there's always an opportunity to reconsider."

"Killing me or anyone else won't bring him back," I tell her. "And we have the death penalty in this state. Just go, and I won't say a word, ever. It's over."

Mary Lou pushes herself up from the chair and bends over, heaving out gasps of air. She's clearly in severe pain. That might be my only advantage. She will react slower to anything I do.

"Death is an inherent risk of this profession, but your friend did kill my brother," she says. "After I take care of you, I'll deal with your friends, Doc and Delaney. Then I'll disappear."

"You did it to yourself," I say, and wonder if those words define my own life.

She aims the gun at me.

I hear a pop, followed by a hiss. Searing pressure to my sternum knocks me backward. I scream and roll onto my stomach, reaching under the mattress. Another muted explosion. My lower back is on fire as I grapple for the gun.

She raises the muzzle again. "This is for Phillip."

I close my eyes, swing my arm out from under the mattress, and, as Maz did, pull the trigger until the gun dry fires. Mary Lou falls forward on top of me, blood pouring onto my face from the wounds on her cheeks and forehead. Gasping for air, I push her off me onto the floor and stare at what's left of her face. I take a step forward, but searing pain from my lower back collapses me onto the bed. A small price to pay for life. The vest did its job.

Chapter 39

I never thought they'd make it to the wedding day. After months of delays due to the investigation and resolving Irina's immigration issue, here we are, with me as the best man. I still laugh at the thought, though I'm thrilled to do it. Maz has morphed from a necessary annoyance to a valued friend.

The text vibration on my nightstand is from Andi: *Up and at 'em. Do you need help with your bow tie? Dress socks match?*

I text back: *It's a clip-on. Did you convince Doc to wear a tux?*

He pushed back but relented. You won't believe how dashing and handsome he cleans up, like a college professor. Be sure to congratulate him.

I dial Delaney. "Hey, what should I kudo Doc for?"

"He's the executive director of the Emily and Patrick Williams Foundation. It will focus on fentanyl awareness, education, and harm reduction."

"Outstanding. I'm thrilled you're putting the settlement money to good use, though I expected nothing different. See you at the church."

I open my computer to a slew of emails from Andi.

Please have the Cox v. Kaddish interrogatories reviewed and on my desk tomorrow. I also left two depositions on your desk. Have them redlined by Monday morning. Are you readying for the Soltis deposition next week? I'm going to let you handle it.

By the way. I tried the Hemingway's coffee. Your recommendation was spot on. It's my new place!

My first deposition as her associate. Despite having taken hundreds of them, my heart flutters. Andi has treated me like a new law school grad, reviewing depositions and handling low-level motions. She said that she normally would never make a hire like me, and it was probationary. After two years of not practicing, it hasn't been easy adjusting to lawyer life again as maybe the oldest first-year associate in Pittsburgh, but every day is a new challenge conquered as I gain her confidence and trust.

With three hours to the wedding, I pour a cup of coffee, head to the back porch, and dial Sam. I can't believe I'm a grandad, but I'm quickly turning into a doting, goo-goo-talking grandpa stereotype.

"How's my grandson doing?"

"The same as last night when you called. Don't you have a wedding today?"

"It's later this afternoon. Put Miles on the phone so I can talk to him."

"He can't speak, Dad."

"He understands. You did at that age."

There's an audible sigh on the other end. "Alexis, my dad's on the line. Bring him over."

After I hear a few gargles and gurgles, I coo, "Grandpa misses you and will be over soon."

"We're putting him down for a nap. Come over tomorrow. We'll set out bagels and lox."

It's surreal, I think to myself. My son's back in my life. I have a grandson. "When are you taking Miles to see his great-grandfather?"

"Soon."

"I want to be there. He doesn't have much time left, and we should get a photo. Three generations."

"A wonderful idea. We'll do it next week. I have to run."

"I love you, Sam."

"Back at you, Dad."

I sip my coffee, navigate to the *Pittsburgh Tribune*, and deep-breathe the cool, almost-fall chill in the air. Leaves from my lone oak tree float to the already blanketed grass, reminding me I need to rake the yard. Cardinals and blue jays flit through branches, chirping and plotting their escape south for the winter.

After months of headlines and national news coverage, the King Fox hubbub has softened a bit. On the advice of my attorney, I'm still declining interviews. Andi has been a regular media fixture. I've also come to a grudging acceptance of Doc hiring Colin Langdon as his lawyer.

I know former Detective Keane survived her injuries but haven't been able to learn anything else. Even Maz won't fill me in. Andi, however, says Keane is in federal protective custody and will cut a deal. Then she'll testify against the cartel and do her time in administrative segregation. After that, she'll disappear into the WITSEC program. Andi also said there are no leads on the shooter who got me with the concrete. He's probably a cartel soldier who is either dead or back in Mexico or Colombia.

After two hours of working on Andi's directives, I put on the best man tux Maz picked out for me from Waggaman's and head to the Sacred Heart Church. Irina never spoke about religious inklings, but the St. Michael pendant always around her neck gave it away.

I walk in as Andi, dressed in an orange silk, floor-length gown, is signing the guest book. She says, "You're looking dapper. I didn't know you cleaned up so well."

I look around, reach into my pocket, and pull out my bowtie. "Can you help with this? I couldn't get it to stay on."

"You and my ex-husband both. I had to dress him from the ground up."

As she pulls my collar over the strap, I say, "Is it sexual harassment to mention how nice you look?"

She laughs. "In the office, yes, but I'm positive there's a statutory wedding exemption, so thank you."

"Hey, you two. It's almost game time." We both turn our heads to Delaney, wearing a pink, flowing bridesmaid gown.

"You might want to get your butts to the front so we can start this show," Maz says, stomping up the center aisle.

"Right behind you," I tell him.

We all follow him to the front and take our places as the organ music starts. Doc hustles down behind us in his groomsman tux. I doubt that his coifed goatee and moussed hair have looked this good in years.

Colin Langdon sits in the front row next to Irina's parents. He'll always be an obnoxious jerk, but because of him, a grand jury no-billed Doc on the two homicides. Colin also got his legal fees paid through social media crowdfunding.

Andi whispers, "I'm glad they agreed to a short-form wedding."

I nod in agreement and look toward the rear as the music starts, and Irina's daughter and Maz's grandson lead the way to the altar. Even Doc's jaw drops. Irina is stunning in her white dress, hair flowing down her back. Towering above Maz, she takes her place next to him.

The vows are simple and short. After they kiss, I turn and look behind me at the few guests of Irina's and the cop types for Maz. What are not present are secrets or fear. No one is following me. It's over.

Acknowledgments

To my wife, Amanda. Thanks for your constant support. Love you. To my wonderful subject matter experts...

Phil DiLucente
Bonnie Hearn Hill
Luke Gerwe
Sabine Morrow
Dale McCue
Marc Daffner
Christopher Moraff
Lisa Wagner Freeman
David Terkel
Bryant Zadegan

The hard-working employees at my publisher, Post Hill Press.

About the Author

*B*rian Cuban, the younger brother of Dallas Mavericks owner and entrepreneur Mark Cuban, is a Dallas-based attorney, author, and person in long-term recovery from alcohol and drug addiction. He is a graduate of Penn State University and the University of Pittsburgh School of Law.

His book, *The Addicted Lawyer: Tales of the Bar, Booze, Blow, and Redemption* is an unflinching look at how addiction and other mental health issues destroyed his career as a once successful lawyer, and how he and others in the profession redefined their lives in recovery and found redemption.

Brian has spoken at colleges, universities, conferences, non-profits, and legal events across the United States and in Canada. His columns have appeared—and he has been quoted on these topics—online and in print newspapers around the world. He currently resides in Dallas, Texas with his wife and two cats.